The WAR CHIEF'S SON

The WAR CHIEF'S SON

ROBERT L. BROWN

Ramona Park Press

© 2014 Robert L. Brown

All rights reserved. No part of this book may be reproduced, scanned, or distributed in any printed or electronic form without permission from the publisher.

RAMONA PARK PRESS
Harbor Springs, Michigan

Printed in the United States of America

Brown, Robert L. (Robert Lewis), 1938-
    The war chief's son/Robert L. Brown. —Harbor Springs, Michigan : Ramona Park Press, c2014.
    p. ; cm.

    ISBN: 978-0-9915924-0-1

    Summary: Beau Lightfoot was born into a world of isolation and poverty in Northern Michigan in the mid-1950s, the son of an Odawa Indian woman and a white father. When he turns 11, the spirit of Pontiac, the great Odawa War Chief, appears to Beau and becomes his guide and advisor, as he navigates high school and wins a football scholarship to the University of Michigan. Unprepared for the 1960s world of big-time football, Vietnam War protests, drugs and sex, but guided by the advice and Native American philosophy of a long-dead War Chief, Beau copes with betrayal and friendship, while trying to win the heart of a young woman far above his social class.—Publisher.

    1. Indians of North America—Mixed descent—Michigan—Fiction. 2. University of Michigan—Football—Fiction. 3. Michigan Wolverines (Football team)—Fiction. 4. Wequetonsing Association (Harbor Springs (Mich.)—Fiction. 5. Pontiac, Ottawa Chief-1769—Philosophy—Fiction. 6. Vietnam War, 1961-1975—Protest movements—Michigan—Ann Arbor—Fiction. 7. Vietnam War, 1961-1975—Protest movements—Illinois—Chicago—Fiction. 8. Ottawa Indians—Philosophy—Fiction. 9. Friendship—Fiction. 10. Man-woman relationships—Fiction. 11. Bildungsromans. I. Title.

PS3602.R72275 W37 2014   2014903382
813.6—dc23   1404

This is a work of fiction. All incidents and dialogue, and all characters with the exception of some well-known real-life figures, are products of the author's imagination and are not to be construed as real. Where real-life figures appear, the situations, incidents, and dialogues concerning those persons are entirely fictional and are not intended to depict actual events or to change the entirely fictional nature of the work. In all other respects, any resemblance to persons living or dead is entirely coincidental.

Cover and interior design by To The Point Solutions
www.tothepointsolutions.com

For Ray Brown

The WAR CHIEF'S SON

My name is Pontiac. Many call me The Greatest War Chief Who Ever Lived. I was born to the Odawa in a village near Fort Pontchartrain in 1718. I united the tribes of the northern forests and led them in war. More than a decade before the American Revolution, we burned forts from Pittsburgh to the Mississippi River and created terror among the English-speaking people. As War Chief of the Great Algonquin Nation, I killed twenty-three men by my own hands.

I died in 1769.

As a spirit, I am helping a son of my people find his way in the modern world. It is a difficult task because Beau Lightfoot is a foolish young man. Although I am disappointed by his reluctance to kill even one person, I have come to love him.

PROLOGUE

Two young warriors lay hidden in the tall weeds at the top of a small rise. Less than two hundred feet away, a small family arranged themselves on a blanket spread in the dappled sunlight. Mary Ann Jenkins enjoyed the soft spring air and felt no hint of impending terror.

The last day of May was beautiful in northern Indiana. The heat of summer had not yet arrived and the gently rolling countryside was a vibrant green. The Wabash River flowed easily and peacefully through the shade of the trees along its banks. It was a perfect day for a family picnic, and Mary Ann didn't allow the concerns of her husband to interfere.

Lieutenant Edward Jenkins, commanding officer of Fort Quiatenon, had heard rumors of Indian trouble nearby and insisted that two troopers come along to protect his wife and their two young daughters. The soldiers were armed and in uniform. They kept a careful lookout but failed to detect anything amiss.

The watching braves were part of a band of Odawa warriors who, under the leadership of the War Chief Pontiac, had come down the Wabash River by canoe during the night. The two Indians were fascinated by Mary Ann's fair skin and blonde hair, but they wouldn't dare touch her without Pontiac's approval. Cat Face, one of the braves, whispered, "You stay here. Keep a close watch and don't let them get back to the fort. I'll go to Pontiac."

Pontiac was meeting with the local tribes of the area—the Kickapoo, Mascouten, and Wea—to tell them about his war and the victories already won. He was trying to persuade them to join his cause and attack the fort, when Cat Face breathlessly approached with news of the family observed outside of the fort. "Should we kill them?"

Pontiac stood completely still for a full minute and then said, "No. Take some warriors to help you, and bring the people to me. Don't kill any of the family." He turned to the assembled chiefs and said, "We will seize the fort without the loss of a single warrior. The English will surrender and everything in the fort will be yours." Chief Blackbird of the Kickapoo asked how this could be possible. Pontiac slowly turned his black eyes toward him and said, "There are weapons other than guns, knives, and tomahawks. Fear is a powerful weapon. I will show you."

Cat Face selected six warriors and left to capture the family. They quietly joined the brave keeping watch, and began to encircle the unsuspecting family. They crawled flat on their stomachs, moving through the tall grass as silently as snakes.

The Jenkins family finished their sandwiches and iced tea. The girls were building a stick house for their dolls. Eddie rested his back against a large oak tree and smiled at his beautiful young wife. Mary Ann was happy she had gotten out of their warm bed at five o'clock in the morning to bake their favorite pie. She opened the sealed section of her picnic basket and the delicious aroma of freshly baked rhubarb pie filled the air. She called in a soft voice, "Who wants some pie?"

Everyone immediately rushed to her side. She said, "Everybody sit down on the blanket and I'll serve you." She cut six pieces, four for her family and two for the soldiers. Since Eddie was always a stickler for proper military procedure, she thought he would want to be the one to invite the soldiers to join them for some pie. "Ed, would you invite the boys to sit with us and have some pie?"

The smile disappeared from her husband's face. He replied in a harsh whisper. "Damn it, Mary Ann. Those men are here to guard us. They're not boys. They're soldiers and they are on duty. No, they may not sit on our blanket and eat pie with us."

Mary Ann's happy face clouded over. She was on the verge of tears. "Oh, Eddie. Please don't be cross with me. I baked the pie because I thought you liked it. I just wanted to make everyone happy."

Lieutenant Jenkins decided to retreat. His wife was about to cry and his daughters looked at him as if he were a monster. He gently touched Mary Ann's hand. "Okay, the soldiers can have some of your wonderful pie. Clarke can sit with us while Shipley stands guard. When Clarke finishes his pie, they can trade places."

Unseen by the family, Cat Face directed the attack with hand signals. He pointed to the three warriors hidden in the tall grass near Shipley and made a sign of shooting an arrow. He raised his arm and looked about. All was ready. He dropped his arm and screamed.

The Indians came from everywhere at once. The first arrow went through Shipley's throat and the next two thumped into his chest. Ed Jenkins, who had been reclining on the blanket while enjoying his pie, tried to scramble to his feet to reach his officer's sword lying on the ground a few feet away. One Indian jumped on him and another slashed his right leg. He collapsed onto the blanket.

Tom Clarke, with his rifle lying at his feet, raised his arms in surrender. Two warriors grabbed the girls, and with a mother's ferocity, Mary Ann defended them with the only weapon she had—she stabbed her fork into the side of one of the braves. He screamed and drew back his tomahawk to kill her. At the last second, he remembered Pontiac's order that the family not be killed. He grunted, pulled the rhubarb covered fork out of his side, and smacked her in the face with his fist.

The attack was over in less than sixty seconds.

The captives were taken to Pontiac and forced to the ground at his feet. Mary Ann was bleeding from her nose and the little girls were whimpering and hiding behind their mother's skirts. Pontiac addressed Jenkins. "You are an officer. Are you the commander of the fort?"

Jenkins replied, "I am the commanding officer of Fort Quiatenon. Your braves killed one of my men and you're mistreating us. I demand that you release my wife and children immediately."

Pontiac ignored his complaints and calmly said, "You will surrender the fort to us."

"We will not surrender! I am an officer of His Majesty's army. If you attack us, we will fight. I ask only that you allow the women and children to leave the fort with a small armed escort. Then, if you wish, we will fight."

Pontiac smiled. "That is not how it will be." He drew his knife and, with a flick so fast it could hardly be seen, made a small cut in Mary Ann's cheek. She screamed and collapsed in the dirt. Jenkins surged forward, but he was restrained by two warriors. Pontiac said, "We will kill the women and children. The men will be scalped alive and then left to die. I'm going to show you what it is to be scalped. Bring the soldier over here and hold him down."

Tom Clarke was dragged forward and held by several braves. Pontiac extended his knife for everyone to see. Tom soiled himself and screamed in terror. Pontiac grabbed a fistful of Tom's hair with his left hand and pulled up hard. With the knife in his right hand he began to cut into Tom's forehead along the hairline. He was able to reach bone with a shallow cut. Tom let out an inhuman scream and fainted. Pontiac continued to cut a neat circle around the top of Tom's head and then stopped. Blood was pouring over Tom's face, head, and neck—but he was not dying. The cuts were not deep and no vital organs had been damaged.

"Lieutenant, that's the first part of being scalped. I'm going to stop for now. It gets worse, but I have done enough to give you the idea. You will carry this man to the fort and tell everyone what you have seen. If you do as I say, your family will live.

Tomorrow morning you will open the gates of the fort and surrender. All arms and supplies in the fort will belong to us. No one will be harmed."*

---

*On the morning of June 1, 1763, Fort Quiatenon, defended by forty-one soldiers and surrounded by more than three hundred Indian warriors, surrendered without firing a shot. The British senior military officers located in Boston felt the soldiers should have fought to the last man. They considered the surrender to be a disgrace to His Majesty's army. The Indians kept the occupants of the fort as captives for a month, and then released them. No one was harmed.

A DAY FOR FAWN

2013

The ground was saturated from the snowmelt and spring rain. Beau's feet created depressions in the soft earth as he walked from his car to the gravesite. After each step, his footprints filled with water. He stooped to feel the water with the first two fingers of his right hand and found it warm. He picked up a handful of moist dirt, brought it to his nose, and smelled the sweet aroma of spring. New green growth was beginning to push through the brown. Yes, it was God's day for Fawn.

It was 2:00 p.m. on a Saturday—and not a proper kind of day to be buried. A person should be buried on a rainy day, with heavy clouds and a north wind. Beau stood beside the open grave, waiting for the last words to be spoken over his sister, his gentle sister who lived her adult life as Sister Mary Francis. She had left this world and was now with Jesus.

Sister Mary Francis would have considered her death to be an occasion for joy, not sadness. God sent this beautiful day to welcome her. The first warm spring days in the far north are surely His finest. The air was moist and cool, but for the first time since winter, there was a hint of warmth. A breeze blew inland from Lake Michigan.

She had asked to be buried in the Indian cemetery next to the Middle Village Church a few miles south of Cross Village. Fawn died quietly in her sleep on April 30th. She was sixty-three years old. The old priest, her friend for fifty years, was there to say good-bye.

Father Marcotte stood next to Beau at the side of the grave and Beau offered his left arm to steady the old man. He was ninety-one years old and bent with age, but his blue eyes held the keen intelligence and peaceful kindness Beau had first seen many years ago. He felt a surge of affection for the old priest. Beau hadn't cried for Fawn, but when he felt the touch of Father Marcotte's hand on his arm, tears began to stream down his face.

The old man patted Beau's arm and whispered, "It may be sad for us but it isn't sad for Sister Mary Francis. She believed."

Beau didn't respond. What could he say? He envied her faith. Fawn had a rough childhood. She deserved the gift of unquestioning belief.

Beau's thoughts were interrupted by Father Marcotte's whisper. "It's a nice turnout, don't you think?"

The number of people in attendance reflected Fawn's life as Sister Mary Francis. Almost forty years ago, just before Beau left for New York, Fawn told him she was going to use the time allotted her by God to do His work. She had lived a quiet life of devotion. Her days were spent in prayer and in helping those in need.

More than two hundred people had come to honor her. It was a large crowd for a small town. Most were local, working-class people. Several were Native Americans and a few were well-dressed out-of-towners. The locals must have wondered who the strangers were and why they had come to this remote village in Northern Michigan to attend the funeral of a modest nun. The out-of-towners stood together in an irregular line.

Bobby Cunningham and his younger sister, Janet, stood to Beau's right. With her brown eyes and wide bright smile, Janet was still beautiful at sixty-two. She had the erect posture of an athlete and her black silk suit complemented her graceful body.

Robert L. Cunningham, Senior United States Senator from the State of Michigan was a big man with the body of a former University of Michigan football player. He worked out every morning in the Senate gym.

When Janet called her brother with the news of Fawn's death, Bobby said he would fly from Washington, D.C. to Harbor Springs to attend the funeral. Janet said she knew he was busy with the Armed Services Committee hearings, and he could just send flowers. Bobby replied that he would leave Washington as soon as possible and would be in Harbor

Springs within forty-eight hours. It wasn't for a woman he hardly knew, it was for Beau, he explained.

Bobby gently returned the telephone to its cradle and called through his open office door. "Beth, would you please get me Eddie in Los Angeles?" No last name was necessary. The senator's executive assistant had Eddie on speed dial.

Eddie said his company had a twelve-passenger jet on its way home from New York. He'd have the pilot swing by D.C. and give Bobby a ride to Harbor Springs.

Eddie Bartucci, Chairman of the Board of Bartucci Natural Foods, arrived at the Harbor Springs airport fifteen minutes before Senator Cunningham's flight from Washington touched down. Eddie had flown in the corporate jet from Los Angeles. Under his leadership, Bartucci Foods had grown from a family-owned Michigan supermarket chain into the largest retailer of organic foods in North America. In 1995, he moved the corporate headquarters from Detroit to Los Angeles.

Eddie stood next to Bobby and Janet. He was trim and tan. His Italian suit was beautifully tailored and his grey hair was dyed jet black. He looked like an actor central casting would select to play the role of an important executive from LA.

To Eddie's right was twenty-nine-year-old, blonde-haired Keri Ann Bartucci, his fourth wife. Beau, always one to appreciate a beautiful woman, allowed his eyes to linger on her shapely form for a moment too long and Eddie noticed. Beau was embarrassed, but Eddie flashed his professionally whitened teeth in a licentious grin and winked.

When the service concluded, Bobby Cunningham gathered Eddie, Beau, and Janet into his powerful arms for a hug. He said, "We could all use a stiff drink. Let's go to my cottage. Bring Father Marcotte along."

Beau held the old priest's elbow to assist him in navigating the few yards of soggy ground separating the cemetery from the parked cars. The old man spoke quietly to him. "I see Mr. Bartucci has arranged for an automobile. Can I ride to the cottage with you?"

Beau slid behind the wheel of his silver Mercedes while Father Marcotte settled into the passenger seat and made a half turn to face him.

At sixty-two, Beau was five feet, ten inches tall and slim. His full head of stylishly cut grey hair contrasted with his light-brown skin and dark eyes. The drive to the Cunningham cottage would cover seventeen miles along country roads. There was plenty of time for conversation. In the Indian manner, Beau waited quietly for the old man to speak.

"Fawn didn't leave a will. She asked me to see that all of her worldly possessions go to the church. Does that meet with your approval?"

"Of course it does, and I'd like to add a contribution of my own. I'll write a check when we get to the cottage."

"That's generous of you, Beau. Thank you very much."

"I'm the one who should give thanks … I can never repay you for everything you've done for me."

The old priest acknowledged Beau's words with a smile, as he produced a battered leather journal. "I have something for you. It's a history of your people, at least the Native American branch of your people. I've been collecting stories for a long time. Some of it came from records kept by the French priests and fur traders, but most is from conversations with old Odawa Indians. The stories have been handed down from one generation to the next, but those stories, like the old people, are disappearing. I'm not a real historian, but I'd like for you to have my journal."

Beau accepted the worn journal and placed it on the console between them. "This is a wonderful gift. Thank you."

Father Marcotte smiled and then appeared uncomfortable.

"What is it, Father?"

"It's about your mother."

There was a long pause. Beau waited patiently while his friend composed himself.

"I was a new priest in Harbor Springs when your mother stopped after Mass to speak with me. She was one of the most beautiful Odawa women I had ever seen and she told me about her unhappy marriage to a white man. She said her husband, John Lightfoot, was a bad man. You must remember that I was young. I believed we were all children of God and there was no such thing as a thoroughly bad man. I hadn't seen her husband at Mass, but she said he was Catholic. I asked her if John would come and speak with me, and she said she would try to persuade him."

Beau broke in. "What happened?"

"Nothing. He wouldn't do it. Ramona came to her priest for guidance, and I tried to help her. I counseled love, patience, and forgiveness. During the next three years we grew to become close friends."

Although now more than sixty years old, Beau still missed his mother. *He was eleven on the morning he woke up to discover she had disappeared. He asked where she was and what had happened but was only told she had run away. He was given no explanation of where she might be or when she would return.* It suddenly felt as if there wasn't enough air in the car. He lowered his window and felt a little better.

Father Marcotte continued. "There came a time when your mother walked into my study with the mark of John Lightfoot's fist on her delicate face."

Beau sat rigid but said nothing.

"Since Lightfoot wouldn't act like a civilized man and meet with his priest, I decided to go to your cabin. I expected to encounter a vile individual, but that wasn't the man I found. I arrived angry but left feeling sorry for him. He said he was very sorry he hit Ramona, but his remorse appeared to extend much further. He seemed to regret his whole life."

Beau couldn't avoid the memories. *His father regretted his whole life. Well, isn't that too damn bad? No one forced him to be a sadistic bully. John Lightfoot had made his own choices and caused a lot of people to regret his miserable life.*

The old priest continued with his story. "We sat at his kitchen table and talked for an hour. You and Fawn were in school. It was just the two of us. He seemed beaten down by poverty, menial jobs, and lack of respect. He said being a sergeant in the Army was the high point of his life." *Beau remembered his dad making everybody, even his wife and kids, call him Sarge. What a bunch of horse shit!* "He said he was going to do better. He asked to be forgiven and said he was going come to Mass every Sunday."

Beau shook his head in disbelief. "I don't think he actually did it."

"He did come to Mass ... for a few weeks. Time went by. Things got better and then got worse. One day, your mother came to my study with her eyes swollen from crying and her lower lip split. Sarge had come home from work, found she had not fixed his supper, and punched her in the face." *Beau remembered that fight and many others.* Father Marcotte was still talking. "I told Ramona I would talk with him again and insist that he treat her with respect. As she left my study, she hesitated in the doorway and turned back to look at me. She said, 'Father pray for me.' "That was the last time I saw your mother. Lightfoot said she had run off, but I didn't believe his story. Only God and John Lightfoot know what really happened."

Beau inhaled a great breath. "Do you think he murdered my mom?"

"I think he killed her by accident. A couple of hard blows from a big man like Sarge could have been fatal. He was probably drunk when it happened. I doubt he intended to kill her. I think he got scared, buried her body in the woods, and told people she had run away." The old man began to sob. "I never believed she ran away and left you and Fawn."

Beau nodded but was unable to speak. He gathered himself and straightened his shoulders. "Do you remember the day Fawn and I came to you? You took us in your arms and made a home for us at Holy Childhood Indian School. You saved our lives. That's part of the story. Don't forget that part."

Father Marcotte managed a smile. "I'll never forget the morning you and Fawn showed up at my front door. You were the most bedraggled kids I had ever seen. I wanted to give you something, but the only thing I had was some hot coffee. I poured a cup and offered it to you. You looked at it and started laughing. I thought it was a strange reaction. Do you remember that?"

Beau remembered everything. The shack where he and Fawn had lived with Sarge was only a few miles north of where he and Father Marcotte now sat, talking.

Half an hour later, they drove into Bobby Cunningham's driveway. The neighboring cottages were still boarded-up for the winter, but Bobby had had people open up his place. They had removed the shutters, turned on the water, and put the elegant old house in shape to receive guests. The shaded green lawn sloped toward the shore of Little Traverse Bay. Beau thought it was just as beautiful today as it was more than half a lifetime ago when he was one of the boys hired to mow the grass and trim the hedges.

The dock had been taken out of the water to avoid being crushed by the winter ice and it was resting on the shore in sections. Beau remembered being seventeen years old and sitting on the end of that dock with Janet Cunningham. They would stay there for a long time, legs almost touching, swinging their feet back and forth with their toes grazing the surface of the water. He'd always liked that dock.

As he looked at the cottage, the bay, the dock, and all of the familiar things from when he was young, Beau felt unready to go inside and be with people. "Father, I'm going to sit by the lake for a few minutes. Please go inside. I won't be long."

The water in the bay was quiet. Beau sat comfortably on a flat stone with his back against a large tree. He thought about Fawn and everything that had happened. After a while, he opened the old priest's journal and began to read.

A CUP OF COFFEE

In the spring of 1742, the Odawa Tribe moved 200 warriors and their families from Michilimackinac sixteen miles south to establish a settlement at Cross Village. From the shore of Lake Michigan for about 100 yards, the land was level before it reached a steep bluff. This area provided space for lodges and gardens. Lake Michigan provided fish and the forest provided game. The Odawa kept some furs for their own needs but most were used for trade. The meat was eaten. Nothing was wasted. Bear fat was particularly prized. It was fried down into oil for cooking and for an emollient which gave one's skin a beautiful shine. The bark of the birch trees was used to make canoes. Maple trees provided sap which was boiled down into maple syrup. A special treat was a meal of pancakes made from corn and beans pressed into cakes, fried in bear oil, and slathered with maple syrup.

Cross Village became the Odawa's second-largest settlement. Pontiac made regular visits to his northern brothers.

The shade provided by the tree had shifted and the sun was shining in Beau's eyes. He had lost track of time while reading most of Father Marcotte's journal.

The old Indian village must have been near where his dad had built their cabin. Beau had purposely forgotten the horrible things that had happened there. But he hadn't forgotten everything. Some memories were good. Beau remembered having a wonderful fantasy life as a boy, and especially enjoying listening to sports on the radio while imagining he was the hero playing in championship football games.

NEAR CROSS VILLAGE, 1959

The announcer was yelling into the microphone in order to be heard above the screaming crowd:

"*Less than twenty seconds remaining to play in the game ... The Big Ten Championship is on the line ... If Michigan fails to score, Ohio State wins it all ... The referee places the football just in from the near hash-mark on the Michigan forty-three-yard line ... Michigan breaks the huddle and lines up with flankers split both left and right ... There's the snap ... Kabaski drops back to pass ... He looks deep ... He pumps ... It's a fake ... He hands off to Beau Lightfoot, going around the right side ... He's got some room ... He's across mid-field ... He's at the forty ... Only one man left to beat ... Lightfoot fakes left and cuts right ... He's in the clear ... He's going all the way ... He scores! ... A fifty-seven-yard run by Lightfoot ... Thanks to Beau Lightfoot, Michigan is going to the Rose Bowl.*"

In his imagination, thirteen-year-old Beau heard the University of Michigan marching band playing "The Victors" as he ran through the woods, faking left, cutting right, and dodging between trees. The sound of the frenzied crowd screaming his name began to fade. He slowed to a jog and eased back to reality. He continued to jog for a few more yards before stopping to wait for his sister.

The school bus had dropped them off at their usual stop and they were walking along the narrow gravel road that ran through the birch and hardwood forest and down a steep bluff toward home. As she came toward him, his sister's step was so light she seemed to float above the ground rather than walk upon it. Her name was perfect. Brown-eyed and beautiful, fourteen-year-old Fawn Lightfoot moved softly through life. Like a deer, there was a delicacy and vulnerability about her. She needed the protection of someone who could be a hero, someone like Beau.

Beau did a lot of pretending. Their mother had been gone for more than two years and, as real life became increasingly unhappy, he spent more time in pretend life. Unlike Fawn, who tended to get mixed up, Beau knew the difference between real and pretend. He knew he had dark eyes and light-brown skin ... half Indian and half white. His mom was a full-blooded Odawa. He thought he might be handsome. His mother told him he was a beautiful boy, but he hadn't heard anything like that for a long time. His build was slight but he was strong. He was fast on his feet and proudly carried the seventh-grade track medal in his pocket.

As they approached their cabin, Beau got a sick feeling in his stomach. Dad was coming home. Tonight might be a bad night. His father acted like he thought he was some kind of a war hero. He seemed to love being called Sarge. A real war hero would take care of his children. Sarge hadn't been home since Monday morning. He'd been working overtime at the sawmill and stayed in town rather than traveling home each night. Today was Friday. He'd draw his pay and have a few drinks before coming home. He'd expect supper on the table when he walked in the front door of the cabin.

Sarge called it a cabin. Beau called it a shack. It was hunkered down in the woods, just back from the shore of Lake Michigan. No other houses were within sight. The natural setting with the level land near the shore; the high bluff; the pine, birch, and maple trees; and the clear, cold water of Lake Michigan would have been beautiful if his father had left things undisturbed. Instead, the wooden shack was unpainted, there was rusty junk strewn in the yard, and the outhouse sagged to its left.

Beau wanted to leave; get away from his dad. He had made plans to run away, but never followed through. He'd be okay. He was a smart kid. He'd figure a way to get along. The problem was Fawn. He couldn't leave his sister and he didn't see how they could survive on their own if he took her with him.

There was another problem that he didn't like to think about. He was scared. He hated being scared. Sometimes he missed his mother so much he felt like a baby. She left him because she had to. He had hidden under his bed covers late that night and heard the yelling and the crying and the sounds of blows being struck. She had run for her life and couldn't take her children with her. He understood.

Now, he was trapped. He had to take care of his sister. The shack was their only home. There was no choice but to make the best of things.

The first task was to make supper. There was almost nothing left to work with. By Wednesday night, they were down to some cornmeal and a few beans. Beau had to hoard these small reserves. For the last two days, neither he nor Fawn had eaten anything at home. They did eat while at school, though. Since Cross Village was too small to have its own school, they rode the bus to Harbor Springs. The Harbor Springs schools received food from the State of Michigan and provided free lunches for needy kids. The school was not able to provide free lunches every day and sometimes it was something Beau and Fawn didn't like. Regardless, they were grateful for the food. On Thursday, bread, peanut butter, honey, milk, and apples were served. Beau told Fawn to take as much of everything as the teachers would allow. Friday's lunch wasn't as good as Thursday's. There were hot dogs that had been warming in a pot of gray water and some unidentifiable mixed vegetables. He caught Fawn's eye to send her a silent message: "We have to eat anything we can get."

As the siblings entered the dark shack, late-afternoon sunlight filtering in through the grime-covered windows illuminated floating dust motes. The air was damp and smelled of defeat.

Beau turned on the one overhead light bulb. The inside of the shack appeared in splotches of light and shadow and a thin layer of dust covered every flat surface. There was only one room. There was a wood stove for cooking and heat. Two beds were shoved against the back wall. The double bed, in which Ramona and Sarge had slept together, was now used by Sarge. The single bed was shared by Beau and Fawn. He and Fawn shouldn't have to sleep together. Sarge said he would get another bed but never did.

Fawn gathered wood and Beau lit the stove. He mixed water with the cornmeal and put it on to boil. He found a lump of lard wrapped in wax paper that had been left in the back corner of the cupboard and added it to the beans as he put them in another pot to warm on the stove. It was the best he could do. There would be no supper for Fawn and he. There might be enough food to satisfy their dad.

Sarge liked to have bread with his meal. There was no bread. He liked to have coffee. There was no coffee. Nothing could be done about the lack of bread, but maybe Beau could make some coffee. He'd heard about people making coffee from acorns. Fawn gathered some acorns while he cleaned out the old metal coffeepot. If there was coffee to go with the cornmeal mush and the beans, the meal might be satisfactory.

Fawn returned with acorns and a bonus of some used coffee grounds she had found in the outside garbage can.

How the heck do you make acorn coffee? Beau was clueless. Should he dry the acorns, grind them up, or remove the shells and just use the meat, or remove the "little hats" and use the rest? Maybe using everything was the best idea ... beat the acorns with a hammer and pour water over the mashed acorns and used coffee grounds and put the whole mess on the stove to boil.

If the coffee wasn't good, Sarge would whip Beau with his wide leather belt. He had never whipped Fawn, but for the past few months Sarge had been looking at her in a funny way. Fawn said Sarge's look scared her more than a whipping.

Beau's worry about the coffee was interrupted by the crunch of work boots on the gravel path that led to the shack. There might be a way to avoid trouble. He told Fawn to get into bed and pretend to be asleep. She pulled the covers over her head just as Sarge walked through the door. His bulk filled the doorway and he staggered when he stepped over the threshold.

Beau tried a cheerful greeting. "Hi, Sarge. How are you?"

"I'm tired. I've been working like a dog to support you kids. Have you got my supper ready?"

"Yes, Sarge. I did the best I could with what we had. I hope you like it." Beau spooned the beans and cornmeal mush onto a plate and placed it on the lopsided kitchen table.

Sarge took a bite and made a sour face. "This stuff isn't fit for a man's supper. Don't we have any bread?"

"No. I'm sorry."

"You're sorry. I work myself to death to take care of you brats, and this is the thanks I get?"

Beau poured a large mug of coffee. "I made coffee. Would you like some?"

"Yeah. But first I'd like to have a drink. Get me my whiskey."

Beau brought the bottle to the table and put it down in front of his dad. Sarge took a look at the bottle and began yelling. "This bottle is almost empty. It was full the last time I saw it. You've been stealing my whiskey, you little bastard."

"No, sir. I didn't touch the bottle. It was like that. There was only an inch left in the bottom."

"Are you calling me a liar?"

"No, sir. I would never do that."

Sarge slowly pulled his big leather belt from the loops in his pants.

"No! Please, Sarge. Don't hit me."

Beau cowered and tried to become as small as possible. He was too old to cry, but if Sarge beat him with that belt, it would hurt so much he didn't think he could stand it.

"Well, for Christ's sake. I ain't even touched you and you're about to cry like a baby. You make me sick. But what the hell can I expect from you, with that whore you had for a mother?"

"Come on, Dad. Don't say that."

"Oh, no! Well, she was a whore, that's what! She was a bitch who ran off and left me to take care of you kids all by myself. And you ... you act like a goddamn crybaby. The way your mother whored around all the time ... some other guy's probably your father." He nodded his head in agreement with himself. "You act like a goddamn sissy. Beau's a sissy name. Your mother said it was French. Maybe it is French. She probably got it from that French priest she hung around with."

Sarge noticed a movement in the blankets on the single bed. "Fawn, I'll bet you thought I forgot about you."

Fawn replied in a timid voice, "Hi, Sarge."

"How come you're in bed, honey? Are you sick?"

Beau tried to catch Fawn's eye to give her a sign to just nod and to say she was sick. She missed his warning.

She said," I'm fine, Sarge."

Sarge walked over to the bed and sat on its edge. He pulled the blankets back and stroked her hair. "Yes, you are fine, Fawn. You're getting to be a fine-looking girl." He began to stroke her arms and shoulders. He undid the front of her blouse and ran his hands down her neck. The fact that Beau was standing a few feet away didn't appear to bother him at all.

Fawn choked out a whisper. "Sarge, please stop."

Beau couldn't breathe. He stood, holding the steaming mug of coffee he had offered Sarge a few minutes ago. Fawn was crying and Sarge was working his hands under her clothing. Beau approached the bed but had no idea what to do.

Sarge snarled. "Get the hell away from me!" When he bent back over Fawn, his shirt pulled out of the back of his pants. He wore his pants low and his lower back and part of the crack of his ass were revealed. The exposed skin was shockingly white, its color a stark contrast to his dirty work clothes and sun-darkened hands and face. He grunted and forced his hands down the front of Fawn's jeans.

Beau still hesitated. He'd imagined a lot of heroic adventures, but now he faced a real situation and he was afraid. If he was going to do anything it had to be now. Should he step back and protect himself or should he help his sister? Was being a hero nothing more than a childish fantasy?

He took a deep breath and moved closer to his father and struggling sister. His trembling hands still held the full mug of scalding acorn coffee. The mug seemed to move of its own accord. Beau poured the entire contents directly on Sarge's snow-white ass.

A POWERFUL WEAPON

Indians loved children. Every child was considered to be a child of the entire village. If parents died or were otherwise unable to provide for their children, a relative or another family in the village would take the children into their home. Within the Odawa Tribe, every child was highly valued. There were no unwanted or neglected children.

2013

Beau blinked and shook his head. Despite the passage of so many years, he remembered every detail of that awful night. He knew he should get up from his comfortable spot against the trunk of the big tree and go inside to be with his old friends in Bobby's cottage—but he decided to spend a little more time with his memories.

NEAR CROSS VILLAGE, 1959

When the full mug of scalding coffee hit his skin, Sarge screamed like a wounded animal. It was loud enough to disturb the Odawa warriors who had spent the past two hundred years resting peacefully in unmarked graves near the shack. Sarge released his hold on Fawn and continued to scream as the burning black liquid flowed down the crack of his ass.

Beau grabbed Fawn and they bolted through the door. They jumped down the three front steps and ran headlong down the gravel path away from the cabin. They had only gone a few strides when they heard the door behind them smash open so hard it came off of its hinges. Sarge bellowed and lunged after them. "Come back here, you little bastards! Stop! Goddamn it, you better stop right now!"

They ran in panic to the rocky shore of Lake Michigan. It was only six o'clock, but since it was late November in Northern Michigan, it was as dark as midnight. They turned left at the edge of the water and scampered over the slippery rocks. Sarge was bellowing and running after them, but he wasn't able to gain any ground. He was a grown man and he was drunk and stumbling; they had the agility of children.

The wind whipped the waves into whitecaps that broke against the shore. A full moon sliced through racing black clouds and then was immediately obscured. A light, cold rain and the lake water were beginning to form a thin coating of ice on the rocks. Beau grabbed Fawn's hand and pulled her along. "Run as hard as you can! He can't keep going. He'll quit."

The children struggled onward—and, in a few minutes, Beau noticed the quiet. He could hear the breaking waves and the wind but no sound from their father. Beau hoped Sarge had stumbled back to the shack and passed out. He stopped pulling on Fawn's hand and allowed their pace to slacken. Fawn trembled. She looked at him in terror and said, "What can we do? Where can we go?"

Beau put his arm around her narrow shoulders and whispered in her ear. "Fawn, it'll be alright. I know a place we can hide. We'll be out of the wind and rain. I'll take care of you."

They walked along the beach until they came to one of Beau's secret hideouts. A large oak tree grew on a low bank at the very edge of the forest. It was about twenty feet from the shoreline, where the woods ended and the sand began. The sandy bank under the tree had been undercut by high water, creating a little cave. The largest of the tree's roots remained, and the children squeezed into the hollowed-out area. It provided shelter from the wind and rain but not from the cold.

They sat against the back wall of the small cave. Fawn was shivering and softly moaning. Beau unbuttoned his flannel shirt and pulled her against his chest to allow her to share his body warmth and to be partly covered by his shirt. She snuggled against him. He stroked her hair and began to feel the tension leave her body. In a few minutes she was asleep. Beau was scared. He was supposed to be the strong one. He had no idea what to do and there was no one to help him.

How can I take care of her? We're freezing. There is no way to start a fire. No food. Nowhere to go. In the morning, Sarge will come after us. He'll be hungover and mean. I'll get a terrible whipping, and I can't stand to think what he'll do to Fawn.

Sitting with his sister's head against his chest, Beau was cold, hungry, and felt utterly alone. Without warning, a shadow fell across the entrance to the hideout. Beau held his breath. The shadow moved closer ... it was a man—but thankfully, not Sarge. Beau felt weak with relief and gasped, "Help! Can you help us?"

The man's voice was distinctive, calm, slow, and confident. "I have come to help you." He bent down, entered the little cave and sat cross-legged in front of Beau. A musky animal smell accompanied him. The visitor was an Indian, although he was unusually tall for an Indian and strongly built. He wore moccasins, fringed buckskin britches, and a fur vest. Tattoos of animals and various designs covered much of his exposed chest and arms, and his brown skin glistened with a thin coating of bear oil. His black hair was cut short and ornaments of beads and feathers hung from each ear lobe. An overwhelming aura of power and authority emanated from him. He fixed Beau with an unblinking gaze from eyes that were so dark they appeared black.

"Who are you?"

"I am Pontiac."

"Who?"

"Pontiac. Chief of the Ottawa Tribe; War Chief of the Great Algonquin Nation. Your mother was of my people. I am your Spirit Father. I will help you."

Beau recalled learning about a great war chief named Pontiac in school, but as far as he could remember, Pontiac had been dead for two hundred years.

"Is this a dream? Are you alive?" Beau said.

"I am no longer of the Earth world. I live in the Spirit world."

"Can you help us? Can you give us food? Blankets? Can you protect us from our dad?"

"I cannot do things in the Earth world, but I can share my wisdom. You can help yourself. You must always remember you are a son of Pontiac. The blood of The Greatest War Chief Who Ever Lived flows in your veins. You are no ordinary man."

"I'm only thirteen. I'm not a man at all!"

"You and Fawn are in trouble. There is no time for you to grow up. It is necessary for you to be a man."

"That's crazy! I'm not a man just because you say it."

"If you think of yourself as a man, you will be a man."

"I still think it's crazy—but let's say I really am a man. What I should do?"

"The person you call your father will wake up and come after you. Wherever you hide, he will find you. He wants to do to Fawn what a man does with a grown woman. This must not be allowed to happen. Fawn is delicate. If this thing happens, she will be lost."

Beau gasped, "Oh God! I know you're right. What can we do?"

Pontiac didn't seem particularly worried. "The solution is easy. Your father is passed-out now. Go back to the shack. Get a sharp knife from the kitchen and cut his throat."

Beau recoiled in horror. "No! Just cut my father's throat while he's asleep? No! I won't do it."

"It's not difficult. I've killed twenty-three men by my own hand—but, if you don't want to cut his throat, I have another idea."

"What?"

"Go to the lakeshore and find a big rock. Have Fawn help you lift it. Carry it to the shack before he wakes up and drop it on his head."

"No! It doesn't matter how it's done. I'm not going to murder anyone."

Pontiac appeared disappointed. "You're causing an easy thing to be difficult. Perhaps The Greatest War Chief Who Ever Lived should not waste his time with a boy like you." Pontiac sat thoughtfully for a moment, and then allowed a small smile to appear on his stern countenance. "There was a time when I got what I wanted by scaring people."

His smile spread and lit up his face, as if he was reflecting on a distant but very pleasant memory. "I think, if we do it properly, it can work ... You are willing to scare somebody, aren't you?"

Pontiac explained that the objective was not merely to scare their dad, but to instill a fear so profound that Sarge would never again dare to bother either Beau or his sister. Beau thought it was a ridiculous idea, but Pontiac sounded confident.

In order to be successful, Fawn's help was required. Pontiac said that an insane person was a potent source of fear. Fawn would be an actress. She would cry hysterically, scream that Beau had gone insane, and beg him not to kill Sarge. Pontiac said screaming and yelling alone would not be sufficient to create the abject terror he felt was necessary to scare Sarge. Beau had to do something to actually hurt his dad. Pontiac asked if there was a gun in the shack.

Beau said, "There is an old shotgun, but it can only shoot one shell without being reloaded."

Pontiac said the shotgun would be fine for his purpose. He revealed the rest of his plan and sat quietly, watching Beau. His black eyes asked, "Can you do it?"

Beau could only manage a whisper. "Yes, I can do it."

Without disturbing Fawn, Pontiac put his hand on Beau's shoulder. The hand felt warm and strong; the gesture of a loving father. Beau was surprised a spirit had physical substance. He was moved by the strong arm of his Spirit Father. With no more words, Pontiac got up, stepped between the tree roots at the entrance of the little shelter, walked to the shore of Lake Michigan, and disappeared.

The rain and wind had stopped. The shack was dark. Sarge must have turned out the oil lamp before he fell asleep. The children were hidden in the tall grass and shadows outside the front door of the shack. Fawn, who could move more quietly than Beau, crept inside and retrieved the shotgun; one shotgun shell; one of Sarge's long, wool, hunting socks; and an empty water glass.

Back at the shore, Fawn filled the glass with cold Lake Michigan water while Beau scooped six pounds of wet sand into the foot of the wool sock, packed it in tightly, and held it in place with a knot. He then broke open the breech of the shotgun, inserted the shell, and snapped it closed.

Everything was ready. Beau trembled as he looked at Fawn. She was steady and, for the first time in his life, it occurred to Beau that of the two of them, Fawn was braver. Or maybe she seemed brave because she didn't understand the risk. No. That wasn't it. Fawn knew the danger. Maybe she understood things better than he did. Maybe, in her mind, everything was clear. There was no longer a choice. She had to be brave.

Beau didn't feel brave. He was so scared that, for a few moments, he thought he might be having a heart attack. He whispered to Fawn, "Maybe we should say a prayer?"

If she felt fear, she kept it well hidden. "Beau, we'll say lots of prayers— after this thing is done."

They moved quietly into the shack. Beau saw Sarge's body in the dim light. He was sleeping in his easy chair, his head back, his mouth open, and he was breathing deeply and noisily. Fawn lit the oil lamp and the interior was immediately illuminated by an orange, flickering glow. She moved to stand beside Sarge and held the glass of ice-cold water above his face. She looked toward Beau and nodded.

He set the shotgun on the floor within easy reach, grasped the hunting sock with both hands, and whispered, "Okay."

Fawn threw the frigid water on Sarge's face and began to scream. His eyes flew open and he struggled to rise from the chair. Beau swung the sock with every bit of his strength. It made a wide arc. The six pounds of wet sand was traveling at a high speed when it struck the center of Sarge's chest. The sound was dull but solid, like a large telephone book being dropped on a bare table.

THWOCK!

The blow caused a reverberation through Sarge's body. He exhaled sharply and didn't seem able to move. Fawn was yelling that Beau had gone crazy and was going to murder him.

Pontiac's plan was for Beau to strike one blow with the sock to temporarily immobilize Sarge and then shoot off his ear with the shotgun. As Beau reached for the shotgun, Sarge raised himself on his left arm and said something. Beau couldn't understand and leaned closer. "What?" Beau said.

Sarge grabbed Beau's leg and croaked, "I'm gonna get you ..."
Beau swung the sock and brought it down on Sarge's left shoulder and the left side of his neck.
THWOCK!
He didn't hear any bones break but he could see that the blow hurt. "You're not gonna get anybody!"
Sarge was gasping, trying to say something, but unable to form the words. His mouth was opening and closing like a guppy. Beau swung the sock again and the heavy sand hit squarely against the right side of Sarge's head. At the moment of impact, he saw Sarge's head jolt to the side. Beau took another big swing and brought the sand down hard on Sarge's knee. It must have hurt a lot because Sarge moaned like a wounded animal. This was very satisfying.

Beau noticed the quality of Fawn's screaming had changed. No longer acting, she sounded sincerely panicked. "Beau, stop! STOP! You're killing him! Don't hit him again!"

He swung the sock above his head and aimed for the left side of Sarge's chest, just above the heart. Fawn grabbed her brother's arm and spoiled his power but the sand still hit with a resounding smack. From only two feet away, Fawn yelled into Beau's face, "That's enough! Do the other thing now and let's get out of here."

Beau dropped the sock and picked up the gun. Sarge was breathing in shallow gasps but he was conscious. His eyes bulged with fear. Beau placed the barrel of the shotgun along Sarge's left cheek and aimed at his ear. Fawn fell back into her acting role and began to cry and scream at Sarge that Beau had gone insane. She begged Beau not to kill Sarge; saying she was sure he would never bother them again if Beau only let him live. She was crying and moaning and begging. Beau thought it was an outstanding performance.

In spite of Pontiac's instructions, Beau had never intended to actually shoot off Sarge's ear. He moved the shotgun to point slightly away from the side of Sarge's head and pulled the trigger. The blast inside the enclosed space sounded and felt like an explosion. A four-inch flame erupted from the end of the barrel and an unimaginable BANG! smashed into Beau's eardrums. The room was immediately filled with the smell of cordite.

At first, Beau couldn't see Fawn through the smoke; then a movement caught his eye. She was heading out the door. He had one more job to do.

The left side of Sarge's head was covered with blood. Sarge was trying to scream, but wasn't making any sound. There shouldn't have been any blood. Beau had aimed away from the side of Sarge's head, but some of the shot must have raked his cheek and ear.

It was important to finish everything exactly as Pontiac had instructed. Beau moved close to Sarge's face, looked him in the eye, and spoke calmly. (Pontiac said speaking quietly would be more frightening than yelling.) "I'll let you live this time—but next time, I'll kill you. I'm taking the gun with me. If you ever come near either Fawn or me, I'll kill you."

Beau tucked the shotgun under his arm, turned, and, without haste, walked out of the shack and closed the door.

Fawn and Beau walked along the narrow gravel road as it climbed the bluff and wound through the familiar woods before meeting the larger road on which they had traveled by school bus hundreds of times. They planned to walk through the night and arrive at the Holy Childhood Indian School in Harbor Springs by morning. Pontiac said many Indian children boarded at the school and Father Marcotte would find places for them. Father Marcotte? Beau had a vague recollection of his mother speaking fondly of a French priest named Marcotte.

As they trudged along the deserted road, Beau's arms began to ache from the weight of the shotgun. He'd hurt Sarge. He could still feel the sand-filled sock smacking into the side of his head. It felt good. The mean old bastard was terrified. Beau had the power now. He was a son of the War Chief. Pontiac had told Beau to hit Sarge once, but he had continued to strike him again and again. If Fawn hadn't stopped him, he might have murdered Sarge.

He suddenly didn't want to keep the shotgun any longer. He stepped a few yards off the road and threw it over the edge of a deep ravine. Beau did not want to meet Father Marcotte with a gun in his hands.

THE ACCIDENT

An important factor in the survival of the Odawa Tribe was the tradition of individuals helping one another. Neither food nor belongings were held as private property. Labor and goods were always freely given to people in need.

Pontiac took pride in helping others. No task was too difficult. No request for help was ever denied.

2013

It was 7:30 p.m. The gentle weight of Father Marcotte's hand on Beau's arm roused him from his memories. He stood up and followed his old friend into Senator Cunningham's house to join the others for a few drinks in memory of his sister, who in her entire life had never touched a drop of liquor.

He thought about the first time he saw the Cunningham's graceful Victorian summer cottage. It must have been about five years after he began living at the Holy Childhood Indian School.

WEQUETONSING, 1964

Beau was cleaning weeds and dead leaves from the base of a short privet hedge. It was basic manual labor but it was outside work and he was happy to have the income. He had tried to get a job on the lawn crew the previous summer but they had turned him down. This year, Father Marcotte put in a word with one of his parishioners and the supervisor of the Wequetonsing Association lawn maintenance department called Beau to offer him a job.

The Wequetonsing Association or "Weque" as it was called by the *cottage* owners, rested on the north shore of Little Traverse Bay. As far back as anyone could remember it had been customary for Weque members to refer to their summer homes as *cottages*. Grand homes with six bedrooms, five bathrooms, and servants' quarters in the rear were called *cottages*.

Located near the northeast corner of Lake Michigan, Little Traverse Bay was five miles wide at its entrance and extended several miles inland before ending against a series of wooded sand dunes. Important families from the great Midwestern industrial cities of Detroit, Chicago, Cleveland, and St. Louis; as well as others from more distant places, spent July and August in Wequetonsing. They fled the oppressive heat and humidity of the cities for the blue waters, lush golf courses, clean air, and cool nights of Northern Michigan. They "summered" in grand white-frame houses situated on large sloping green lawns shaded by tall trees. There were artesian wells on some of the lawns and small streams flowed to the bay. Flowers lined the streams and sidewalks.

Maintenance of the lawns and gardens in this summer Eden fell to Beau and his fellow workers. In addition to their duties of pruning, mowing, trimming, raking, watering, and sweeping the crew was trained to observe proper relations with the Weque people. *Say hello. Smile. Be polite. Respond when addressed but otherwise be quiet. Do your work in an unobtrusive manner.*

Of course, the invisible workers gossiped about the Weque people. Beau heard that the cottage next to where he was weeding was owned by the Cunningham family from Bloomfield Hills. Mr. Cunningham was an executive with General Motors. There were two kids about Beau's age. His fellow lawn workers said the boy was a big bull of a guy and the girl was skinny and kind of good-looking. Beau, on his knees cleaning around the base of the privet hedge, could not have imagined the Cunningham's influence on his life.

As he continued to work, his thoughts were interrupted by the sound of people coming out of the Cunningham's front door. He was on the side of the hedge away from the house and could observe the family through the small branches.

It was fun to spy on the owners. Two boys were setting up lawn chairs in the front yard. One guy was more than six feet tall and very muscular. He had a brush cut and was wearing a tank top to show off his powerful physique. Beau leaned to his left to get a better view. The fellow was so solidly built that he didn't seem to have a neck. His head sat on a triangle of muscle that began at his ears and sloped down to his shoulders. There was something unusual about him but Beau couldn't determine what it was. A woman came out of the house with a pitcher of iced tea. She called the boy Bobby and asked him to get a small table for the pitcher.

When Bobby returned outside with the table, Beau got a good look at his face and realized what was unusual about him. Bobby Cunningham had the body of a strong man and the face of a young boy. He had a sweet smile.

The woman offered some iced tea to the other boy who was helping with the lawn chairs. Bobby called him Eddie and sat down next to him.

Beau pretended to clean around the hedge while secretly observing the people. The woman must be Mrs. Cunningham. The big guy was Bobby Cunningham and Eddie must be his friend.

Nothing much happened for twenty minutes. They sat in the shade, drank iced tea, and talked. Beau turned his attention back to clearing debris from the base of the hedge when a commotion caused him to look up.

Two girls in tennis dresses bounded down the front steps. There was excited talk about the tennis tournament at the Little Harbor Club. Mrs. Cunningham gave the girls glasses of iced tea and everyone sat down. One of the girls was shapely, blonde, and bouncy. They called her Pinkey. *The other girl must be the Cunningham's daughter. She's the one the guys described as being kind of good-looking.* Her name was Janet. She was tall for a girl and had soft, light-brown hair that she pulled back into a ponytail. Her eyes were dark and her smooth skin was lightly tanned. Her short tennis dress revealed a great deal of her long, graceful legs. To Beau, this girl was a heck of a lot more than skinny and kind of good-looking.

There was something about her that struck him hard. (Even years later, he wasn't able to say exactly what it was.) Maybe it was the way she stood and the confident way she walked. Janet had the easy movement of a natural athlete. But, perhaps, it was something else. Maybe it was the way the summer sun brought out a few freckles on her cheeks and nose. Maybe it was her quick laugh and wide, bright smile.

Beau had to catch his breath. He hid behind the hedge and tried to pull himself together. When he looked up, he saw a man, most likely Mr. Cunningham, walk out of the house and hand a football to Eddie. Janet got two younger boys from the cottage next door. Sides were chosen for a game of touch football. There was one big boy, one girl, and one little boy on each team.

Beau, "the invisible man," watched through the base of the hedge. What a scene. This beautiful place. This family. These young people running and playing and laughing. He wanted to stay and watch but it was time to go home. Actually, it was past quitting time and he was the only yard boy still working. He had to leave right away or he wouldn't be invisible.

Beau lived in a small room with a cot, a table, and a chair at the Holy Childhood Indian School—but he wouldn't be able to stay there much longer. Everyone was required to leave at age sixteen. Beau was seventeen, but Father Marcotte had arranged for him to work at the school and continue to live there until he finished his senior year at Harbor Springs High School. The two-mile walk from the lawn maintenance tool shed to his home at Holy Childhood felt lonely. He couldn't get the Cunningham family out of his mind.

The next morning, Beau walked through the village of Harbor Springs and along the shore of Little Traverse Bay on his way to work. It was a beautiful morning, but he didn't notice. He was still thinking about the Cunninghams and wishing he was part of a family. He felt like he didn't really belong anywhere.

As he walked, he heard the soft sound of moccasins. There was an unmistakable aroma of bear oil. Chief Pontiac was walking beside him. Beau was anxious to speak with his Spirit Father but, as was proper for a young man dealing with a great chief, he waited for Pontiac to speak.

Pontiac made a small gesture toward the bay and said, "Let's sit by the shore." After they were seated, he continued. "I am going to provide you with some rules to help you along the path of your life. I thought you might forget my rules if I gave them to you all at one time. I've given you only one rule, and I see you have already forgotten it."

Beau didn't understand. "What did I forget?"

Pontiac fixed him with a stern look. "I told you to always remember you are not an ordinary man. You are a son of The Greatest War Chief Who Ever Lived. You must not walk around with your head down, feeling sorry for yourself. That is my first and most important rule. Do you promise never to forget it again?"

"Yes. I promise."

"Good. Now lift your head and open your eyes. Look at the beautiful world you have been given."

Beau looked around. It was seven o'clock on a cool summer morning. Everything was still and clear. The sky was a soft blue. The water of the bay was perfectly smooth. From where he sat with Pontiac, Beau could see Harbor Point, a finger of wooded land that curved about three quarters of a mile into Little Traverse Bay to form the natural harbor for the village of Harbor Springs. Large summer homes lined the shore on the point's quiet harbor side and its unsheltered Lake Michigan side. The Coast Guard maintained a sturdy, brick lighthouse at the end of the point. Harbor Point was suspended in the air. The clear, smooth blue of the water merged into the soft, clear blue of the sky. They were as one. There was no place where the water ended and the sky began. The point wasn't an ephemeral thing that might easily float in the air. Harbor Point was heavy. No matter. The trees, the sandy shore, the big houses, and the brick lighthouse floated in the early morning sky.

Both Beau and Pontiac sat silently for a few minutes. Beau looked with wonder at the water and the sky and the floating point of land.

Pontiac spoke in a quiet voice. "My second rule is to always experience and appreciate the natural world. Draw strength and peace from it. God's world is all around you. It's there for everyone—but most people don't see it." Pontiac paused and fixed his dark eyes on Beau.

Beau said, "Yes, I understand. The first two rules are to remember who I am and to appreciate God's beautiful world."

Pontiac gave a nod of satisfaction. "Good. The third rule is also important: If a person asks for your help, you must give it. It makes no difference how difficult the task is. If asked, you will give."

"Will the person I help, help me when I need it?"

"He will help you or he will not help you. You can only control your own actions."

Beau looked quizzical. "These rules ... are they like the Ten Commandments or something like that?"

Pontiac took a moment before replying. "During my time in the Earth world, the French priests spoke to me about the Ten Commandments. I respected the priests and listened carefully but I don't think the commandments are meant for Indians." Pontiac continued. "The three rules, which I have given, are to help you live a good life. There are a few more. I don't have ten but you probably wouldn't be able to remember that many."

"I'll never forget."

The place where Pontiac had been sitting next to Beau was empty. A breeze created small ripples in the water. The sky and the water were no longer one. The wooded point of land still protected the harbor but it was no longer floating in the air.

Beau stood and continued walking to work.

The work day seemed to last forever. Finally, at exactly 5:01 p.m., Beau was on his way to the Cunningham cottage. When he got there, he noticed one leaf at the base of the privet hedge, and dropped to his knees to pick it up and to spy on the Cunninghams. Everything appeared unchanged from the previous day. Mrs. Cunningham, Bobby, Janet, Pinkey, and Eddie were sitting on lawn chairs, drinking iced tea, and talking.

Soon Mr. Cunningham walked down the front steps with a martini in his hand and a football under his arm. Janet ran next door. It seemed like it was going to be a replay of yesterday.

As Beau, the invisible man, watched from behind the hedge, Janet returned with only one boy and said, "Dickey has gone home to Chicago. We're a man short."

Eddie said, "We need one more person to have even sides for a game."

Bobby looked toward Beau. "There's a kid over there, working on the hedge. Maybe we can get him to play."

Janet looked at Beau and shrugged. "Sure. Why not? I'll ask him." She took a couple of steps toward Beau before being brought up short by her father's loud voice. "Jesus Christ, Janet. Don't invite the help to play games. Try to remember who the hell you are."

She gave her father a look of disgust. "Oh, Dad. That is such bullshit. I know very well who I am and I'm old enough to make my own decisions."

Mr. Cunningham turned to his wife and muttered something. Whatever it was, it didn't appear to bother Janet. She walked right up to Beau and said, "Hi."

A shiver of electricity ran up Beau's spine. He straightened up and said, "Hello."

"We need another guy for touch football. Do you want to play?" said Janet.

It was difficult for Beau to speak. After a moment, he finally stammered, "No— I— I can't play. I'm the yardman."

Janet smiled.

Oh my God, she has a beautiful smile, thought Beau.

"That's silly," she said. "You're no yardman. You're a kid, just like us. Come on, let's play some football."

I'd like to play. It'll be like the pictures I saw in Life *magazine: the Kennedy family playing touch football on the lawn of their beautiful summer home in Massachusetts. It'll be just like that: a large, shaded front lawn with the Kennedys playing touch football with their friends ... No, it won't. It'll be like the Kennedy kids playing football with their lawn boy. I'm wearing dark-green work pants and a matching green shirt.*

"I can't play."

"Why the heck not? We need another player."

"These clothes. I can't play in these clothes."

Janet laughed. "Is that all? We've got a few things you can wear. You can do a quick change in the garage. Okay?" She reached out her hand. "Come on."

Janet Cunningham touched him. She took Beau's hand and pulled him toward the garage. Then she let go of his hand and headed for the house while calling back over her shoulder, "I'll get a pair of shorts and a T-shirt for you to wear."

What could she find to fit him? Bobby was twice his size. The other guy wasn't as large as Bobby but he still outweighed Beau by fifty pounds.

Before he had time to worry, Janet came bounding into the garage with shorts and a T-shirt. He took them and stood awkwardly until she left the garage and closed the door. They fit quite well. He walked out of the garage and into his new life, wearing a white T-shirt and a pair of maroon shorts with "Kingswood – Field Hockey" neatly stenciled on the left thigh.

It wasn't much in the way of an actual football game. There was a lot of running around and falling down and laughing. Afterward, they sat on the grass to rest and talk.

Janet told Beau they played touch football almost every afternoon. She said they were going to need him to even out the teams and invited him to come over after work.

Their games usually ended around six o'clock. They would sit on the lawn and talk for fifteen or twenty minutes and then the Cunningham family and their guests would go inside to "dress for dinner." Beau would walk back to Holy Childhood.

After a week of this routine, there was a change. Bobby didn't go into the house with the others. Instead he asked Beau if he would stick around for a few minutes to spot him while he lifted. Beau had no idea what that meant but said, "Sure."

Beau followed Bobby around the house to the backyard. There were dumbbells sitting on the grass. A heavy barbell was held by vertical stands on either side of a narrow bench. "These are nice," Beau said. "They look brand-new."

"Yeah," Bobby replied. "My dad bought them for me when we came up to the cottage for the summer. I've got a set at home and another set at school."

"Why do you have so many?"

"Dad wants me to have weights available wherever I am." Bobby spoke as if it was the most logical thing in the world.

Beau replied, "I see."

"Eddie usually spots me, but he's getting ready for the Friday night dinner dance at the Little Harbor Club."

"Is he taking Janet?"

"No. He's taking Pinkey."

Beau knew it was absurd, but he felt relieved. "I thought Janet was his girlfriend. She seems to really like him."

"Of course, she likes him—but not in the way you mean. We know each other too well for that stuff. Eddie has been my best friend since we were little kids, and Janet always did everything with us. We're all too close for any girlfriend or boyfriend business. Eddie doesn't need any more girlfriends. Every girl he meets falls in love with him."

Bobby went over to the bench and positioned himself underneath the barbell. "Come on over and spot me."

"What should I do, Bobby? I've never done this."

"This lift is called a bench press and I really need a spotter for this one. On the other lifts, if I can't hold the weight, I can drop it on the ground. On this one, I'd be dropping the barbell on my chest.

"Stand at the end of the bench by my head. I'm going to lift the barbell off of the brackets and pump it up and down. If my arms start to shake and it looks like I can't hold the weight, you grab the barbell and help me get it back on the brackets. Got it?"

"Yeah, I think so."

Bobby laughed. "Good … because if you screw up, this thing will probably crush my chest."

He began to pump the barbell up and down. Each time he raised the weights, he let out a sharp exhale of breath. "FOOF three … FOOF four … FOOF five … FOOF six …" Bobby's upper body was glistening with sweat. His arm and shoulder muscles strained and his face grimaced with determination.

A voice came from behind the boys. "Hey, powerhouse, how's it going?"

Janet had broken the spell. She walked over to Bobby and patted his bicep. "Very impressive. If I ever need somebody to leap over a tall building in a single bound, I'll know who to call."

She turned to Beau. "Tomorrow is Saturday, sailboat races. No touch football. Bobby and Eddie are racing. I'm going to sit on the end of our dock and watch the races. You don't have to work on Saturday, do you?"

"Just a half day. I'm off in the afternoon."

"Why don't you come by about three o'clock and watch the races with me?"

I can't think of anything more boring than sitting on a dock and watching a sailboat race. It's impossible to tell who's winning and who's losing. But, Janet asked me. Of course I'll come. If she asked me to sit with her to watch the paint dry on her house, I'd be thrilled.

The next afternoon, Beau found Janet sitting on the end of the narrow wooden dock that extended eighty feet into the bay from the shore in front of the Cunningham's cottage. The dock was painted white and someone had placed pots of red geraniums at ten-foot intervals along its length. The end of the dock was only about two feet above the water; Janet was dangling her feet in the cool bay. She patted the spot next to her. "Sit down and put your feet in the water. It's really nice."

It was more than nice to sit next to Janet. She was wearing a pair of red short shorts that exposed so much of her lovely smooth thighs that Beau quickly looked away. Her feet were swinging back and forth, just grazing the surface of the lake. Her light-brown hair had been fluffed up, combed back, and held in place with a headband that matched her shorts. Her skin had a faint aroma of spring flowers. They sat in companionable silence for several minutes before Beau decided he should try to start a conversation. What the heck could he say to a girl like Janet? Nothing came to mind, but he couldn't sit there forever like rock. He took a deep breath. "Bobby told me you've been friends with Eddie for years."

"Yeah. The Bartuccis are our neighbors in Bloomfield Hills."

"That's his last name ... Bartucci?"

"Yeah. You've heard of the Bartucci Supermarkets? It's the largest grocery chain in southern Michigan."

Beau, of course, had not heard of Bartucci Supermarkets, but he was determined to hold up his end. "Oh sure, that Bartucci."

There was another lull in the conversation. Beau looked from his seat at the end of the dock back toward the Cunningham cottage. "Your family has a beautiful place."

"Thanks. We're very fortunate. My dad does everything for us. He has a tough-guy act and he can be a pain in the neck, but I have to give him credit. He started with nothing and now he's Vice President and General Manager of Pontiac."

Beau wasn't ready for that one. "He's general manager of what?"

"Pontiac. He's the General Manager of the Pontiac Division of General Motors."

"Oh."

"Anyway, the trouble with Dad is that he takes himself and Bobby much too seriously. I figure that's why he needs a loving daughter … to tease him and bring him back down to Earth."

Her gently swinging leg brushed against Beau's. She was talking about her family and her father's obsession with Bobby becoming a football star at the University of Michigan. She said Bobby and Eddie were taking an extra year of high school at a private prep school in Maryland. Beau tried to listen.

Her legs continued to slowly swing back and forth, with her red polished toenails sometimes barely touching the surface of the water and sometimes just missing. When they did touch, they created little rings that radiated outward into wider and wider circles, and then gradually disappeared. Janet must have noticed his lack of concentration because she let her leg swing to the side and gave him a gentle kick. "Tomorrow is my birthday. We're going to have a beach party. I want you to come. Meet us at the cottage tomorrow night about nine o'clock."

~

The next afternoon, Beau took some of his lawn maintenance earnings and walked into the village of Harbor Springs. His first stop was Rosenthal's Dry Goods. The eighty-year-old sales lady's technique was to "get all over" a customer as soon as he walked through the front door. She greeted Beau with her customary, "May I help you?"

Beau wanted assistance. "Mrs. Gridley, would you help me pick out an outfit to wear to a beach party with some kids at Wequetonsing?"

A few minutes later, he left with a pair of casual pants, a shirt, a sweater, and Mrs. Gridley's assurance that his new outfit would be appropriate for the beach party.

His next stop was Hovey Drugs, where he selected the nicest box of chocolates in the store. With shopping now complete, he began to walk back to Holy Childhood to get ready for Janet's party. There was plenty of time. He strolled down Main Street, enjoyed the beautiful summer day, and thought about Janet.

Beautiful, rich, Janet Cunningham is being friendly to me. Why? She acts as if she really likes me. But, she's a friendly, confident girl who appears to like everybody. It's probably nothing more than that. Her father certainly doesn't approve of her socializing with me. Is she paying attention to me in order to defy her dad? She goes to a fancy private school. Maybe the teachers at a place like that tell the girls it's their duty to be kind to people with brown skin. Who knows? Janet Cunningham is the most wonderful girl I've ever known. I can't understand what the heck she sees in me, but she seems to like me. I guess I'll go back to Holy Childhood and get ready for the party.

At nine o'clock, Beau walked up to the Cunningham cottage with the box of chocolates in his hand. There were about twenty people standing on the front porch. Most were kids he had seen around Weque but he did not know them. Janet ran up to him, accepted the chocolates, and said, "That's so sweet of you." Then she gave Beau a quick kiss on his cheek.

Before he could recover from the shock of her kiss, she pointed to the driveway. "Look at what Mom and Dad gave me for my birthday." It was a bright-red Pontiac convertible with tan leather seats. Janet squealed," What are we waiting for? Let's go!"

She jumped behind the steering wheel. Bobby got in beside her and Pinkey, Eddie, and Beau piled into the backseat. The other kids climbed into four other cars and everyone headed toward the deserted Lake Michigan beach north of town. When they arrived, they built a big fire and spread blankets on the sand. Although no one was old enough to legally drink, there were several cases of cold beer. They sat around the fire, roasted marshmallows, sang songs, and drank. Mostly they drank.

Beau did not drink. Father Marcotte had warned him that alcohol was poison to Indians. The white kids from Wequetonsing apparently received no similar warnings and were downing bottles of beer as if there was no tomorrow. Bobby was already tipsy. He suggested a drinking game called Indian signs. Then he looked at Beau, "No offense, man."

Beau assured Bobby he was not offended. He sat beside the fire and looked around. Everyone was getting drunk. Some couples were lying on blankets and passionately kissing. There were several attractive girls. One of them, her name was Lucy or Louise, sat down next to Beau. She sat very close. *She'd probably let me kiss her*, thought Beau. It was tempting but he couldn't do it. He wasn't going to kiss a girl in front of Janet.

Janet was sitting on the other side of the bonfire. She was talking with her friends, laughing, and going through bottles of beer at a prodigious rate. He imagined walking over to her. He would casually sit down next to her and ease his arm around her. He would gently turn her face toward him and kiss her sweet lips.

As Beau was enjoying his tender thoughts, she actually turned and looked in his direction. He immediately looked away. He could have secret wishes, but for a boy like him to do it, to actually kiss Janet Cunningham, was unthinkable.

The party was on a wide sandy beach. The sky was clear and the stars appeared to hang close to Earth. There was a full moon and the tall pine trees cast shadows in the moonlight. Beau followed Pontiac's rule and appreciated the natural beauty.

Since Beau was the only kid not drinking, the party was becoming tiresome. One of the boys said he heard a new song that was really excellent. It was something about a hermit named Dave who saved money by keeping a dead whore in his cave. Beau thought it was disgusting. The boy said there were ten verses but he couldn't remember the words. He overcame this minor hurdle by singing loudly and repeating the first verse over and over again.

Beau was wondering how much longer the party was going to last when Eddie staggered up to him and said, "The beer is all gone. Let's go home. Help me round up everyone."

Eddie, Bobby, Beau, and Janet met at Janet's car but they couldn't find Pinkey. Bobby said, "I think Pinkey is down on the beach making out with George Watson." Janet's head appeared to be loosely attached to her neck. She attempted to say something but nobody could understand her.

Eddie said, "Pinkey will be okay. George will bring her home." He made a quick appraisal of Bobby and Janet and said, "Beau, we're all smashed. You drive."

"I can't drive."

"What do you mean, you can't drive? You're cold sober."

Beau was embarrassed to admit he couldn't drive a car—but he wasn't able to think of a believable excuse. "I mean that I can't drive. I don't know how to drive a car."

"You're seventeen. Don't you have a driver's license?"

"No."

"How do you get around?"

"I walk."

Eddie shook his head in disbelief. "No shit. That's a bummer. Well, fuck. Bobby, you drive. Big son of a bitch like you can probably hold more beer than any of us. I'll sit in the front seat and make sure you stay awake. You guys, get in the back."

The road along the lakeshore was narrow with a lot of curves and bumps. Bobby drove slowly and cautiously. A car sped right up to their rear bumper and flashed its lights. The car blew its horn and cut around Bobby. Two boys leaned out of the windows, gave Bobby the middle finger, and shouted, "WHERE'D YOU LEARN TO DRIVE? GET OFF THE ROAD, ASSHOLE!"

Eddie slapped the flat of his hand on the dashboard. "BOBBY! RUN THOSE BASTARDS OFF THE ROAD AND WE'LL BEAT THE LIVING SHIT OUT OF THEM! ... LET'S GET 'EM!"

Bobby stomped on the gas pedal and the rear tires spewed gravel as Janet's new car accelerated.

It happened within the first two minutes.

They come over a small rise at high speed. The road in front of them made an easy left turn before it narrowed at the point where Five Mile Creek crossed under it in a large culvert.

Bobby touched the brakes and they slew around the left turn then he stomped on the accelerator. An instant later, there were headlights from an approaching automobile and he slammed on the brakes. The cars converged right at the spot where the road narrowed. Bobby tried to squeeze between the oncoming car and the drop-off into the creek. They nearly made it. The front wheels cleared but the back end of the car fishtailed. The back left side, where Janet was sitting, smashed into the front of the oncoming car. They spun off the road, down the bank, and into Five Mile Creek.

The first thing Beau noticed was the quiet. There had been the blare of horns, the squeal of brakes, the rat-a-tat of gravel, and the awful crash. Now, there was only silence. He was lying with his legs in the cold water of the creek and his head was in a patch of wild mint growing in black soggy mud. There was blood dripping down his face from a cut on his head. He might be okay. He struggled to his feet. Five Mile Creek was five miles from town.

What about his friends? Maybe they needed help right now. He heard someone yelling.

"Beau, you okay?" It was Eddie.

"Yeah."

"Help me get Bobby out of the car."

The car was resting at a steep angle on its side with the hood in the creek and the rest of it on the bank. Bobby was wedged behind the steering wheel. Eddie and Beau pulled on his arms and shoulders and worked his body back and forth until he came free. He was breathing and they couldn't see any injuries, but he wasn't responsive. Eddie and Beau dragged Bobby to a level spot and stretched him out on his back. Eddie took off his jacket and put it over Bobby's chest.

While Eddie covered Bobby, Beau looked for Janet. It was too dark to see much. "Janet ... Janet, where are you? Can you hear me?"

"Beau. Over here. I'm hurt. Help me. Over here."

Beau rushed to her side. Her face was covered with blood and her left arm was bent at a sickening angle. He knelt beside her but didn't know what to do. Eddie came up next to him. Beau heard police sirens in the distance.

Janet let her head settle on the ground and closed her eyes. Eddie put a hand on Beau's shoulder. "This is serious trouble. They'll charge Bobby with drunk driving and causing an accident. That's mandatory jail time. It'll ruin his life. Our dreams of playing ball together will never come true. Bobby will go to prison. It'll destroy his family. You've got to help. We'll say you were driving. You haven't had anything to drink. It will be much less serious for you than it would be for Bobby. Will you do it?"

The sirens were getting closer.

"Please, Beau. Do it for Bobby. Do it for his family."

"I didn't cause this. I don't want to lie to the police. It's not fair to put the blame on me."

"I know it's a hell of a lot to ask, but I'm asking for Bobby because he can't ask for himself. I wouldn't ask at all if I could see any other way out of this mess. Please, Beau. Please say you were driving. Please say you'll help. Do it for Janet."

Beau closed his eyes. He took a deep breath and tried to think—but his panicked mind felt out of control. He held a small birch tree for support and blinked a couple of times. *"If a person asks for your help, you must give it. It makes no difference how difficult the task. If asked, you will give."*

Beau answered, "Yes, I was driving."

Eddie said, "I'll tell Bobby. You tell Janet."

The police car and the ambulance were arriving. Beau bent down to Janet. He wasn't sure if she was conscious but he whispered in her ear. "Bobby wasn't driving. I was driving."

As the police and paramedics scrambled down the bank toward them, Janet opened her eyes and nodded.

~

On the way to the police station, Beau listened to the deputy talk on the radio with the sheriff. Static distorted the sheriff's replies but Beau could understand the deputy. *"Auto accident with injuries ... two cars ... four kids and an older couple ... girl seventeen or eighteen ... lacerations on face ... some broken bones ... Woman about seventy ... head injury ... Don't know how serious ... Little Traverse Hospital ... Yeah, kids were drunk ... not the driver ... no other serious injuries ... one boy was going into shock but the medics brought him around ... he said his father is an executive with General Motors ... we'll meet you at the Sheriff's Office."*

Bobby threw up once in the squad car and again after they arrived at the station.

By 5:00 a.m., the boys were in the Emmet County Sheriff's lockup. The deputy allowed Bobby to telephone his dad before putting him in a cell with Eddie and Beau. The medic patched up the cut on Beau's head but he had a terrible headache and wanted to get some rest before Mr. Cunningham arrived. He lay down on the cot in the cell for about thirty seconds before being rousted.

"Sheriff Eastman is here."

Beau was led into a small interview room. The walls were concrete block painted gray. There was one window; not reflective glass or anything fancy, just a regular window that overlooked an asphalt parking lot. The furniture consisted of a metal table and three chairs. Beau expected Emmet County Sheriff John Eastman to be like Barney Fife. He was wrong. Sheriff Eastman was fifty-three years old with steel-gray hair, a trim physique, and the erect posture of a former military man. His summer uniform was starched and sharply creased. His black shoes had been shined and buffed to a high gloss. He sat in one of the chairs and motioned for Beau to take a chair on the other side of the table. The sheriff didn't appear to be a man Beau should lie to.

In a surprisingly quiet voice, Sheriff Eastman said, "You're in serious trouble, son. I want you to tell me what happened and I want you to tell me the truth. Do you promise to tell the truth?"

"Yes, sir."

"Whose car was it?"

"It belongs to Janet Cunningham."

"Why were you driving?"

"Because I don't drink, sir. The others had been drinking and we thought it would be safer if I drove."

"I see ... When my deputy asked to see your driver's license, you couldn't find it. Do you have a driver's license?"

Beau was sure Sheriff Eastman would be able to check. "No, sir."

"You were driving another person's car. You don't have a driver's license. You caused an accident and two people are seriously injured. You understand you are in a bad situation, don't you, son?"

"Yes, sir."

"Do you understand that if you are not being truthful with me, it will make things worse for you?"

"Yes, sir."

"Tell me what happened."

"It was all so fast. Everything is just a blur to me. The other car and I tried to pass right at the place where Lower Shore Drive goes over Five Mile Creek. The road narrows at that spot and we sideswiped each other."

They were interrupted by a commotion in the outer office. Mr. and

Mrs. Cunningham burst in. The sheriff opened the interview room door and stepped out.

He said, "I'm John Eastman," and put out his hand.

Mr. Cunningham shook his hand. "I'm Buck Cunningham. This is Mrs. Cunningham."

Mr. Cunningham glanced around and saw Bobby and Eddie in the jail cell and Beau in the interview room. Mrs. Cunningham ran to her son.

"Bobby, are you hurt?" she cried.

"No. I'm okay, Mom."

"Are you hurt, Eddie?" she asked.

"I'm okay, Mrs. C."

"How did this happen?" asked Mr. Cunningham. "Was Janet driving?"

"No. Beau was driving," said Bobby.

"Where is Janet?" said Mrs. Cunningham. "Is she hurt?"

"The yard boy was driving?" said Mr. Cunningham. "He caused this?"

"OH, MY GOD! WHERE'S JANET?" screamed Mrs. Cunningham.

Mr. Cunningham ran through the open door of the interview room. He grabbed Beau by the front of his shirt. "YOU LITTLE BASTARD! LOOK WHAT YOU'VE DONE!" He drew back his right arm to slap Beau, but before he could strike, the sheriff caught his wrist.

"BUCK!" yelled Mrs. Cunningham. "JANET ISN'T HERE!"

"She's at Little Traverse Hospital," said Sheriff Eastman.

Mrs. Cunningham was crying. "How badly is she hurt?"

"We don't know yet, ma'am," answered the sheriff. She has serious injuries but the medics don't think it's a life-threatening situation."

Mrs. Cunningham was crying harder. "We're going to the hospital. OH JESUS, BUCK ... HURRY!"

After the Cunninghams left, Sheriff Eastman turned to Beau. "I don't think you're acting in your best interest, son. Rather than talking any more right now, I'm going to have the deputy put you back in the cell. I suggest you use what's left of the night to think about the story you're telling."

When the Cunninghams returned at 9:00 a.m., Beau was waiting in the jail cell with Bobby and Eddie. Mrs. Cunningham looked tired and drawn. "Janet has a broken clavicle and some bad lacerations on her face," she said. "They've set her broken bone and stitched up the cuts. After she has had time to heal, we're going to take her to the finest plastic surgeon …" Mrs. Cunningham began to sob. "… and have him fix my little girl's beautiful face." She sat down and put her head in her hands.

Mr. Cunningham gently patted her on the back. When Buck Cunningham turned toward the boys, Bobby asked if Janet had been awake when he saw her.

"Yes. She was groggy but awake."

"Were you able to talk with her about the accident?"

"None of it is very clear to her." He hesitated, turned away for a moment, and then looked directly into Bobby's eyes. "The only thing she remembers is that Beau was driving much too fast."

Bobby swallowed hard and moved on. "What about the people in the other car?"

"The man wasn't hurt. The steering wheel protected him. They kept him in the hospital last night for observation and released him this morning. The woman has a concussion. She was unconscious for a long time. She's seventy-two. That adds to the risk."

Beau asked Mr. Cunningham if the woman might die.

"Yes, Beau, it is possible she will die. We certainly hope she'll recover, but the doctors can't predict the outcome."

Beau said, "Can't they do something?"

Mr. Cunningham replied, "The neurosurgeon said they might operate to remove a piece of her skull in order to give her brain room to swell."

Beau cringed. "That sounds awful."

Mr. Cunningham nodded in agreement. "It does sound awful, but the surgeon said that if her brain doesn't swell too much, they won't have to do it. They're going to wait for a while before making a decision. Head injuries are unpredictable. She could have a complete recovery."

Buck turned to the sheriff. "May we take Bobby and Eddie home? They were only passengers. I presume they aren't being charged with anything."

Sheriff Eastman appeared to choose his words with care. "We are not charging either of them at this time. They are free to go. We're charging Beau Lightfoot with reckless driving and driving without a license.

If the woman dies, we'll amend the charges to include vehicular manslaughter."

The deputy released Bobby and Eddie and they left with Mrs. Cunningham. Buck stayed behind to speak with the sheriff.

"Sheriff Eastman, I'm sorry I lost my temper this morning. There is no excuse for acting as I did. I wasn't myself."

"Apology accepted. I understand."

"Sheriff, I've come to know Beau Lightfoot quite well. I think he is a fine young man ..."

Beau's cell was right next to them. He could hear every word. *He has come to know me. Thinks I'm a fine young man. What bullshit. He doesn't know me at all.*

Mr. Cunningham continued. "... Beau has had a difficult life. I want to do everything possible to help him."

"That's kind of you."

"John. May I call you John?"

"Sure."

"John, I've retained a lawyer for Beau. As soon as he is able to finish some business in Detroit, he'll be on his way here in one of General Motors' planes. He said he should be able to get to your office by noon tomorrow and asked me to request that you not question his client before he arrives."

Sheriff Eastman picked up a clipboard and a ballpoint pen.

"What's the lawyer's name ... Buck?"

"Buford Gerard."

Beau noticed that the unflappable Sheriff Eastman did a double-take.

"The Governor of the State of Michigan is going to be this kid's lawyer?!"

"Former Governor, John. He's just a lawyer now."

Eastman nodded and said nothing.

"As I was saying, we plan to be here by noon tomorrow. Would you be kind enough to contact the Emmet County Prosecutor and arrange for him to meet us?" Buck Cunningham rubbed his face with both hands. "John, I'm dead tired," he said. "If you don't have anything more, I'm going home to get some rest."

That night, as Beau lay on his cot, he realized that Fawn and Father Marcotte would have heard about the accident by now and were undoubtedly worried about him. There was nothing he could do right now, but he would get a message to them as soon as he could. He remembered all of the times Father Marcotte had urged him to pray. He didn't do it often but this seemed like a good time. He offered a prayer for the recovery of the woman who had been the passenger in the other automobile. He prayed for her and for himself.

The next morning, Emmet County Prosecuting Attorney Andrew Alexander arrived, wearing his best blue suit and new black wingtip shoes. He was about thirty years old and looked eager, the way a golden retriever looks eager just before you throw a stick for it to fetch. Andrew went into the sheriff's private office to have a cup of coffee and wait for Beau's lawyer to arrive.

The wait was short. Buford Gerard swept through the front door, accompanied by his attractive young female assistant and Buck Cunningham. He introduced his assistant to everyone; complimented Sheriff Eastman on his modern office; and told Andrew Alexander that, through the legal grapevine in Detroit, he'd heard some good things about him. Finally, he asked the sheriff for a private room where he and Mr. Cunningham could confer with his client.

As they entered the interview room, Mr. Gerard paused just inside the doorway. He spoke in a low voice to his assistant. "While I'm in here with our client, I want you to speak with Mr. Alexander. No confrontation. Keep everything cordial. Remind him our firm's clients are major corporations and we almost never accept criminal cases. We are only involved in this matter because the father of two of the young people is a vice president at General Motors. Take Mr. Alexander into your confidence and admit we're out of our area of expertise. Tell him we will appreciate any guidance he feels it would be proper for him to provide.

"Find out everything you can about the evidence they have and how he views this case." Mr. Gerard paused and cleared his throat. "And, Leslie, without being obvious, use some of your feminine wiles to get a handle on what he's like as a person."

After she left to meet with the prosecutor, Buford Gerard turned and shook hands with Beau. He said, "Buck has a couple of things to say and then he is going to leave us."

"Beau," Mr. Cunningham said, "Mr. Gerard will help you out of this trouble. I'm going to pay all of your legal fees and take care of any other financial matters. You don't have to worry about anything. What you must do is to trust Mr. Gerard and do exactly as he directs."

"Thank you, Buck," said Buford. "You should leave us now. Beau and I need to talk."

Mr. Cunningham promptly left the room. Beau thought he looked relieved to be leaving.

After the door was closed, Mr. Gerard said, "Before coming over here this morning, I checked with Little Traverse Hospital. The woman is doing better. The brain swelling is beginning to subside. In a few days, if it becomes clear she is recovering—and I certainly hope that's the case—our position will be much better. Our best strategy is to wait and see how she progresses over the next few days. In the interim, your job is to be patient and to be quiet. You must not say anything to anyone."

"Yes, sir."

"We're going to do everything possible to help you. You have a good friend in Buck Cunningham. He wants me to take care of this and he doesn't care what it costs. Do you have any questions?"

"Don't you want me to tell you what happened?"

"I want you to respond to my questions. I think there may be some things that I don't wish to know." He paused and looked at Beau. "Anything else?"

"Yes, sir. The woman in the hospital. What's her name?"

"Gosh, Beau, I don't know. I'll find out for you."

"Thanks, Mr. Gerard."

"I'll be back in two days."

"Mr. Gerard, would you do me a favor?"

"Of course."

"Would you have your assistant go to Holy Childhood School in Harbor Springs and tell Father Marcotte and my sister, Fawn, that I'm okay?"

"I'll send her over this afternoon. If there is nothing more, I'll see you on Thursday."

Buford Gerard left and Beau was ushered back to his cell. He wondered what Mr. Gerard was going to do during the next two days. Probably play some golf; drink a few martinis on the Cunningham's front porch; and treat Leslie, his snappy little assistant, to a fancy dinner at the Colonial Inn. There was no need to wonder what he would be doing. He would be lying on his cot and staring at the ceiling of a jail cell.

Time barely moved. A day felt like six months. How could anyone endure years in prison? It would be worse than death.

Thursday afternoon finally arrived. Buford Gerard steamed into the sheriff's office with Leslie in his wake. "Deputy, would you please bring Mr. Lightfoot into the interview room so we can confer in private?"

As soon as they were in the interview room, Mr. Gerard said, "Beau, I've just come from the hospital and I've got good news. Mrs. Larson is doing much better. That's her name, by the way, Mrs. Larson. Anyway, the doctors expect her to recover. It may not be a complete recovery but they're confident she's out of danger."

Mr. Gerard motioned for his assistant to wait outside and shut the door. "Leslie is going to call the judge to request an expedited hearing," he said to Beau. "I believe our request will be granted. Mr. Alexander is on his way to meet with me. Andy is an ambitious young fellow. His dream is to become a judge and Leslie has led him to believe that in my opinion he will make a fine judge. Andy's a smart boy. I don't think we have to draw him any pictures. He'll understand I can be a valuable friend. I am confident we'll be able to negotiate a plea agreement.

"Your job is simple. You speak only to the judge. He will read the charges and ask if you understand. Then he will ask how you plead. Yes, you do understand the charges. You plead guilty. You are very sorry for what you have done. That's it! Is everything clear to you?"

"Yes, sir."

"Good. I'll see you at the hearing tomorrow and we'll put this matter behind us."

At two the following afternoon, Beau was brought into the courtroom. It was small but, other than that, it looked exactly like the courtrooms he'd seen in the movies. The jury box was unoccupied. Two old men were the only spectators.

The hearing proceeded exactly as Mr. Gerard had predicted. Beau pled guilty to all charges. He said he was sorry for what he had done. *So far, so good.*

Then Beau began to get a bad feeling. Things were going wrong. The judge asked Beau to stand for sentencing and delivered a lecture that sounded as if he believed Beau was the scum of the Earth. Beau stood silently and listened as the judge heaped scorn upon him.

The judge finally finished his lecture and got to the sentencing. "I hereby sentence you to forfeit your driving privileges for a period of three years; to pay a fine in the amount of $10,000; and to be incarcerated in the State Penitentiary at Jackson, Michigan, for a period of eighteen months."

The courtroom was spinning. Beau's knees gave way. Mr. Gerard grabbed his arm to keep Beau from collapsing.

The judge continued, "The incarceration portion of the sentence is suspended." He banged his gavel. "This court is adjourned."

Buford Gerard smiled and gave Beau a pat on the back. "It's all over. Buck Cunningham will pay the fine and he'll pay whatever compensation has to be paid to Mrs. Larson. A suspended sentence is a sentence you don't have to serve. It will come up again if you get into trouble within the next few years, but I know that's not going to happen. I'll give you a ride to the Cunningham's cottage. They're cutting their vacation short and want to see you before they leave for Bloomfield Hills."

The Cunninghams were waiting for Beau on the front porch. When he walked up the front steps, a remarkable thing happened. Everyone stood, and Buck Cunningham extended his hand. "I'm glad things turned out well for you," he said.

Mrs. Cunningham gave Beau a hug. She didn't say a word but when she withdrew there were tears in her eyes. Janet's left arm was in a sling. She patted Beau with her right hand. Bobby wrapped both of his powerful arms around Beau and whispered in his ear, "I'll never forget this. You're my blood brother, man." Then he stepped back and spoke in a normal voice. "I'm going to miss you, Beau. Take good care of yourself."

Janet wanted to go down to the dock and take one last look around before they left. She asked Beau to join her. As they walked, he took a close look at Janet. She had a five-inch laceration along her forehead about a quarter of an inch below her hairline and another, about four inches long, ran diagonally across her left cheek. He felt like crying when he looked at those two ugly lines of stitches on her lovely face.

She saw his distress. "They're going to fix me. That's one of the reasons we're going home now. Mom's going to take me to California. There's a plastic surgeon in Beverly Hills who works on all of the movie stars. They say he can work miracles."

My God. She's so brave. I don't know what to say. I want to say she will always be beautiful to me. I want to say I love her but I know I can't say that.

He took a deep breath, and asked about Eddie and Pinkey.

"Pinkey returned home the day after the accident." Janet smiled as she continued. "She said going down the beach to make out with that geek George Watson and missing her ride home with us was the best thing she's done in her entire life.

"Eddie went home on Tuesday. He said he wanted to have a few days with his family before he had to leave for school." As she spoke, Janet moved closer to Beau. She rested her good arm on his shoulder. "Taking the blame for Bobby is the most courageous thing ..." Her eyes filled with tears and she shook her head from side to side. "You could have gone to prison for something you didn't do ..." Her voice broke and she paused to regain control. "Our family will never forget what you've done. We're going home—but I'll write to you and let you know what I'm doing and tell you what's up with Bobby and Eddie. I want you to write to me. I want to know how things are for you."

Beau stood at the end of the dock with this lovely, brave girl's arm around his shoulder, and looked out across the blue water of Little Traverse Bay. For now, there was nothing more to say.

THE DEER AND THE RABBIT

Indians do not share the whites' opinion that only a human can possess a soul. Indians view themselves as sharing the world with other living creatures. Animals are killed only to provide the necessities of life; never for mere sport.

Animals have much to teach and are treated with respect. Like people, animals have spirits and Indians sometimes speak with those spirits.

2013

The sharp sound of a hand slapping against leather startled Beau. He looked up as Eddie yelled, "Beau! Think fast!" A football flew at Beau, hit him on the chest, and bounced to the floor. It was the ball from the 1968 Minnesota-Michigan game. Coach Blieschroeder had given the football to Bobby Cunningham in recognition of his outstanding play. Eddie must have taken it from its display stand on the bookcase and tossed it at Beau.

Eddie walked over to Beau and put his arm around him. "There was a time when you wouldn't have missed that one. I guess none of us are as quick as we used to be. Anyway, I came to get you for dinner."

After an excellent meal and a couple bottles of wine shared with good friends, the sadness of Fawn's funeral gradually lifted. Once Beau began to relax, he was hit with a wave of fatigue. Since everyone was going to spend the night at Bobby's cottage, Beau excused himself and climbed the stairs to Bobby's old bedroom. Bobby and his wife had occupied the master bedroom for more than twenty years; so Beau was sleeping in the room Bobby had when he was a young man.

Beau's eyes were drawn to a framed photograph on the dresser. It was a black-and-white photo of the football team. The inscription along the bottom read: "University of Michigan—1968 Big Ten Co-Champions."

That was a great football team. They should not have been co-champions; should have stood alone as Big Ten Champs. Hell, they should have been national champions. In the photo, Eddie, with his usual big grin, was holding the football and standing in the center of the front row. Bobby stood next to him. Even after everything that happened, they were still friends. Best friends for life.

Bobby was a rock-solid tackle and Eddie was an audacious quarterback with the greatest throwing arm Beau had ever seen. It was Eddie who had convinced Beau to try out for the Harbor Springs high school football team. Eddie had said he didn't play for the love of the game or the comradeship with his teammates. He played to attract girls. Girls liked football players. Eddie liked girls. Therefore ... Eddie saw no reason why it wouldn't work for Beau.

HARBOR SPRINGS, 1964

In Harbor Springs during the 1960s, summer didn't slowly merge into fall. Everything changed on one day. Before Labor Day, the town was busy. The sidewalks were crowded with wealthy cottage owners and their beautiful children. Late-model American-made automobiles occupied every parking space on both sides of Main Street, and the shops were filled with women wearing brightly colored Lilly Pulitzer resort outfits.

On the day after Labor Day, it felt like someone had flipped a switch to off. The cottage families were gone. There was plenty of parking. There were open tables in the restaurants and the summer shops were empty. Peace and quiet. Harbor Springs reverted to being an ordinary small town. A hint of cool weather was in the air and the sun set earlier in the evening. School started.

When Beau left his room at Holy Childhood on the morning after Labor Day to head for high school, he remembered Pontiac's advice to appreciate the beauty of the world around him. He walked east for two blocks along Main Street and enjoyed the cool air. In many ways, Harbor Springs was its most beautiful after the summer residents returned home.

He turned north and headed toward the boardwalk that climbed the steep, wooded bluff that divided the town into two parts. The high school and most of the houses were located above the bluff. The businesses, churches, and some homes were clustered below the bluff around the harbor, and along Main Street.

Both sides of Main Street were lined with large trees with branches that arched over the street and met in the middle. The houses along the east end of the street gradually gave way to shops and small commercial establishments. There were no stop lights or parking meters.

About two hundred feet beyond the last store, Main Street appeared to end at the front steps of the Catholic church. In reality, it turned left, but that wasn't apparent until you were very close. The visual effect of the white-frame church standing squarely at the end of the street was like a Norman Rockwell painting of an idealized New England town.

The Holy Childhood Indian School located behind and to the north of the church had served as Beau's home for the past five years. Many Indian children, some orphans, others temporary borders, were housed and educated within the walls of the school's large, brick building. The good Sisters taught the children through eighth grade and provided what Father Marcotte called a "solid Catholic education." The eighth-grade graduation ceremony marked the end of formal schooling for many of the children, but for some such as Beau and Fawn, it was a prelude to a transfer to the public high school.

As he climbed the boardwalk toward high school, Beau recalled the anxiety he had felt three years ago when he entered the school as a freshman. Now, as he walked up the wide front steps and through the double doors of Harbor Springs High School, he carried himself with the confidence of a senior. He hadn't received a letter from Janet yet, but he wasn't discouraged. Janet and her mother had gone to Beverly Hills to consult with the famous plastic surgeon who promised to employ state-of-the-art medical technology to reduce the scars on her face to a minimum. Janet would write as soon as she could find the time.

Beau was in love with Janet—but he was also an eighteen-year-old boy. A worshipful love for a young woman, many social classes above him and hundreds of miles away, didn't fulfill his immediate needs. Thoughts of sex intruded on his mind almost constantly.

Some of the high school girls gave signals they would be receptive to him, but they weren't the ones he wanted. The good ones, the attractive popular girls, regarded him with a mixture of disinterest and scorn. He understood there was no reason for the desirable girls to have positive feelings toward him. He was a complete zero at school, a boy from the Indian school, and a kid who always worked and never participated in extracurricular activities.

The situation was understandable but unacceptable. Beau was willing to try anything, including Eddie's idea of attracting girls by playing football. He would be one of the smaller players on the team but he was a fast runner. He'd planned to try out for the football team on the first day of school but it was too late. Since he had been working in Wequetonsing until the day school opened he was uninformed about school activities and didn't know the team had been practicing for two weeks and the first game would be played in four days. Beau was disappointed and resigned himself to being an ordinary student.

On the morning of the second day of school, he took his assigned seat in Mrs. Kring's algebra class. Seating was alphabetical and there were no Ks in Advanced Algebra. Joyce Johnson sat next to Beau Lightfoot. Any girl who came within ten feet of Beau caused instant arousal, but she was something special. She was wearing a white sleeveless blouse. Beau was stunned! Joyce was feminine perfection. Her face, her arms, her neck, her shoulders, her ... *Oh, my God!* He could look through the arm hole in her blouse and see her bra. He could see a little bit of the tops of her tits. Perhaps if he leaned to the side and got a better angle ...

"Beau, would you please go to the blackboard and give us your solution to problem three?" Mrs. Kring's voice disrupted his concentration. She wanted him to walk to the front of the classroom. Beau knew the answer—he always did his homework—but he was in no condition to walk to the front of the class.

"Mrs. Kring, I'm sorry. I haven't done my homework."

Mrs. Kring gave him her standard lecture about the importance of personal responsibility. She pointed out that a person who failed to do his homework was only hurting himself. Finally, mercifully, Advanced Algebra class came to an end.

Beau held his math book over his crotch as he walked to his locker. His friend Tommy Webb was waiting. As usual, Tommy was free with advice. On the subject of girls and football, he was in total agreement with Eddie. "Beau, it's like the song says, 'You gotta be a football hero.' I'm serious. The only way you're going to get a fine woman like Joyce Johnson is to be on the football team."

"Tommy, it's too late to sign up—and, besides, I've never played football."

"Yeah, and you've never had a girlfriend either … have you?"

Beau thought the theory of attracting girls by playing football was wishful thinking, but the image of Joyce Johnson in her sleeveless blouse was more than he could stand. "Maybe you're right. I'll talk to Coach O'Donnell after school."

O'Donnell looked skeptically at Beau. "How much do you weigh?"

"One hundred and fifty-five pounds, sir."

"How tall are you?"

"I'm five feet, eight and three-quarters inches, sir."

Coach O'Donnell looked Beau up and down; obviously unimpressed.

"Coach, I'm fast. I bet I can outrun anybody on the team. Please give me a chance to show you what I can do."

"We've already been practicing for two weeks but, what the hell? Our squad is a little shorthanded. I'll let you try out. We'll see how fast you really are."

Practice that afternoon went well. Beau was the fastest man on the squad. At the conclusion of practice, Coach O'Donnell gathered his players on the field for a pep talk.

"Boyne City is coming into our stadium on Friday—in two days. And, you know what? I feel sorry for them. They have never played a team as tough as you guys. We're the Harbor Springs Rams and we hit hard!

Football isn't a contact sport—it's a *collision* sport. We're going to win this game because we want it more. We block harder and tackle harder and run harder than they do. When we run, we don't bob and weave. We don't make fancy moves. You lower your head and shoulders and blast 'em! You explode into 'em! You run right over 'em! You put 'em on their backs and punish 'em for trying to tackle you! *That's* Ram football! That's how we're gonna win!"

Beau thought Coach's speech was over the top, but as he looked around at the other players; he saw they were buying it. Their boyish faces were contorted into manly scowls, their hands were clenched into fists, and their bodies leaned forward. Beau was reminded of a scene in a John Wayne movie where the Marines were getting ready to storm an enemy beach.

Maybe football is like war. It's clearly serious business; nothing like the games I played on the Cunningham's front lawn. Coach says it's a game for men, not boys; a game that requires determination and courage; a game that encourages a player to inflict pain on his opponent. I remember from last year's European History class that a famous English guy wrote that the character of England's future leaders was forged on the playing fields of Eaton. That must be how it is with high school football.

As the team headed into the locker room, Coach O'Donnell called Beau aside. "Beau, I want to use your speed against Boyne City. You just joined the team and don't know anything, but I'm going to put in a special play for you. It's a misdirection play and it might give you a chance to break away. We'll run through it a few times tomorrow to make sure you know what to do."

Beau didn't feel his feet touch the ground as he ran to the locker room. Coach was putting in a play just for him! This was great! The atmosphere in the locker room was upbeat. The boys were keyed up, shouting in the showers, snapping towels, and kidding around with each other. And why not? This was an undefeated team with the potential to be conference champions. Of course, they hadn't actually played any games yet this season, but what of it? These boys were ready.

Before dressing in his street clothes to go home, each boy was weighed in by the assistant coach. Beau weighed in at one hundred and fifty-eight pounds. Over the summer, he had bulked-up with three pounds of solid muscle. He felt good. In addition to being clean and tingly from the shower, his skin felt tight. Probably from those extra pounds of muscle. He let his dark hair stay wet and combed it with a neat part on the left and a small wave on the right. His street clothes were the same ordinary shirt and pants he wore to school that morning—but now they looked different... better... more filled out.

When Beau walked out of the locker room and headed toward Holy Childhood it was already getting dark outside. He took the boardwalk that ran down the bluff from the high school to the lower part of the village and Holy Childhood. The boardwalk was four feet wide and solidly constructed. It cut diagonally most of the way down the bluff; then near the end, it turned straight and descended in steep steps to the bottom. Beau had been up and down the boardwalk so many times he was able to navigate it without conscious thought. Indeed, his mind was consumed by football glory and Joyce Johnson's sleeveless blouse. As he approached the turn where the steps headed straight down, he wasn't paying attention to his surroundings. Then, when he was on the top step, he realized someone was below him. It was Sarge. Sarge was on the fourth step and heading up. There was no way for Beau to avoid him. Two seconds ago, Beau was thinking about what a tough guy he had become; now his stomach hurt. He looked at his father and sternly said, "Sarge." No hello, just his name.

Sarge jerked his head up, saw Beau, and stopped.

Beau didn't trust himself to say anything else. He felt he had said Sarge in a reasonably forceful manner—but he didn't think he could say anything more without his voice betraying his panic. He too stood still.

"I don't want any trouble," Sarge said as backed down a step.

Beau remained silent. His heavier weight didn't seem as formidable as he had imagined earlier.

Sarge turned and retreated. When he reached the bottom of the stairs, he began to walk fast and turned left on Third Street.

Beau had been holding his breath. He inhaled with a gasp. Sarge was gone. He was a tough guy again. *Well, alright!*

The Boyne City game carried the extra excitement of being the season opener. Fourth period classes were cancelled in order to hold a pep rally in the gymnasium. The marching band played, the best-looking girls jumped up and down in their short cheerleader skirts, and each member of the varsity football team was introduced to wild applause. Any lingering doubts Beau had were erased.

Home games were played at night and the blazing stadium lights added drama. When the game got underway, Beau sat on the bench and waited for his opportunity. He screwed his eyes closed and wished with all of his might that Coach would put him in the game. As he waited, he thought of Coach O'Donnell's words, *"Lower your shoulder. Blast into 'em! Punish anyone who tries to tackle you!"* He would do it. Football was war. If anyone tried to stop him, he would blast 'em.

In the third quarter, Coach O'Donnell put Beau in the game. The special play called for Beau to take one step to his left, receive a handoff from the quarterback, and immediately cut back to his right. The blocking was good. A hole opened in the line, and as Beau sprinted into it, he saw Boyne City's All-Conference linebacker, Jim Neiswander, step into the gap. *This is it!* Beau thought. He lowered his shoulder and blasted the six-foot, two-hundred-and-twenty-pound Neiswander.

BLAM! The football was knocked from Beau's arm and flew into the air. Beau was slammed backward and bounced off of the ground. It felt like an automobile had driven into him. He staggered to his feet with his helmet turned so that he was looking out of its ear hole. He took one step and fell on the ground. An assistant coach ran out and helped Beau to the sideline. Beau slumped on the bench and glanced at the field. Jim Neiswander looked fine ... not at all like a player who had just been punished.

Beau sat by himself at the end of the bench and began to feel dizzy. He lowered his head to avoid passing out. As he sat with his head between his knees, he noticed the feet of the man next to him. The fellow was wearing moccasins rather than football cleats. The distinctive smell of bear oil penetrated the fog of Beau's brain and he slowly lifted his head. His Spirit Father, Chief Pontiac, was sitting beside him.

Pontiac looked amused. "That was a stupid play, Beau."

"I tried my best to do what Coach O'Donnell told me to do."

"Your coach is not a smart man. I fought English officers like him. They believed only in frontal attack. They never changed tactics; no flexibility, no imagination. I defeated them by using our strengths of stealth, speed, and deception. You must be who you are. A rabbit must act like a rabbit and do rabbit things. If a rabbit tries to behave like a bear, it will go badly. A deer can have a good life being a deer. If it begins to act like a buffalo, it will be in trouble.

"You are a small, fast player. You must learn how to run. Learn from the deer and the rabbit. Go at sunrise to the field at the edge of the forest and wait quietly. The deer and the rabbit are the best runners in the forest. Observe them and learn."

"I will, Spirit Father. I'll watch what they do and learn from them."

Pontiac nodded. "I like this game you are playing. Pay attention to everything about the deer and the rabbit. If you learn to run like a deer and dodge like a rabbit, you will be a good player of football."

Pontiac gave Beau a fatherly pat on the back and walked from the brightly illuminated sideline into the shadows. Nobody noticed.

~

Beau was hugging the ground, silent, hidden in the tall weeds. It was 5:00 a.m., and as Pontiac had instructed, Beau was in a field at the edge of the forest. From a distance, the field appeared to be covered with rich, golden wheat more than two feet tall and ready for harvest. Upon closer inspection, however, it was a field of weeds that had been parched by the summer sun.

There was no sunlight now. It was dark and cold. Save for the slightest glow in the east, the fall sky was as dark as one of Father Marcotte's black robes. Low-growing sticker plants hidden beneath the weeds attached to Beau's clothing and poked his skin. Heavy dew clung to every weed and soaked into his clothing as he waited and tried to remain perfectly still. Beau thought Indians were supposed to be good at this sort of thing but, as far as he was concerned, this business of observing wild animals was definitely uncomfortable.

This was Beau's third attempt to observe the deer. Pontiac's instructions sounded easy: "Go at sunrise to the field at the edge of the forest and wait quietly."

On Saturday morning, Beau arrived at sunrise. The deer immediately saw him and walked back into the forest. Beau realized he shouldn't go *at* sunrise but rather arrive *before* sunrise and be in his hiding place when the sun rose.

On Sunday morning, he arrived earlier—but he failed to consider the wind blowing from behind him toward the deer. The first animal came out of the tree line, lifted its head, took a couple of sniffs, and retreated back into the trees.

It was now Tuesday morning, and Beau had learned nothing about the running ability of deer or the agility of rabbits. There was no time for more mistakes. He figured he would need a few days to work on his improved techniques before the game on Friday. He wanted to be ready for the game, but in his heart he knew it wouldn't matter because Coach O'Donnell had not forgiven him for fumbling the ball. The fumble allowed Boyne City to take a temporary lead but, in the fourth quarter, the Harbor Springs Rams scored a touchdown and were able to win by a score of 12 to 7. Beau felt awful but had hoped Coach would understand. After all, it was his first game and everybody makes mistakes sometimes.

Beau decided the honorable thing to do was apologize to Coach O'Donnell on Monday. Wrong again. O'Donnell turned red in the face and screamed at Beau. "You're sorry? That's just swell. You almost cost us a ball game and now you're sorry. You have a record of one carry—and one fumble! That's a one hundred percent failure rate. Think about that pitiful record and get out of my sight."

O'Donnell was a mean-spirited, profane, and unforgiving man. The nurturing coach who installed a special play for Beau was gone. O'Donnell viewed the fumble as a personal insult. During practice, he acted like he'd forgotten Beau's name, calling him either "little shit" or "little bastard."

As Beau hid in the wet weeds, waiting for a deer to emerge from the woods, he thought about the unfairness of the abusive treatment he'd been receiving. He consoled himself by remembering Pontiac's opinion that O'Donnell was not a smart man. You don't get to be The Greatest War Chief Who Ever Lived without being right about people. The sky was beginning to brighten in the east. In a few minutes, the sun would come over the horizon and, he hoped, deer would appear.

They came without a sound. At first, they were mere shadows. Slowly, as the sun began to rise above the horizon, the shadows were replaced by light and the exquisite details of their forms were revealed. There were six deer: a buck, three does, and two fawns. The wind was blowing from behind the deer and when the buck sniffed the air he didn't detect danger. Beau was close to them, but well hidden.

The deer were both delicate and powerful. Their bodies were designed for speed: thin legs and strong shoulders and haunches. Beau watched intently as they grazed on the clover that grew along the edge of the field. He then noticed something else: their eyes. Their large, dark-brown orbs showed an intense alertness that surpassed any eyes Beau had ever seen. The deer seemed to be keenly aware of everything. Beau watched them graze peacefully for several minutes; then he remembered he was there to watch them run. He jumped to his feet and yelled, "HEY!"

Their tails shot up, the white undersides acting as flags of warning, and they were off. They quickly bolted into the forest and disappeared from sight. Even though it was over in a few seconds, Beau saw everything—and what he saw during those few seconds changed his life.

The deer had reacted instantly. There was no hesitation, no moment of panic, not a split-second of indecision. They had been surprised but, because of their constant alertness, they were ready. Immediately choosing their best path, they ran at high speed toward the dense woods. They ran with their heads up, their keen eyes looking well ahead rather than at the ground close to them. They ran fast but with control. They maintained balance and leaped over obstacles that blocked their path. If it was faster to go over than to go around, they went over. Was it too high? Could they safely make the jump? Calculations, decisions, and actions were immediate.

Wow! Beau would remember everything: alertness, speed, power, vision, balance, instant decision making, leaping ability, and control. The deer had shown him how to run. Pontiac was right. Beau would let their skill guide him.

After several days, Beau had not been able to find any rabbits to observe. Maybe he was too tired from his full schedule of school followed by football practice and chores at Holy Childhood to make a proper effort.

Anyway, it didn't matter because Coach O'Donnell wasn't going to let him play in Friday's game. Practice continued to be miserable. The team was tense and Coach's temper was awful. He wouldn't even speak to Beau.

The team bus departed at noon on Friday for their first away game in Pellston. The marching band, cheerleaders, and Pep Club followed in a second bus. Cars and trucks carrying townspeople lined up behind the buses, and the caravan began its thirty-minute drive north to Pellston. Both the high school and the town of Harbor Springs had high expectations for their team.

Pellston High School served a poor rural community and had no athletic facilities to compare with the Harbor Springs stadium and lighted field. The Pellston Hornets played their games on Friday afternoons. There was neither a stadium nor seating of any kind. A thirty-six-inch high snow fence stood fifteen feet back from the sidelines on each side of the field and spectators parked their cars along the outside of the fences. Most people watched the games while standing. Any fans wishing to sit, sat on the front fenders of their cars.

When the Hornets took the field, car horns blew in appreciation. Beau thought the Hornets looked like a rag-tag outfit. Their uniforms and their school colors were brown and gold. How could any school have brown and gold as their colors? Their team had fat guys and skinny guys; tall guys and short guys; and, unlike other teams in the league, several Indians. The Hornets also had something that hadn't been obvious during the pre-game warm-up: their coach had taught them solid fundamentals. These guys could play ball.

The tone of the game was set on the first play from scrimmage when Pellston fullback George Tahquamenon blasted through the middle of the Harbor Springs line for an eighteen-yard gain. The Rams couldn't get on track. They made errors, fumbled, and were unable to establish any positive momentum. Beau was secretly glad he wasn't playing. Some of the people from Harbor Springs quietly backed out of their fence-side parking places and left before the game ended.

The final score was 32 to 0. The Harbor Springs players were a dispirited bunch.

Beau didn't arrive home from the game until seven o'clock. He grabbed a quick bite to eat in the Holy Childhood School kitchen and headed upstairs to his room. Father Marcotte was sitting on the side of his bed. "I heard about the game and thought you might be feeling a bit down. I've got something that might lift your spirits." He held out an envelope and, trying to suppress a smile, backed out of the room.

The envelope was a rich cream color with a thin line of maroon piping along the edge and Janet Cunningham's monogram embossed on the back flap. Beau sat on the floor, leaned comfortably against the side of his bed, and opened her letter:

> Dear Beau,
> The plastic surgeon is confident he can help but he advised waiting a few more weeks to allow time for healing before beginning treatment. My classes at Kingswood School are starting off quite well. I'm disappointed I can't play field hockey but my injuries make it impossible.
> Bobby and Eddie have a wonderful football team in Chevy Chase. Eddie threw three touchdown passes and they won their first game 42 to 6.
> Love,
> Janet

What did she mean? Janet loved her parents, her brother, Eddie, her girlfriends, and probably a lot of people he didn't even know. She must have meant she loved him in that way ... or maybe it was something more?

How should he sign his letter to her? He couldn't write "Sincerely Yours." He wanted to handle everything correctly, but it was difficult to sort things out. Where was the line between friendly and too forward?

Saturday morning was wasted in an unproductive search for rabbits. He couldn't continue to search all day because Saturday was his day to clean and scrub the Holy Childhood School kitchen. It took almost five hours to do a thorough job, and it was dusk by the time he was satisfied with his work and sat on the outside kitchen steps for a breath of air. As usual, his friend, a big mongrel dog from the neighborhood, was waiting for him and hoping for some table scraps. Beau provided a few bits of meat that his canine friend promptly chomped down.

He absentmindedly patted the dog's head and gazed at the large play area that the school maintained for the children. The dog and Beau spotted the rabbit at the same instant. It was sitting in the middle of the ball field—no nearby cover. Beau grabbed at the dog but was not quick enough. His friend was off like a rocket.

As soon as the rabbit sensed the dog, it turned and ran—but it didn't have a chance. The dog was much too fast. It was going to be awful; this couldn't have been what Pontiac wanted Beau to witness. The dog quickly caught up to the rabbit and was about to grasp it with his jaws when the rabbit came to an abrupt stop. The dog skittered five yards past his target and fell over while trying to make a sharp turn for another pass. The rabbit ran but the dog quickly closed in on it again. At the last instant, without diminishing its speed, the rabbit made a ninety-degree turn and the dog continued his pursuit in a straight line that took him twenty feet past his quarry.

This rabbit was not going to be caught! His elusive running prowess was impressive. The dog kept attacking at supersonic speed. The rabbit stopped, started, slowed, accelerated, and made impossibly sharp turns. After approximately twenty missed attempts, the dog finally stopped. He stood with his head down, tongue hanging out of the side of his mouth, panting for breath, and legs shaking. The rabbit calmly squeezed through the fence and hopped away.

Beau would remember every move.

It was uncertain whether or not Beau would ever have an opportunity to use his new skills in a football game. Coach O'Donnell was not warming up to him and Beau dreaded practice.

The team lacked the snap they had before the Pellston defeat. The season seemed like it was about to head downhill; something had to be done to turn things around. Finally, after watching yet another uninspiring performance by his first team halfbacks, Coach grabbed Beau's arm. "Beau, I'm going to give you another chance. If you fumble again, I will strangle you with my bare hands!"

Beau managed to avoid any fumbles in the ensuing practices—his new techniques were paying off. Avoiding fumbles was easy because he didn't allow would-be tacklers to smash into him head-on. If they got him at all, it was by glancing tackles or by grabbing some part of him as he shot past.

On Friday night, Beau was given the chance to test his skills against the Mancelona Iron Men. The Rams had trouble stopping the Mancelona offense—but the Iron Men couldn't stop Beau Lightfoot. What a great feeling! He ran like a deer and dodged like a rabbit. Defenders lunged for him and grabbed air. Beau ran for five touchdowns—and the Rams prevailed 33 to 20.

Every morning for the next twelve years, Beau would faithfully spend fifteen minutes visualizing himself running like a deer and dodging like a rabbit. After these quiet visualizations, he always felt spiritually connected to the deer and rabbits. In some unexplainable way they became part of him.

His running was spectacular and he improved with each football game. Touchdowns rained down. Each week brought another victory for the Rams.

More important to Beau, each week brought a letter from Janet.

> *I have a new haircut with bangs in the front to hide the scar on my forehead. Kingswood will be staging a musical comedy and I'm going to try out.*
>
> *Bobby's football team is tearing up the East Coast preparatory school league.*
>
> *Love,*
> *Janet*

Beau took pains when writing his letters; usually it took several drafts before he was satisfied. He wanted to tell Janet of his athletic success but he didn't want to appear to be boasting. After several failed attempts at choosing the proper words, he decided to share newspaper articles from the local sports writers. Each week Beau wrote a short letter he felt fit the casual, friendly tone he sought, and he included headlines he had cut from the sports pages. For several weeks, Beau's and Janet's letters silently passed each other in the mail:

HARBOR SPRINGS UPSETS MANCELONA 33 TO 20
SECOND STRING HALFBACK SCORES FIVE TOUCHDOWNS

I got a leading part in the Kingswood School's musical comedy. In Chevy Chase, Eddie is setting records for pass completions.

HARBOR RAMS BEAT GAYLORD 27 TO 7
BEAU LIGHTFOOT RUNS FOR FOUR TOUCHDOWNS

I will soon be taking the Scholastic Aptitude Test as part of my college application process. I'm a little worried, but hope I will do okay.
I love getting the newspaper headlines and want Bobby to see how well you are doing. I'm going to enclose the clippings with my letters to him. The Chevy Chase football team is undefeated.

HARBOR SPRINGS CRUSHES EAST JORDAN 45 TO 6
LIGHTFOOT SENSATIONAL – SCORES SIX TDs

My mother and I have gone back to Beverly Hills to the plastic surgeon. He is treating my scars with a process called dermabrasion. It's like smoothing them down with sandpaper, and it hurts like crazy.

HARBOR SPRINGS TOPS GRAYLING 32 TO 13
BEAU LIGHTFOOT UNSTOPPABLE

Eddie has been named to the Scholastic Magazine High School All-American Team. Bobby was listed as one of the best high school linemen on the East Coast. The famous University of Michigan coach, Gary Blieschroeder, is coming to Bloomfield Hills to talk with Daddy. It looks as if the dream of Bobby playing football at Michigan is going to come true. My scars don't hurt anymore and my new hairstyle, with the bangs, is kind of cute.

HARBOR SPRINGS EDGES CHARLEVOIX 20 to 19
LIGHTFOOT SCORES THREE TOUCHDOWNS AS RAMS WIN NORTHERN MICHIGAN CLASS C CONFERENCE TITLE

My SAT scores turned out to be excellent! I am going to apply to Wellesley, Duke, and the University of Michigan. The big news is that there has been a major blow-up between Daddy and Bobby. They were yelling at each other over the telephone. It has something to do with football scholarships. Daddy is steaming mad and refuses to talk about what happened. I telephoned Bobby but all he said was that when he got things worked out, he'd let me know.

Although Janet's letters were important, Beau did not neglect his social life. After scoring a combined nine touchdowns against Mancelona and Gaylord, it was clear to everyone that he was the best running back Harbor Springs had ever seen. Beau's social life was due for a change and he was ready.

The number one item of business was Joyce Johnson. Beau dispatched his friend Tommy Webb to speak with her. The plan was for Tommy to meet Beau before Advanced Algebra class and give him the scoop. Assuming Joyce's reactions were favorable, Beau would strike up a conversation with Joyce and ask her for a date. He waited impatiently for Tommy's report. When Tommy finally did meet Beau in the hallway, he spoke with a distinct lack of enthusiasm. "Beau, it doesn't look good."

"Why? What's the matter?"

"Joyce says she's interested in the life of the mind. She thinks football is a brutal sport and will never date a football player."

"That is bad news. Did she leave any opening at all?"

"No. I'm sorry, Beau."

"That can't be right. Tell me exactly what she said."

"Come on, Beau. Just let it go. I don't want to repeat what she said."

"Tommy, you have to tell me. You probably misunderstood her. Tell me her exact words."

"I honestly can't remember every word, but she did say she thinks football players are macho shitheads."

Their conversation was interrupted by the insistent sound of the bell summoning students to their next classes. Beau had to go into Advanced Algebra and sit right next to Joyce. This was unfair. Joyce had been the reason he decided to play football. Now, he discovers she hates football players and he has to sit right next to her.

He nodded hello to Mrs. Kring and took his seat. He looked at Joyce and she pretended not to see him. His gaze wandered to Pam Illsey. She looked sensational in her new pink sweater. He cast his eyes further down the row to Gail Hedrick, whose blonde hair contrasted beautifully with her blue blouse. Both girls, who three weeks ago would have ignored him, nodded and smiled.

On the Monday after the Rams wiped out East Jordan, Coach O'Donnell called Beau into his office. He asked Beau to close the door and sit down.

Coach cleared his throat and leveled his usual intimidating glare at Beau. "You haven't been running the way I told you to."

Oh, brother! The man's insane!

As O'Donnell leaned forward across his desk, a giant smile transformed his face. "You've been running one hundred times better than the way I taught you to run. You're the best halfback I've ever seen. A coach, if he's lucky, has a player like you once in his lifetime."

All Beau could manage was a simple, "Thank you."

Coach O'Donnell said he knew Beau was a good student, but didn't have a family to provide money for college. He needed a football scholarship and Coach wanted to help him get one. With Beau's permission, he was going to contact some college coaches and see what he could do.

Beau took a good look at the man on the other side of the scuffed, gray-metal desk. He hadn't taken the trouble to really see Coach before today. There was a plastic name stand on the front of the desk. "Coach Jim O'Donnell." His name was Jim: a man with a cheap watch and threadbare slacks—a real person and a man who wanted to help him. This hard-ass guy, who wore short-sleeve white shirts in November, actually cared about him.

Jim O'Donnell said he would get back to Beau as soon as he had something to report.

The conversation with Coach O'Donnell lifted Beau to the top of the world. During the next two weeks, Beau Lightfoot piled up touchdowns and Jim O'Donnell contacted football coaches at every college in the state of Michigan. Soon after the end of the season, the *Detroit Free Press* published its All-State High School Football Team and Beau Lightfoot was named to the Class C First Team.

When Coach sent for him, Beau knew it meant good news. Coach folded his hands on top of his desk and sat back in his off-kilter swivel chair. "I've worked hard on this. Contacted everybody I could think of. We only got one offer. It's not much, but at least it's something."

Beau couldn't believe what he was hearing. "Everybody else turned me down? Why? I'm an All-State halfback. What did they say?"

"They all said the same things. You're too small. You only played one year in Northern Michigan and haven't faced first-rate competition. Class C high schools don't produce top players."

Beau was disappointed but, at least there was one offer. "Tell me about the offer we did get."

"It's from Ferris State in Big Rapids. The scholarship will only cover your tuition. I tried to get them to do more. I wanted to do better for you, Beau. I'm sorry."

"Coach ... you found a scholarship for me. It's not exactly a blue-chip deal, but it's a scholarship and I'm grateful for your help."

"Are you going to accept the Ferris State scholarship?"

Beau shook his head. "I don't know. I want to talk it over with Father

Marcotte." Father Marcotte, with his intelligence, honesty, and simple goodness, was the man Beau trusted above all others.

Beau told Father Marcotte about his desire to attend college; his hope for a full scholarship; and his disappointment in the meager, tuition-only scholarship Ferris offered. After more than two hours, they arrived at three possible alternatives.

Under plan one, Beau would ask Mr. Cunningham to help him secure an assembly line job at General Motors so he could save as much money as possible and go to college after two or three years. Plan two was to join the Army, save most of his pay, take advantage of whatever college benefits were available in the Army, and attend college after his discharge. The third choice was to accept the Ferris State scholarship and enroll next fall. The latter appealed to Beau, but Father Marcotte said it would be a hard road. A scholarship that paid tuition would help, but college was expensive. Beau would need money for his room, meals, books, supplies, fees, clothing, laundry, travel to and from Big Rapids, and something extra for an occasional pizza or movie. Beau had saved some money from his summer employment but it wouldn't last very long. Father Marcotte said he would try to help, but he had no personal assets and there were already substantial demands on the church's funds.

If Beau decided to attend Ferris State, he would have to make his own way. Father Marcotte got out some paper and a couple of pencils and they listed estimates of likely expenses and possible sources of income. After figuring and refiguring, it looked like it could be done—but it would be a tight squeeze. In addition to being a student, Beau would have to have a good job every summer, play varsity football to maintain his scholarship, work twenty-five to thirty hours per week during the academic year, and pinch every penny.

It didn't sound like any fun. Facing reality was harsh. Beau didn't like any of the three plans and spent the next few days in a funk. On the fourth day, a letter from Bobby Cunningham arrived.

Bobby apologized for not writing sooner and hoped things were going well for Beau. He said he had some good news.

Yeah, swell, thought Beau. *Good news for Bobby. It's always good news if you're Bobby Cunningham. But, Bobby's a friend. Might as well read the darn letter.*

The Chevy Chase football team had finished the season without a loss. Bobby had a good year. Eddie had a stupendous year. College coaches were all over them: Miami, Ohio State, Southern Cal, Texas, and Notre Dame ... all of the big football powers. Bobby had twelve offers of full scholarships; Eddie more than twenty. The Cunningham and Bartucci families could easily afford college expenses, but Mr. Cunningham said all big-time football players were on scholarships; so Bobby and Eddie should have scholarships too.

It was a rush to have famous coaches calling him almost every night. Of course, the solicitations didn't mean anything to Bobby and Eddie because ever since they were six years old they planned to play football together at the University of Michigan. Now, they were going to do it.

Coach Blieschroeder telephoned with Michigan's offer. He dispatched his top assistant, Coach Smith, to visit the boys in Chevy Chase, while he drove to Bloomfield Hills to meet with Mr. Cunningham. Coach Smith was a friendly guy. He asked to be called "Smitty," and said he would be straight with the boys. He was authorized to offer each of them a scholarship that would cover all reasonable college expenses but nothing more. He made a point of saying Michigan was a high-class outfit and did not give money under the table or make special deals. He said the coaching staff projected Bobby as a starter by his junior year and they thought Eddie could be the quarterback to lead Michigan to a national championship. After Smitty finished his pitch, he smiled and leaned back. It was his last smile for a long time. Things went downhill fast.

Bobby said both he and Eddie would accept Michigan's offer—with one condition: an all-expense scholarship also be provided to their friend Beau Lightfoot. The previously friendly Smitty reacted badly. He said there could not be a scholarship for Beau, and reminded Bobby that Michigan didn't make special deals. Bobby said he wouldn't go without Beau. Smitty replied that the Michigan coaching staff knew about Beau, a hundred-and-sixty-pound scat back from a tiny high school—not University of Michigan material.

Bobby was adamant; he would not sign without Beau. Smitty said if Bobby's mind was made up, Michigan would just take Eddie. Eddie began to talk about his love for the mild climate in Southern California. Smitty appeared stricken and asked Eddie what the hell he was trying to say. Eddie said it was simple, he wouldn't go without Bobby Cunningham and Bobby wouldn't go without Beau Lightfoot. Smitty said their demands were impossible. They talked further, but there was no give. In the end, Smitty left in a huff.

Later the same day, Mr. Cunningham telephoned to tell Bobby about his meeting with Coach Blieschroeder. He said they established a wonderful rapport. Within a few minutes it was as if they were old friends. Bobby told his father it was nice that he and Gary Blieschroeder hit it off so well, but the Michigan deal was off. He explained the deal breaker was his insistence on a full scholarship for Beau Lightfoot. Buck Cunningham started yelling about Bobby acting stupid and throwing away his future. It was a hell of a blowup. No need to go into the details. Suffice it to say, the call ended with the telephone being hurled across the room.

Bobby heard nothing for two days; then a phone call from Gary Blieschroeder. It turned out that the full, all-expenses covered scholarship for Beau Lightfoot, which Smitty said was absolutely impossible, was possible after all.

Beau should be on the lookout for a large blue envelope with a yellow block-style M on the back flap. It would contain the University of Michigan student application forms, the details of his scholarship, and a letter of welcome from Gary Blieschroeder.

A STRANGE NEW WORLD

The University of Michigan was established in 1817 on 1,920 acres of land donated by the Odawa, Chippewa, and Potawatomi Tribes for a "college at Detroit." It was subsequently moved from Detroit to Ann Arbor, and by 1866, became one of the largest universities in North America.

2013

Janet peered over Beau's shoulder as he looked at the old scrapbook that he had found lying on Bobby's dresser. She pointed to a faded black-and-white picture of two football players. The smallish fellow with a handsome face and smooth chestnut-brown complexion was an impossibly young Beau Lightfoot. Next to Beau was his roommate, Thaddeus D. Kowalski. He was only slightly taller than Beau but twice as wide.

People said Kowalski was built like a fire plug: short but solid.

Beau smiled as he recalled the first words Thaddeus had said to him. "Hello, I'm Thaddeus D. Kowalski. I'm called TD. TD stands for touchdown."

ANN ARBOR, 1965

The names Thaddeus Kowalski and Beau Lightfoot were posted on a dormitory room door on the sixth floor of the South Quadrangle student residence building. Someone had crossed out Thaddeus and written the letters TD. Beau hesitated before opening the door. Everything was new to him. He'd just experienced his first ride in an elevator. He'd never been in a building of more than four stories. Now he was about to meet a stranger with whom he would live for several months and, on top of everything else, he was exhausted from an eleven-hour bus ride.

His journey began early that morning. Fawn and Father Marcotte were there to see him off. He had not thought he would ever leave his sister but Fawn said she wanted him to go. She smiled as tears ran down her cheeks but her words were unequivocal. "For a boy who has nothing, to attend The University of Michigan with all expenses paid, is a life-changing opportunity. It's a gift to you through the grace of God and you have to accept it. I'll be fine. Father said I can be a teachers' assistant at Holy Childhood. I'll have my own room, meals at the school, and work I enjoy." She gave Beau a quick hug and then stepped back. "Get on the bus, little brother. Go out there and make us proud. I'm gonna be watching."

As he hoisted the suitcase containing all of his possessions onto a little bus, Father Marcotte pressed $20 into his hand, gave him a pat on the back, and said a quick "God bless." Father Marcotte was the best man he knew. Beau would do anything for him; even attempt to embrace Catholicism.

Beau looked out the back window and watched his sister and his best friend standing on the sidewalk and waving. Soon the bus went up East Hill and out of sight. It transported Beau the ten miles from Harbor Springs to the small town of Petoskey, where he transferred to the large Greyhound bus for the trip to Ann Arbor.

The Greyhound was idling at the station when they arrived. Beau climbed aboard and saw only five or six other passengers. He took a seat next to a window and was resting his head against the glass when a tall Indian walked down the aisle. There were plenty of empty seats but the man sat next to Beau.

What's the matter with this guy? There is no reason to crowd in next to me like this.

When the man spoke, his voice was unmistakable. "Hello, Beau."

"Hello, Spirit Father. I didn't expect to see you on a bus."

Pontiac, a man who did not waste words, merely nodded.

Beau said, "Where are you going? Do people in the Spirit World usually travel by bus? Why aren't you dressed like a chief? In those jeans and buckskin jacket, you look like an ordinary guy." A look into Pontiac's eyes would tell anyone that, regardless of his attire, he was no ordinary guy. Beau stammered, "I mean you kind of blend in ... a little."

Pontiac smiled. "Beau, so many questions. People in the Spirit World are not required to travel by bus. I dress as I wish to dress. I'm only traveling as far as Boyne Falls or Gaylord. I'm here to speak with you. I'll get off the bus when I am finished."

Beau sat quietly and waited for Pontiac to continue.

"This bus is taking you to a world that is new to you. It's a strange place with new people, unfamiliar customs, and rules you won't understand. I've given you three rules to help guide you along the path of a good life. Do you remember them?" He stopped speaking and looked inquiringly at Beau.

"Yes, Spirit Father. Of course, I remember."

"Good. I have three more rules to help you find your way. The first rule is to be brave. I mean, more than physical bravery. I mean the kind of bravery you need in order to try your hardest and not be held back by fear of failure or humiliation. The only person who never fails is the one who doesn't try.

"The second rule is to think for yourself. There will be people who attempt to influence you. A time will come when everyone will hold a certain opinion and you feel pressure to agree with them. Do not follow the crowd. Decide things for yourself.

"The last rule is to love everybody you can. Love is the only thing in the world that you can give without limit to one person and still have plenty left to give to others."

Beau maintained a respectful silence until he was sure Pontiac was finished. "I like the rule about love. Father Marcotte says you should love your enemies."

Pontiac's face darkened. He looked like he had just taken a bite of a lemon. "Beau, I mean no disrespect to a priest, but that is the dumbest thing I ever heard. You should love everybody who is worthy of your love. I didn't say to love anybody who happens to cross your path. Love is for your friends, your family, good people. It is not for enemies. Perhaps a priest can love his enemies, but Indians can't afford such foolishness. Enemies are to be crushed. I thought you would know that." As the Greyhound slowed for its stop at Boyne Falls, Pontiac said, "I'll get off here. Do you understand the three new rules?"

"Yes, Spirit Father. Be brave, think for myself, and love everybody I can."

Pontiac climbed down from the bus and disappeared into the small rundown building that served as a combination bus stop and coffee shop.

After a bus ride with stops in every little town between Petoskey and Ann Arbor, Beau was finally standing outside the door to his room. He thought of Pontiac's warning that he wouldn't know the rules of this new world.

Heck, he didn't even know how he was expected to enter his own room. *Should he knock on the door? Would they laugh at him for being timid? Should he just open the door and walk in? Would that be considered rude?* Beau gave one quick knock, opened the door, and was face to face with the most beautiful man he had ever seen.

The guy was well over six feet tall and had such deep black skin it appeared to shine. His shorts and T-shirt revealed an incredible physique. Every muscle was clearly defined. His appearance was one of great strength combined with fluid grace. This was Michelangelo's *David* come to life with black skin, a wide smile, and gleaming white teeth.

Beau extended his hand. "I'm Beau Lightfoot. Are you Thaddeus?" He had been expecting to meet a boy. Not a man.

The man shook Beau's hand. "I'm Marcus White." He gestured with his head. "That little short stuff over there is Kowalski."

Kowalski grabbed Beau's hand and said, "I'm Thaddeus D. Kowalski but people call me TD. TD stands for touchdown."

Beau sat on one of the beds while Marcus and TD filled him in. They both went to Carver High School in Pittsburgh. Marcus was a junior at Michigan and a first-team defensive end. TD, like Beau, was a freshman; but unlike Beau, he'd had a choice of a dozen offers. TD had scored thirty-three touchdowns as a high school senior and was one of the most coveted college football recruits in Pennsylvania. He was less gifted academically and had to struggle to qualify for admission to the University of Michigan. Marcus had taken on the role of a big brother to help TD adjust to the academic and social demands of a big university.

Beau didn't know it at the time, but during the next few years, Marcus White would become an important person in his own life. Marcus doubled the number of thoroughly good people Beau knew. Now it was two: Father Marcotte and Marcus White.

Beau hadn't imagined a real person could have such a perfect body. He had never met a Negro before or, as he had heard was now the preferred term, a black person. Neither Marcus nor TD appeared to notice any difference between each other or that Beau was half Indian. A sophisticated person knew that attitude about race was not an appropriate topic of conversation; especially with people one had just met. Beau, however, had no hesitation in asking TD and Marcus about their feelings.

Marcus answered, "As TD knows, there's still plenty of discrimination in America ... but not among football players. Football is an ultimate meritocracy. You can either play ball or you can't. It doesn't make any difference who your daddy is or the color of your skin. I think of our team as a warrior brotherhood."

TD agreed. "Marcus is pre-med. He uses words like *meritocracy* but he's okay."

After a while, Marcus said he had to go, but before he left he gave Beau some important academic advice. "For one of your elective classes, take Sociology 101. There are always lots of girls in Sociology."

TD watched the door close behind Marcus and immediately began to tell Beau about his friend. It was obvious that Marcus was TD's hero. He seemed to have an unlimited supply of Marcus White stories and Beau paid attention to the first three or four.

Marcus grew up poor, was raised by a devout Baptist grandmother, became religious himself, was a straight-A student, didn't drink, didn't take drugs, didn't swear, and was one of the two best football players ever to come out of Carver High School. (Beau assumed the other all-time best player from Carver High was TD.)

The Marcus White stories continued; but rather than paying attention, Beau observed his roommate. TD was a friendly guy, tightly wound, and a bundle of strength and energy. Beau had to suppress a smile. *This guy is obviously a powerful athlete but there's something about his energy and unrestrained enthusiasm that reminds me of a puppy.*

TD began to laugh at his own story. "So the religious stuff was getting out of control. Marcus would drop into his stance and, just before the play began, he would ask the guy across the line if he accepted Jesus Christ as his Savior. Remember, this was in a darn football game. The guy usually replied with something nasty. When the ball was snapped, Marcus would swing his strong right fist straight up from the ground and smite the guy a righteous blow to the solar plexus. Then, he'd spin him around, whack him a couple of more times, knock him down, and bang his head on the ground. Marcus was real fast. The whole thing would take him less than two seconds.

"Then he'd ask again, 'Do you accept Him now?' I wasn't there, but they say most guys saw the light."

Beau was skeptical. "TD, did that really happen?"

"I don't know. It might be an exaggeration, but it's a hell of a good story and, knowing Marcus, it is possible."

~

The white athletic socks with the dark-blue M stamped on their sides turned out to be the best part of Beau's first day as a freshman football player. He had planned to stop at a store on the way to practice and buy some socks and a T-shirt but TD told him the athletic department furnished those things. Beau wondered out loud if they would provide a couple of sets so he would have a pair to wear while the other was being washed. TD had laughed. "This is big-time college football. The equipment manager will give you clean socks, a T-shirt, and a jockstrap before every practice."

That was excellent news. In high school, Beau had to wear his athletic clothes all week and wash them himself on the weekends. He had to admit, by day three they were pretty gamey. "Big time" meant clean clothes every day and he didn't have to do the washing. It also apparently meant he would have to wear somebody else's jockstrap. *Oh, well. If that's the way the big guys do it ...*

The socks with the dark-blue M made everything real; and they felt good on his skin when he put them on. Beau really was a student at the University of Michigan!

Two hours later, when he took them off after his first team practice, they were hardly dirty. Practice wasn't bad; he just wasn't allowed to do much. About fifty players were on the freshman team and the coaches lavished their attention on the prize recruits like Eddie Bartucci and TD Kowalski. They had no time for the likes of Beau Lightfoot.

His academic career, on the other hand, was off to a fine start. As Marcus had predicted, lots of girls took Sociology 101. The professor said he would go around the room and have each student stand and give his or her name; home town; and, if the student wished, a bit of personal information. About half of the kids provided something personal.

As they worked their way down his row, Beau decided he would be among those who declined.

"Gail Shanley. Fort Bragg, North Carolina. I live in North Carolina now but I've moved all around the world. I'm what you might call an Army brat."

"Susan Bradley. Grand Rapids."

"TD Kowalski. Pittsburgh, Pennsylvania. I'm a football player."

"Beau Lightfoot. Harbor Springs, Michigan."

As the introductions moved past him, Beau relaxed. A girl three seats beyond his got to her feet. *Oh my goodness! What an absolute smash! She was a small girl, probably only a couple of inches over five feet tall, with beautiful clear skin and a wonderfully feminine body.* She said she was Rebecca Goldman from Long Island, New York, and people called her Becky.

Becky caught Beau watching her so he quickly looked away. He was in love with Janet Cunningham, and Janet was at the University of Michigan. He shouldn't be looking at another girl. Of course, he couldn't be sure how things would go with Janet—and one of Pontiac's rules was to love everybody you can. He could make some room for Becky Goldman.

Beau decided to speak to Becky after class but four or five other guys were crowded around her. They'd probably leave in a minute or two but he couldn't wait. His schedule was jammed: classes; football practice; a quick dinner; required study period with the other football players until nine o'clock; and, finally, some free time.

By nine o'clock, Beau was so tired he could barely move; but, of course, no amount of fatigue could keep him away from Janet. She had been accepted at several colleges but the pull of Michigan was too strong for her to resist. Many of her Kingswood friends were going to Michigan, Bobby and Eddie would be there, and her father loved the university.

Beau managed to see Janet two or three nights every week; not alone, of course. Bobby and Eddie were usually there, and sometimes other friends. They met at the undergraduate library around nine thirty to study together and always ended up in the coffee shop drinking Cokes and talking. Janet spoke excitedly about the Chi Omega Sorority and said that since her mother was a Chi Omega, she would probably have a good chance of being accepted as a pledge.

Beau didn't understand much about what Janet called 'the Greek system." It had to do with Greek letters used for the names of the various fraternities and sororities. The whole thing seemed silly, but Janet was into it. She said she would have a good chance of being accepted. Beau felt it inconceivable that any door in America would not open for Janet Cunningham.

She said she thought it would be neat when she was a sister in Chi Omega or some other good sorority and her boys—Bobby, Eddie, and Beau—were fraternity men. She had heard about the fabulous parties at the fraternities. They could all go to each other's parties. It would be really super.

One night, as the group of friends prepared to leave the coffee shop, Beau drew Janet aside. "Do you think a fraternity would accept me?"

"Don't be silly. You're a great guy. Any fraternity would be lucky to have you for a brother."

"Does it cost extra money to be in a fraternity?"

"I don't know. It probably does cost something but I don't think it's very much."

"Which fraternity do you think I should join?"

"That's up to you, Beau. There are lots of good ones. Bobby and Eddie have friends in Sigma Alpha Epsilon and I'll bet they'll pledge there. SAE is good, but it's a jock house. You might want to think about something else. Beta Delta is really classy; cool guys, not jocks; student leaders; those kinds of guys. Anyway, I shouldn't tell you where to pledge. You'll pick a good house."

Later that same night, Beau walked five doors down his dormitory hallway to the room shared by Bobby and Eddie. Bobby was out but Eddie knew how to go about joining a fraternity. He said there wasn't much to it. The frats were having open houses next Sunday afternoon. All you had to do was pick those you liked and show up at the front door. They would invite you in, show you around the fraternity house, introduce you to some of the brothers, and try to convince you to pledge.

It sounded easy.

On Sunday afternoon, Beau joined a large group of young men as they left South Quad and prepared to rush the fraternities. Some of the boys with rooms on his floor had told him it was important to dress correctly: nice slacks, shined shoes, and a jacket. Since his only slacks were chinos, he washed them, creased them with his fingers, flattened them out on his desk, and pressed them overnight under some heavy textbooks. He shined his shoes and put on his jacket—a blue nylon windbreaker.

He saw that the other guys were wearing sport coats. He had misunderstood—but it didn't make any difference since Beau didn't own a sport coat.

The group began to disburse as each young man headed toward the fraternity that appealed to him. Since Beau was only rushing because Janet thought it was the thing to do, he headed toward Beta Delta because Janet had said she thought it was classy. He might as well go to the frat she liked.

His route to Beta Delta took him along Washtenaw Avenue and past several other fraternity houses. Each house was larger and more beautiful than the last; until he was walking past graceful mansions set well back on splendid wide lawns. A gently curved sidewalk led to the front door of one the grand houses. The door was open and a couple of freshmen were going in. The Greek letters of the fraternity were above the door but, of course, they were unfamiliar to Beau. The fraternity was less than a block from Chi Omega and the house looked inviting. It would probably be fine. At worst, it could serve as a practice rush before he arrived at Beta Delta. Beau turned down the sidewalk and headed for the open door.

A nice-looking fellow invited him in and offered to show him around the house. After what seemed a cursory tour, he was escorted to a large living room and introduced to a guy named Johnny McAlister, who said he was rush chairman. Beau said hello and they talked for about one minute. McAlister asked Beau where he went to high school and what he planned to study at Michigan. His quick eyes took in Beau's brown skin and nylon windbreaker. He made a small gesture to the clean-cut fellow who had greeted Beau at the front door. "It was a pleasure to meet you, Beau," said McAlister. "Thank you for stopping by our house. Good luck with the rest of your fraternity rush."

It was over before Beau understood what had happened. It was a good thing this fraternity was only for practice.

It only took ten minutes to walk to the Beta Delta house; not long enough. Beau needed at least an hour to get ready. The front door was closed and his hand was unsteady when he reached for the brass knocker. Pontiac had said to be brave, but Pontiac never faced anything like this.

It didn't turn out to be difficult at all. Beau was given an unhurried tour of the fraternity house and the brothers were friendly. His tour guide was a fellow named Rick Johnson, who seemed to take a sincere interest in Beau. After the tour, they moved into a room with bookcases and dark wood paneling. The fraternity brothers and the freshmen stood in small groups, talking and smoking cigarettes. Someone offered Beau a cigarette and Beau explained he didn't smoke. One of the brothers laughed and said, "It's okay not to smoke—but you do drink, don't you?"

Beau's response that he didn't drink brought disapproving looks from some of the brothers, but no comments. These guys weren't giving him the bum's rush. They appeared to be making an extra effort to give him a fair opportunity. He wondered why they would afford him this special treatment. When Rick Johnson said, "I understand you know Janet Cunningham"—then Beau understood. *Of course, Johnson knows Janet. Several of the guys probably know her.*

Beau had gotten that far in the process as a courtesy to Janet, but now it was time to get serious. Rick introduced Beau to a self-important senior who must have been designated to ask the questions. "So Beau, if you don't mind my asking, what does your father do?"

How should he answer? There was Lightfoot, the abusive drunk; Marcotte, the Catholic priest; and Pontiac, who had been dead for more than two hundred years. Beau thought about his answer for a beat too long. "My dad was a military man. He passed away quite a few years ago."

"Was he in the Army?"

"Yeah, you could say he was in the army."

"Was he in a war? What rank did he have?"

"He was in a big war. He was a chief."

"A chief? Is that like a Chief Petty Officer in the Navy?"

"Yeah, something like that."

The senior looked disappointed. Chief Petty Officer must not have been good enough. Beau considered saying his father had been a general but that was an awfully big lie and they might have been able to look it up. He felt a hand on his elbow. It was a new guy. Rick Johnson had disappeared.

The new frat brother guided Beau out of the library in the direction of a couch in a back corner of a room he called the great hall. The brother maintained a cheerful conversation as he steered Beau toward two boys seated on the couch. "Here are a couple of fellows I'd like you to meet." A diminutive young man wearing a western-style suit and a turban politely stood and extended his hand. The fraternity brother said, "Beau, this is Garamella Patel. Garamella, this is Beau Lightfoot."

Garamella shook Beau's hand and said, "I am having pleasure for meeting you."

The other boy reminded Beau of Jethro Bodine of *The Beverly Hillbillies*, a popular television show. This guy didn't bother to stand, but the fraternity brother continued his polite introductions. "This is Joe Bob Mason. Joe Bob, this is Beau Lightfoot." Joe Bob made a halfhearted wave and said hi.

The brother indicated that the three of them should sit on the couch and get acquainted. He said one of the other fraternity brothers would be back later. Since no one knew what to say, the outcasts hunkered down on the couch and quietly waited. Beau felt uncomfortable but the instructions had been clear. He was to sit on the couch until someone came for him. As he began to feel more and more foolish, he heard the sound of a raised voice coming from the library.

"WHAT DOES MY FATHER DO? WHAT THE HELL KIND OF QUESTION IS THAT?"

There was a response but it was too quiet for Beau to hear it.

"YEAH. WELL, MY FATHER IS A PRIVATE BUSINESSMAN … VERY PRIVATE."

Another unclear response.

"IT'S A *PRIVATE* KIND OF BUSINESS. THAT MEANS THE KIND OF BUSINESS IT IS, IS NONE OF YOUR FUCKING BUSINESS!"

Soon another freshman was led to the couch and introduced to Garamella, Joe Bob, and Beau. Mitch Caputo was about Beau's size and was swarthy, with slicked-back hair, and a manner obviously calculated to signal that he was a tough guy. He would soon become one of Beau's best friends.

Beau asked Mitch about his angry answers. Mitch explained he had overheard Beau being asked about his father and saw what happened when Beau failed to provide the kind of answer they were looking for. Mitch knew he didn't have an answer that would be acceptable. He figured his trip to the losers' couch was inevitable and there was no sense in putting up with any bullshit along the way.

Mitch stared at Beau with unblinking dark eyes. It was a good effort. Mitch was almost able to pull off the tough-guy glower but he didn't quite make it. He put his hand on Beau's arm. "Guys like you and me don't belong on the losers' couch. Let's get out of here."

Beau said, "The frat brother said to wait here until one of the other brothers came back for us."

Mitch smiled. "No disrespect intended, but you don't know much. It's lucky for you that I'm here … No one is coming back to this couch. They're going to let you sit here forever. Come on; let's get the fuck out of this joint!"

Beau didn't know if it was okay to just get up and leave, but Mitch headed for the door so Beau followed. As they walked out, one of the nice-looking, friendly fellows called out to them, "Good-bye. Thanks for rushing Beta Delta."

Mitch threw a response over his shoulder. "Yeah, sure. Adios dip shit!"

As they walked back to campus, Mitch and Beau discovered their rooms were on the same floor. Mitch said he thought Beau was a good guy who needed somebody to give him a little guidance. He said he knew the score and would show Beau how things really worked in Ann Arbor. The first thing to understand, he said, was that guys like them were not ever going to be allowed to join a fraternity and they shouldn't embarrass themselves by trying. Beau was disappointed, but he could see Mitch was right.

Mitch was unlike anyone Beau had ever known. In addition to his tough-guy persona, Mitch was open and likeable. Beau could use the help of someone who knew how things really worked. By the time the boys reached the front door of South Quad, a friendship had begun.

Beau was feeling depressed. Although he didn't care that his fraternity rush was a complete bust, Janet thought fraternities and sororities were the greatest and now he was going to be an outsider.

And the other parts of his college life weren't turning out any better. His classes were more difficult than he anticipated. He'd been a good student in high school but an A at Harbor Springs High School translated to a C- at the University of Michigan. Freshman football wasn't merely going badly—it wasn't going at all. The coaches weren't giving him an opportunity to show his stuff. They only paid attention to the thoroughbreds, not a little pony like Beau Lightfoot.

Accompanied by unhappy thoughts, he trudged across campus to Sociology 101. When he was halfway there it started to rain. Wet and miserable, he slumped into his chair and waited for class to begin. He was sinking into a depression and needed something to help him regain his equilibrium. The aisle between the rows of chairs was tight. He was slow to straighten up to make room and, when an impatient student turned her back toward him and edged her way past him to get to her seat, he was presented with the quickest and most potent pick-me-up imaginable ... a beautifully turned female fanny. In a world containing such wonders, how could he have ever questioned the existence of God?

Becky Goldman, upon whom He had granted His grace, slipped in front of Beau to take her place three seats down the row. She was wearing a black-and-white checked wrap-around skirt that was held together with a large silver safety pin that appeared to be both ornamental and functional. A black sweater accentuated her lovely curvaceous figure. Her auburn hair fell to her shoulders and then curved out in a whimsical upward flip.

It was imperative for Beau to meet this coed. The last time he thought about speaking to Becky, she had been surrounded by boys and he couldn't get near her. He decided on a new plan. He'd pass her a note. It was straight out of junior high school but it seemed like a good idea. He tore a page from his notebook and wrote: Becky, would you have a Coke with me after class? Beau Lightfoot (the guy three seats to your right).

He folded the paper and passed it down the row. She unfolded the note, read it, and wrote two words on it. When the professor looked in her direction, she quickly covered it with her textbook.

What did she write? I've made a fool of myself. She's not going to return the note until the professor looks away. I'm sure she wrote two words. No thanks. Get lost. Forget it. Sorry buddy. No way.

The student seated next to Beau poked him in the side and handed him the note. *Oh, man. I'm such a jerk. This is going to be embarrassing but it's too late now.* Beau unfolded the paper and read the two words Becky had written: Ice tea.

Becky flashed a 10,000-megawatt smile from across the table in the diner. Beau, true to form, was nervous and unable to think of appropriate conversation. His only thought was that he'd love to unpin the safety pin that held her skirt together. Although he was not a smooth talker, he did have enough sense to let that thought remain unexpressed.

Becky was relaxed and made everything easy. She told him about her background: grew up on Long Island; oldest of three children; father a medical doctor; mother a teacher; a politically and socially liberal family, with a strong interest in The Arts; years of music lessons for Becky, who played the cello and planned to try out for the symphony orchestra at Michigan.

She paused to give Beau an opportunity to say something about himself and, when he failed to do so, she tried a few leading questions. He told her a bit but she apparently sensed his reticence and moved on to another subject.

Didn't he think Dr. Rubinstein, their sociology professor was excellent? Beau agreed he was indeed excellent. He had never thought about such things. Professors were professors and he was a freshman. His job was to write down whatever they said and hope he could understand and remember enough to pass the examinations.

Becky, on the other hand, seemed to be comfortable judging her professor's ability. She was also apparently interested in discussing what was said in class. "Didn't you think the concept he explored today was profound?" She peered at Beau over the top of her glass. She obviously expected Beau to say something.

"Yes. It sure was ... very profound."

Becky had found her stride and was gathering momentum. "How one sees things depends on where one is standing. The more I think about that idea, the more I realize it is absolutely true. The words he used, by the way, 'perception is a function of position,' are just too clever. You better write them down. That concept is definitely going to be on a test."

Beau could only stare at her from across the table. Becky Goldman was a small girl but she was leaving him in the dust.

Suddenly, she stopped talking, looked intently into Beau's eyes, and rested a hand on his arm. "You're Native American, aren't you?"

Beau had never heard the term before, but he liked it because Native American implied respect and acknowledged that the Indians were here first. He told Becky he was half Odawa and half white. She studied him for a moment and said she thought the white half was probably French.

He began to say something, but she silenced him by tightening her grip on his forearm. "You're about to say something dumb, and I don't want you to say it."

Beau was startled. "Are you some kind of a mind reader?"

Rather than answering, she proceeded to say exactly what he had been thinking. "You were going to ask if having an ice tea with a half-breed was a problem for me."

He tried to respond, but could not find the right words.

She continued. "Let's turn things around. I'm a Jew. Does that cause you to have a problem being with me?"

Beau was shocked at the idea. "Becky, how could you say such a thing? Of course not! I can't imagine any guy with a pulse having a problem being with you."

She said she wished that were true, but she had experienced plenty of prejudice and guessed he'd probably been on the receiving end of some mistreatment too.

This girl was open about her feelings and had a sincere kindness that broke through Beau's defenses. Things had been building up so much that he felt he had to confide in someone. He told her about his frustrations and especially about his humiliation when he tried rushing the fraternities. "Why did they ask what my father did? What does that have to do with anything?"

"For those guys, the answer to that question means everything. It's a contest of sorts. Some people put others down to feel good about themselves. Maybe you're the wrong race or religion. Or if that's not an issue, then they have more money than you; or if you have a lot of money, their money is better because its old money. There will always be people who think they are better than you because their grandfather donated a building to the university fifty years ago." She paused to take a deep breath. "The only way to beat these jerks is to refuse to play their game. You have to be brave enough to do what you want to do and not hold back because of fear of humiliation. You have to do your own thinking and not allow the opinions of these self-appointed superiors influence you."

A tingle danced up the back of Beau's neck. "You just said I should be brave and do my own thinking."

"Yes. I think those are good rules."

"They are good rules. Where did you hear them?"

"I didn't hear them anywhere. I pay attention to what's going on in the world. I just know things."

Beau had no doubt Becky Goldman knew things. He had been so engrossed in their conversation that he had lost track of time. Their glasses were empty and he was late for football practice. As they said good-bye, Becky said it had been fun and they should do it again.

Becky Goldman was a friend, but she didn't join Beau when he hung out with Janet, Bobby, and Eddie because she wasn't interested in either sports or in joining a sorority. Mitch Caputo, on the other hand, glommed onto them like a barnacle on a passing ship. Eddie said Mitch was a greasy little bastard but he couldn't help but like him. Janet said she found Mitch unsavory but, in his own way, kind of cute. He was always doing favors; clearly trying to work his way into the inner circle.

Beau didn't know Mitch's true background. Mitch told different stories at different times: Mitch's father was serving a ten-year sentence in Jackson Prison for aggravated assault. Mitch's father was a poor but honest immigrant who worked as a maintenance man at Henry Ford Hospital. Mitch's father had been rubbed-out by the Purple Gang and Mitch had been raised by his grandmother. Mitch was sometimes a Sicilian guy with a vague association with organized crime. At other times, Mitch was an ordinary Italian kid from Detroit. He claimed to have lethal skill at hand-to-hand combat and to have been a professional card player. He was an expert in many subjects and generous with advice.

At one point, Beau heard Mitch advising Eddie on the proper way to beat up a person. "Never hit anybody with your fist. Your hand has lots of delicate bones. Think about it. You're going to smash all those little bones against some moke's hard head? No way. Especially you, Eddie. You're the quarterback; your hands are valuable and you've got to protect them."

Beau was concerned Eddie was seriously listening to Mitch, until Eddie caught Beau's eye and winked.

Mitch continued, "If you do hit a guy, use your forearm and elbow. That's heavy bone and you won't hurt yourself. The thing you want to do, one way or another, is get him on the ground and then stomp him with your foot. Feet can do real damage."

Eddie appeared to think Mitch was harmless entertainment; Beau wasn't so sure.

When Janet suggested they all go to a fraternity party, Mitch, the tough guy, immediately backed away. Beau understood Mitch's quick exit, but Janet said she thought it would be fun, and Beau wasn't going to disappoint her. She said the Beta Lambda Fall Dance was a big deal on campus and, if you knew people, you could go to the party without being a member. One of the Beta Lambda brothers had told her she could come to the party with some friends. The only requirement was she bring an equal number of boys and girls.

Beau was painfully aware of the social distance separating him from Janet. Of course, Janet Cunningham knew people. She had been quickly accepted into the Chi Omega Sorority and it seemed as if every fraternity man on campus either already knew her or couldn't wait to meet her. Beau, on the other hand, was nobody. But, nobody or not, he was going to the Beta Lambda party with Janet.

They needed three girls. Janet was one and she would bring her Chi Omega friend named Dizzy. That would make two. Janet wondered if Beau knew anyone he could ask to join them. Yeah, Beau knew someone.

When they arrived, the party was in full swing. The Beta Lambda house looked like a large eighteenth-century English hunting lodge. It commanded the top of a small rise and the "friends of Janet" group climbed two sets of concrete steps in order to reach the front door. They weren't on dates; instead it was just three boys and three girls going to a party together.

A five-piece band was playing and dimmed lights created pools of deep shadows. The furniture and carpets had been removed from the entire first floor to create space for dancing. Beau hadn't had much experience dancing, but he was naturally graceful and Becky said he probably had some good Indian dancing genes. He was able to pick up the moves easily. He danced with Becky, Dizzy, and once with Janet.

Dizzy was from Venezuela and her proper name was D'Isabella Hernandez. She had beautiful, long, black hair and wore four-inch heels. Her skirt was full at the bottom and flared when she twirled during the fast dances. She moved with speed and confidence. Beau was impressed. Dizzy Hernandez was quite a girl.

Just as Beau finally began to relax and enjoy the party, he heard a commotion coming from the largest of the downstairs rooms. A distressed female voice cried, "PLEASE DON'T! STOP IT! LET GO OF ME!"

A male voice followed. "Come on, Paul. Leave her alone."

There were sounds of a struggle.

Beau ran toward the disturbance. He didn't know if he was running to rescue someone or merely to see what was happening. A big guy, probably about six feet two inches tall and more than two hundred pounds, had a girl by the neck and was bending her backward and kissing her. She struggled but he kissed her hard on the mouth and grabbed her ass with his free hand.

A boy was trying to pull the big guy's arm from around her neck. "Cut it out, Paul! Let her go!"

When Paul finally released the girl, he ran his hands roughly over her breasts as she pulled away. Her face was red and she was gasping. The boy attempted to comfort her by putting his arm around her shoulders. He said something to her but she threw his arm off and left him looking helpless.

One of the Beta Lambda brothers touched Beau's arm. "That guy is Paul Doyle. He's bad news. Keep your girl away from him."

Beau thanked the boy for the warning and immediately panicked. Where's Becky? He'd been dancing with Dizzy and now he couldn't find Becky.

He checked everyone standing near Paul Doyle and, to his relief, Becky wasn't there. Because of the dim light and shadows, he had missed her on his first look, but finally located her standing near the fireplace on the far side of the room. Her eyes were fixed on Doyle and she was staying away.

Some other unfortunate coed didn't keep a safe distance from Doyle and was getting the treatment. Paul gave her a good going-over before she pulled free and ran crying into the bathroom that had been designated as the ladies' room for the party. Beau wondered how this bully was able to grab all of these girls. Why didn't they just avoid him? Then Beau understood what was happening. Doyle was strategically stationing himself near the bathroom. The girls had to pass by him. Becky appeared to be safe so Beau decided to warn Janet and Dizzy to stay away from Paul Doyle.

He located Dizzy but couldn't reach her because of a crowd of enthusiastic dancers. She was heading toward the bathroom! He fought his way across the crowded room but didn't make it in time.

Doyle was partially blocking the bathroom door. Dizzy said, "Excuse me," and attempted to slip past him. Doyle reached out to grab Dizzy but rather than pulling away, as he must have expected, she moved into him and, from a distance of about two inches, screamed into his face, "IF YOU TOUCH ME, I'LL BREAK YOUR FUCKING ARM!"

He backed up a step and affected a look of mock horror. "My, my, don't we have a dirty little mouth?" he said. But he didn't touch her.

Beau's relief didn't last long. Janet was headed toward the bathroom and Doyle grabbed her. Beau made it to her side and tried to pull her away but Doyle was twice his size and too strong to handle.

Janet struggled and gasped, "Get Bobby!"

Beau found Bobby in the next room but before they got back to Janet, Eddie was already there. Rather than trying to pull Janet away, Eddie kicked the side of Doyle's left knee. The knee gave way. Doyle released Janet, turned to his left, and fell toward Eddie. Eddie put his whole body behind a forearm/elbow strike to Doyle's face. The blow was perfectly timed and its force was magnified by the momentum of Doyle's falling body.

Doyle was down and out. Out cold. Eddie moved in for a few kicks but Bobby stopped him. A girl screamed. The band stopped playing. Someone turned on the lights. Paul Doyle's body didn't even twitch. Blood flowed from his nose and mouth. Someone yelled to call the paramedics. Someone else said, "Call the police."

Bobby Cunningham climbed onto a chair so he could be seen. His powerful voice cut through the confusion. "HOLD IT! EVERYBODY, LISTEN TO ME. Most of you know this bum lying on the floor. He's probably assaulted half of the women at this party." Bobby paused. The room became quiet. "The man who put him down is Eddie Bartucci. You don't know Eddie, but he's a damn good man." Bobby pointed to the unconscious Doyle who was lying face down. "It's not worth causing trouble for a man like Eddie Bartucci because of a bum like this. Somebody, call the paramedics. When they arrive, I want everyone to say that Doyle got drunk and fell down."

One of the girls said, "That's not right! We shouldn't lie."

Bobby agreed. "Of course you shouldn't lie. I wouldn't ask you to lie. This fellow hurt himself falling down the stairs."

Someone in the back of the crowd argued, "But he didn't fall down the stairs."

Bobby picked up Doyle as easily as if he was a rag doll. The crowd silently parted to make room. Bobby carried the limp body up the stairs that went to the second floor. Beau was standing at the bottom step and saw Bobby turn and face back down. Paul Doyle's large body bounced down the stairs. His head came to rest at Beau's feet and some blood spattered on Beau's shoes. There wasn't a sound in the Beta Lambda house. Beau stood frozen in place until he felt the gentle pull of Becky Goldman's hand.

"I think this would be a good time to go home," she said.

A BROTHERHOOD OF WARRIORS

Pontiac persuaded the northern tribes to put their disputes aside and unite in common cause against the English. With warriors from many tribes, he forged a formidable fighting force that won major victories throughout the Great Lakes region and terrorized their enemy.

2013

Janet wandered around the bedroom, poking through memorabilia from decades past. She picked up a small, tarnished trophy and read the inscription: *Little Harbor Club Junior Girls Tennis Champion, Janet Cunningham*. Bobby had kept her trophy for fifty years. She moved to the bookcase and shuffled through a pile of old photographs. She selected one and brought it to Beau.

"I love seeing these old pictures. This one must have been taken when I visited Dizzy in Venezuela. That would have been the summer after we were all freshmen. The boys were so handsome—and so young. Look how young Dad is. He was a lot younger when this picture was taken than we are now. It's hard to believe he's been gone almost ten years ... I miss my dad."

Her brown eyes filled with tears and Beau put his arm around her. He knew fatigue and the strain of Fawn's funeral had taken an emotional toll. "Your dad was big and loud and as subtle as a chainsaw. I thought he was a mean guy until I got to know him and realized all the bluster wasn't really him. He kept it well hidden but he was a man with a loving heart. Once I came to understand your father, I loved the guy."

Janet managed a small smile. "He looked happy, didn't he?"

Beau nodded. "I was there when the photograph was taken. He was so proud of Bobby and Eddie. I don't think it's possible for a man to be happier."

Janet wiped her eyes and handed the photograph to Beau. "I'm going to the bathroom. I'll be back in a minute."

He rested the photo on his lap. Two young, smiling athletes preserved forever at the peak of their abilities and a beaming Mr. Cunningham with an arm around each of them. Bobby and Eddie were wearing the dark-blue sweaters with 1969 in yellow numbers across the front that they had earned at Michigan their freshman year.

Beau remembered every painful detail of the night the picture was taken: the lingering daylight of the Northern Michigan July evening, his work as a car parker/drink server/cleanup boy at the Cunningham's' cocktail party, the way his white busboy coat made him invisible to the guests, and the overheard snatches of conversations.

"... so we sent Janet to visit D'Isabella in Venezuela for six weeks ... Hernandez family is very prominent ... will broaden Janet's education to see another part of the world ... keep her away from that boy from Harbor Springs." He also overheard Mr. Cunningham's casual dismissal of a suggestion that since Beau had also earned his freshman numerals, he should be included in the photograph: "Bobby got a scholarship for the kid but that's as far as it is going to go. There's no reason to have him in the picture. He'll never play a down for Michigan."

Yeah, Beau remembered. His feelings toward Buck Cunningham were not loving. Now, looking back from the perspective of time, Beau felt ashamed of his attitude. He had felt sorry for himself—the poor boy with nothing while others had so much. He had thought only of his own petty concerns while the world at large was getting ready to explode.

ANN ARBOR, 1966

Far away from the shaded lawns of Wequetonsing and the cool waters of Little Traverse Bay, the summer of 1966 was long and hot. A portion of the civil rights movement was turning away from the nonviolent protests of Martin Luther King, Jr. to militant leaders like Stokely Carmichael and H. Rap Brown. Lyndon Johnson's civil rights program was stalled in Congress and, among the urban young, black impatience approached spontaneous ignition.

Civil rights leader James Meredith was murdered in Mississippi. Blacks were shot from the windows of passing automobiles in Benton Harbor, Michigan, and Dayton, Ohio. In Milwaukee, national guardsmen were called to protect civil rights demonstrators from an angry mob.

In this atmosphere of racial hostility, street violence, looting, and arson spiraled out of control. The worst rioting occurred in Chicago and Cleveland, two cities that traditionally produced significant numbers of Michigan football players. Chicago's West Side and Cleveland's Hough neighborhood were like war zones.

At the same time, another war half a world away was intensifying. Vietnam, a country that only a few years ago most Americans would have had difficulty locating on a map, became a major battleground. In the seven months through the end of July 1966, two thousand six hundred and ninety-one Americans had been killed there and U.S. planes had bombed North Vietnam all the way to the Chinese border.

Although some opposition to the war began to appear, most Americans approved the actions of the Johnson Administration. Secretary of State Dean Rusk argued the war was necessary to halt worldwide communist aggression and Secretary of Defense Robert McNamara predicted that the war would be over within a year.

The burden of increased draft calls fell on the poor and the nonwhite. Young men from upper and more educated classes found numerous ways to avoid military service. When Beau Lightfoot began his sophomore year at the University of Michigan, he joined the ranks of 2.4 million other American men of draft age who were protected by student deferments.

Beau's concerns were more personal: renewing his growing friendship with beautiful Becky Goldman; progressing toward his dream of earning a college degree; moving from the freshman football team to the varsity; and, most importantly, being with Janet Cunningham while she was away from the decidedly unhelpful influence of her father.

Varsity football players arrived on campus two weeks before the start of classes and Beau was bursting with enthusiasm. He had heard about Gary Blieschroeder's killer practices and he wasn't going to be one of those players who ended up bent over with his hands on his knees, gasping for breath and unable to move.

TD came through the hellish practices without any problem but Bobby and Eddie had difficulty. Bobby's large size, coupled with the late-August heat, conspired to make the first practices too much for him to handle, and Eddie hadn't bothered to stay in good condition over the summer. Beau, on the other hand, could run all day.

By the third day of practice, Beau got a sense of how things were going to be. Eddie and Bobby were lining up with the second team and TD with the third. Beau was assigned to the scout team. He didn't know what the scout team was but it probably wasn't good because he was spending a lot of time standing around and watching other guys practice.

The second-string offense was running passing drills against the first-team defense. Bobby Cunningham's assignment was to block Marcus White. He couldn't do it. Marcus beat Bobby to the inside and Coach Blieschroeder got red in the face and screamed at Bobby. On the next play, Marcus beat Bobby to the outside. Blieschroeder's face went from red to purple. He walked up to Bobby and asked what the hell was wrong with him. On the next play, Marcus pulled the overanxious Bobby off balance and beat him up the middle. Blieschroeder demoted Bobby to the fourth team.

It must have been the worst day of Bobby's football life. He was the last man out of the showers and everyone except Beau had already left. Beau walked beside his friend for the several blocks up State Street to the Michigan Union to join the rest of the team for dinner.

Bobby moped along for a couple blocks before he said anything. "It was a bad day for me, but what bothers me the most is that it was a bad day for our team."

"How was it bad for the team?"

"Didn't you see when Marcus was beating me on every down, all the black players were hooting and hollering and enjoying every minute of a white kid being made to look like a fool?"

Beau had noticed the black players jeering at Bobby but he couldn't think of anything to say that might help his friend feel better.

Bobby continued, "This stuff about our team being color-blind—some kind of warrior brotherhood—it's all bullshit. The black players stick up for blacks and the white players stick up for whites."

Beau wondered how a fellow with light-brown skin like his would fit into the blacks-for-blacks and whites-for-whites arrangement.

"I hate to even go into the dining room for our damn dinner," added Bobby. "The blacks will all be sitting together and the white guys will be at the other tables. The men on our team are segregating themselves. It's no way to build a ball club."

When Beau and Bobby entered the dining room, the setup was exactly as Bobby had predicted. Then something remarkable happened.

Marcus White slowly rose from his chair at the all-black table. Every place at his table was occupied but there were some open seats at the white tables. When Marcus stood, the lively banter at his table came to a stop. In addition to being respected as a two-year starter and one of the team's captains, Marcus had the kind of gravitas that could silence a room.

He waved to Bobby and Beau. "Come over here and eat dinner with me." He looked at two of the men seated next to him and nodded his head toward one of the white tables. "Would you fellows mind moving over to that table? I'd like to have these boys next to me." Everyone did as they were told; no argument, no hesitation.

Marcus patted Bobby's arm. "You're stronger than me and almost as fast. You're gonna be a real good tackle. I whipped you like a rented mule today because you've got a few things to learn about pass blocking. You shouldn't 'fire out' like you do on a running play ... back up, trade space for time ... keep your head up ... keep your feet moving ... stay balanced ..."

Beau watched a black man, a senior and a star player, help a white boy who had been on the varsity for three days. Bobby was wrong about the warrior brotherhood being a fantasy. Through the grace of Marcus White's presence, the brotherhood was real.

The heat of August faded into the early days of September. The grueling twice-a-day practice sessions were over and the team was rounding into shape for the first game. A feeling of excitement and anticipation surrounded the campus as the regular students began to arrive. Cars lined the streets as suitcases and boxes and lamps from home and typewriters and portable television sets were unloaded and carried into students' rooms. Freshmen appeared uncertain while upperclassmen shouted greetings to friends. There was one particular returning student Beau was anxious to greet.

As soon as football practice ended, he showered, dressed, and hurried to Chi Omega to help her move in. He should have known Janet Cunningham would not be lacking assistance. Three guys were toting boxes and clothes on hangers and a stereo and small pieces of furniture from the Cunninghams' Pontiac station wagon into Janet's room. Beau was disappointed that helpers were already on hand but forgot about it when Janet rushed up and gave him a kiss on the cheek. She looked great. Her brown hair had been lightened by the summer sun and her smooth skin was tanned. The scar across her cheek didn't tan and stood out as a thin white line which was visible because the day of moving had worn off some of her makeup. She was usually meticulous about covering her scar because both she and her mother felt it ruined her looks. As far as Beau was concerned, nothing could ruin the looks of Janet Cunningham.

"Beau, I hate for you to see me like this. I'm a mess."

She was wearing jeans, a T-shirt, and some old tennis shoes. A mess? Any other girl could be wearing a coordinated young-sorority-girl-arriving-at-college-outfit that cost $300 at Jacobson's department store and would still suffer from comparison with Janet.

She smiled at something behind Beau and he turned to see Eddie Bartucci and Mitch Caputo walking toward them. Janet waved them over. "Well if it isn't the star quarterback and his faithful sidekick, Sleezeball."

She gave Eddie a kiss on the cheek, then drew back a step and offered her hand to Mitch.

Mitch said, "Come on Janet, be nice. I came over to invite you to a party. I know some people who are having a big war protest party tonight. There will be a ton of people. It'll be a blast!"

He hesitated a second and then spoke to Beau. "Your girlfriend, Becky Goldman, will be there. I've heard she's a serious antiwar person."

Beau wished Mitch hadn't referred to Becky as his girlfriend in front of Janet. He snuck a sideways look at Janet and it appeared she either didn't notice Mitch's comment or didn't care. He could never be sure what Janet was thinking.

Mitch, of course, didn't pause to consider the effect of his words. He was talking about the party when he stopped in mid sentence. D'Isabella Hernandez had stepped through the Chi Omega front door wearing a pair of red shorts and a tank top. Beau figured she bought the shorts in Venezuela because he didn't think shorts that skimpy were sold in the United States. Busy Washtenaw Avenue ran in front of the sorority house and Beau was amazed Dizzy didn't cause a multi-car accident.

Janet winked at Beau to signal that she had observed the "Dizzy effect." She said, "I hate the war. I'll come to the party. Would it be okay if I brought Dizzy along?"

Mitch said he felt confident Dizzy would be welcome.

Since Mitch had said Becky was going to the party, Beau called to ask if she would like for him to walk over with her. It was held in a worn-out rental house on Williams Street. When Beau and Becky arrived, the place was already jammed with people. The air was saturated with the pungent aroma of marijuana and the clear, sweet voice of Joan Baez singing "Where Have All the Flowers Gone" floated from the stereo.

Becky was energized and immediately joined a group of people in intense conversation about the horrible war in Vietnam. Beau stood uneasily at the edge of the group. He didn't join the discussion because he hadn't thought much about the war. He did, however, notice that many of the young women were not wearing bras.

As Beau was trying not to gape at this sea of unencumbered female breasts, or at least not to let anyone observe him staring, Eddie approached the group. Seeing Eddie always helped Beau feel more at ease, although he couldn't help but notice Eddie's eyes had an unnatural glow and his clothes reeked of marijuana.

"Hey, Beau. How do you like this war protest business?"

"I don't know. I'm not sure why I'm here. What do you think? Are you against the war?"

Eddie looked thoughtful; at least he appeared thoughtful for a man who was half-stoned. "I think we have to draw a line and stop those commie bastards. They're knocking over one country after another like a bunch of dominoes. We've got to stop them somewhere, and I'd sure as hell rather fight them over there than here."

Beau thought Eddie's attitude didn't square with attending a war protest party. "If you feel that way, why are you here?"

Eddie answered with the famous Bartucci smile. "Are you kidding? This is an excellent party—great dope, a bunch of good-looking liberated type girls who already have their bras off. I don't know what more a young man could desire."

Eddie was just being Eddie but sometimes it was easy to become tired of him. Beau gave him a friendly slap on the back and turned to look for somebody else. Not seeing anyone he knew, he made his way into the kitchen where a dozen kids were crowded around a keg of beer. He looked for some soft drinks but couldn't find any and he wasn't going to ask somebody for a Coke and have them think he was an oddball. He hated being different from other kids but he'd promised Father Marcotte he wouldn't drink any alcohol. He'd keep his promise, but he wasn't happy about it. He had even asked Pontiac's advice on the matter. Pontiac's opinion was succinct. "Drinking whiskey makes you stupid."

So, he wouldn't drink but he wanted to fit in and nobody had said anything about smoking a little dope. Beau decided he was going to try some marijuana; not tonight, but sometime. His thoughts of social acceptance through pot were interrupted by a movement. Dizzy had materialized beside him with two empty plastic beer cups. "Are you just going to stand there or would you like to do something useful?"

Beau blinked and said, "Sure."

Dizzy handed the plastic cups to him and said, "Grab a couple of beers for Janet and me and bring them out on the porch."

The front porch had a swayback look and its twenty-year-old gray paint was almost completely worn away. Dizzy and Janet accepted their beers and sat on the unstable wooden railing that encircled the porch's front and left side. Beau started to sit with them but thought better of it and remained standing.

The party was crowded and loud but if he leaned toward the girls, it was possible to talk. "Hey, Janet. Is your brother here?"

"He didn't want to come. He was kind of funny about it; said he was tired from football practice and didn't want to get involved in any student protests."

Beau spoke to both of the girls; raising his voice in order to be heard. "What do you guys think about the war?"

Dizzy answered, "You have to leave me out. I promised my father I'd remember I'm not a citizen and Vietnam is none of my business."

Janet said, "I didn't promise my dad anything but he never hesitates to give me his enlightened opinions. He thinks those commie sons-of-bitches need to be taught not to mess with the U S of A and the best way to do that is to blast the shit out of them."

I don't give a good goddamn what Buck Cunningham thinks about the war or anything else, but I would like to know how Janet feels.

Janet said the war made her sick. She was in the midst of explaining the immorality of a large industrial country destroying a third-world civilization and killing innocent people, when a heart-stopping squeal blasted from the stereo. Someone had dragged the needle across the Joan Baez record and removed it from the turntable. A moment later, the sound of the number one song on the popular charts, Sergeant Barry Sadler's "Ballad of the Green Berets," filled the air. A loud male voice began to sing along with the record.

Janet and Beau looked at each other. Realization was simultaneous ... Eddie! By the time Beau was able to push his way into the living room and near the stereo, Eddie was under attack.

Becky Goldman, her face red as a boiled lobster's, was slapping at Eddie and screaming. "YOU THINK THIS IS A JOKE? YOU BASTARD!

THOSE FUCKING GREEN BERETS ARE MURDERING LITTLE CHILDREN AND YOU THINK IT'S A JOKE?!"

Eddie, twice Becky's size and a varsity athlete, covered his face and cringed before her frenzy. She yanked his record from the turntable and sailed it through the open window, across the small front yard, and into the middle of Williams Street. She turned back to face the retreating Eddie and collapsed in sobs.

The party became silent. Beau put his arm around Becky and Eddie quietly disappeared.

As Beau walked with Becky, she explained her deep commitment to the antiwar movement. Everything about the war was upsetting to her, but a new weapon called napalm was a particular horror. She said it was a hellish mixture of gasoline, benzene, and polystyrene packaged into bombs that exploded into jellied fire that burned at 2,000 degrees and clung to human flesh.

Napalm was manufactured by the Dow Chemical Company in Midland, Michigan, a town less than a two-hour drive from Ann Arbor. She felt students everywhere in America should stage anti-Dow Chemical protests and the first one should be held in Michigan. Becky was a member of a group organizing a protest at Wayne State University in Detroit. Students from every college in Michigan were going to participate and she wanted Beau to come.

He said he probably would go with her but he'd like a few days to decide. His reaction produced a decided chill and Becky walked through the front door of her student residence hall without pausing to allow an opportunity for a good-night kiss.

The Vietnam War was far away and didn't affect Beau. His student deferment would protect him for the next three years and by the time he graduated the war would be over. As a loyal American he supported his country. He didn't understand the reasons for the conflict but since the President of the United States said it was necessary, it must be necessary.

When he arrived back at South Quad, he didn't feel like going directly to his room and going to bed. He stopped in the common room to watch television and get his mind away from his conversation with Becky. He flopped onto a comfortable chair with the intention of spending an hour relaxing in front of the big, new color TV. A news program was showing dreadful images of napalm being dropped by U. S. warplanes and burning Vietnamese people. He lowered his head and covered his face with his hands. After a long time, he got up and went to his room.

During the next couple of weeks Beau pushed the brutal images of war to the back of his mind and concentrated on his immediate goal of making a place for himself on the varsity football team. It wasn't going well.

The team appeared to have avoided the racial divisions that were tormenting many college football teams during the troubled fall of 1966. The first two games were played at home and, as expected, Michigan coasted to lopsided victories. Coach Blieschroeder made sure Bobby, Eddie, and TD were given playing time during the fourth quarters of both games. Beau was on the bench and available but there had been no move to put him on the field.

He feared he had been permanently relegated to the scout team—a team of scrubs that ran the favorite plays of Saturday's opponent all week in order for the first-team defense to practice against. Beau and the rest of the scout team had worked harder than usual during the past week as they tried to run the complex offense of UCLA. The Wolverines were traveling to Los Angeles for Michigan's first real test of the season. Thursday's practice was easy; just loosening up and running a few plays; no hitting. In spite of his lowly status on the team, Beau was enthusiastic. They would be flying to California on Friday morning. He'd never flown in an airplane or been to California. Heck, he'd never been out of Michigan. It was going to be a wonderful adventure. He had no idea they weren't going to take him.

The list of players who had made the traveling team was posted in the locker room after Thursday's practice. Everyone crowded around to read the names. Thaddeus D. Kowalski, Robert Cunningham, Edward Bartucci, Jr.—but no Beau Lightfoot.

Beau said nothing and allowed no emotion to show on his face. He quietly sat on the bench in front of his locker with a towel draped over his head and studied the floor, until he felt the strong arm of Marcus White on his neck. Marcus gave him a perfect smile that showed all of his white teeth and said, "I thought you might be feeling disappointed so I decided to stop by and talk with you for a minute."

Beau couldn't believe Marcus—a defensive star and one of the team captains—was concerned with the feelings of a lowly scrub, especially on the eve of a big game. "Thanks, Marcus. I am disappointed. I'm not getting anywhere and I don't know if it's worth the effort. I honestly feel like giving up."

Marcus shook Beau, gently by Marcus's standards, which caused Beau's head to snap back. "Listen to me, boy! Maybe someday you'll get to play for this team—or maybe you won't. The important thing is to keep your scholarship. Life doesn't provide guarantees for poor boys like you and me. A college degree is a door opener; it gives people like us a chance to make something of our lives. If you quit, you'll go back to that small town you came from and before you know what hit you, you'll be forty years old and still mowing rich people's lawns. I'm gonna give you some advice ... be grateful for what you have and don't worry about what you don't have."

Beau watched the UCLA game on the television in the South Quad common room. Becky said she would come over and watch the game with him. She didn't show up until the fourth quarter but she was there in time to see Marcus's devastating tackle that caused a fumble and stopped a potentially game-winning UCLA drive.

Michigan held on to win by a score of 21 to 17. Beau was ecstatic. Becky said she was very pleased but Beau knew she didn't really care about the outcome of a football game.

Becky had come to talk with Beau about the anti-napalm, anti-Dow Chemical Company protest at Wayne State. They were anticipating a large rally with college students from all over Michigan attending. The event was scheduled for a weekend in the middle of October; she wanted Beau to promise he would participate in the demonstration and bring along all of his friends. He had misgivings but had already put her off once. It was difficult to say no to Becky Goldman. He said yes.

Later, when Beau walked Becky to her dormitory, she not only allowed him a good-night kiss, she lingered for several.

As promised, Beau asked his friends to join him at the protest. Janet gave an immediate and enthusiastic yes. He didn't ask Dizzy because she had already made it clear she wouldn't be involved in any protests. Bobby said he wasn't interested. TD said he couldn't spare time away from his studies and Eddie declined because he said he had promised himself he wouldn't go near Becky Goldman for the rest of his life.

When he asked the least thoughtful of his friends, Mitch Caputo, he received the most thoughtful response. Mitch reminded Beau that he was a man who "knew the score" and he considered it his job to tell Beau how things really worked. He said it was essential to know the history of previous antiwar protests. In March 1965, faculty members of the University of Michigan organized a teach-in to focus attention on the Vietnam War. Over the opposition of Michigan Governor George Romney, three thousand students and faculty met in Angell Hall to participate in lectures and debates. The teach-in attracted national media coverage and by the end of the academic year, teach-ins had spread to more than a hundred college campuses.

Beau thought it was cool that teach-ins had originated at Michigan—but the next thing Mitch said scared him to death. In the fall of 1965, thirty-one students were arrested at a draft board sit-in and Michigan Selective Service officials revoked their student draft deferments. National Selective Service Director Lewis B. Hershey backed the Michigan officials and threatened to use reclassification as an ongoing weapon against student dissidence. Mitch said the anti-napalm protest Beau was considering, would turn out to be a four-step deal. "One, you demonstrate at Wayne State; two, you get reclassified and drafted; three, you get shipped to Vietnam; four you get your ass shot off."

Mitch's answer was no thanks. His advice to Beau was to stay away from Wayne State and avoid all antiwar protests.

With no family to financially support him, if Beau lost his deferment and was drafted, he wouldn't ever be able to return to the University of Michigan. On the other hand, he promised Becky he would participate. He wondered if protests accomplished anything. The whole thing made his head spin.

Beau remembered Pontiac's advice and decided to allow the calm beauty of the natural world to help clarify his thoughts. The most beautiful place he knew was on the northwest side of Ann Arbor where a dam captured the waters of the Huron River to form a small lake. Beau walked on a path that ran through the woods on the south edge of the lake. Other than for a railroad track that ran along the north shore, probably the main line to Chicago, the area around the lake was undeveloped. The water was calm and the woods were quiet. He sat on the trunk of a fallen tree and thought about his dilemma. Without doing any critical thinking, he had been a vague supporter of America's war in Vietnam. However, after listening to Becky, he wasn't sure what to think.

"Beautiful spot, isn't it?"

Beau was so startled he almost fell off the trunk as he jumped to his feet and turned to see who had spoken. It was Chief Pontiac.

"Spirit Father, you've come at a good time. I need your advice." Beau explained the war in Southeast Asia, the antiwar demonstration, napalm, his promise to Becky, his risk of losing his student draft deferment—and then he asked Pontiac what he should do.

"Do you remember the rules that I gave you?"

"Yes, Spirit Father. Of course, I remember."

"Wasn't one of the rules to make your own decisions?"

"I understand, Spirit Father, but I'm uncertain. I need your help."

"I'll help you think about things, but in the end it is you who must decide."

Pontiac sat on the fallen tree trunk and indicated for Beau to sit beside him. He removed a pipe from a fringed buckskin bag he was carrying over his shoulder and carefully packed it with tobacco. He took care to get his pipe properly burning before beginning to speak. "You should first think about the war. Is the United States defending itself? Are the Vietnamese threatening to invade your country? Are they trying to take American land? Are they stealing your treasure?

"You should also think about your war leader, President Johnson. Did he fight bravely in past wars? Does he have a good plan to win this war? The war has been going on for quite a while; is his plan working?

"Finally, you should think about the protest. Napalm is a horrible weapon. Will this protest stop its use? You have much to lose. The protest may be somewhat stronger if you participate. Is that amount of additional strength worth the sacrifice you may have to make?" Pontiac placed his hand on Beau's back. "I have given you questions. The answers and the decisions must be yours."

Beau felt as if a great weight had been lifted from his shoulders. It was clear. Once he understood the questions, the answers were in front of his eyes. It wasn't right to delay. He had to tell Becky immediately.

"I know I promised, but I'm not going to go to the protest."

Becky raised her hands to her face as if she were defending herself from a physical attack. "I was counting on you. We need you. Everybody's got to help. My God! They're burning children to death and you're not going to do anything?!"

"Becky, please try to understand. It's easier for you. If I get arrested, I'll lose my deferment and be drafted. It's too much to risk. I'm really sorry."

She gave Beau a disdainful look. "Some people feel the good of humanity is more important than their personal concerns. I understand now that you are not one of those people."

Her face left no room for doubt. His relationship with Becky Goldman was over.

Beau missed having beautiful Becky as a girlfriend but he was able to spend time with his true, although probably unattainable, love, Janet Cunningham. Janet was usually accompanied by Dizzy and Dizzy was showing a friendly interest in him. He thought there were some possibilities but knew he better be careful.

Beau was being careful with everything. He was diligent with his studies and uncomplaining about football. He often thought of Marcus's advice to be grateful for what he had and not to worry about what he didn't have.

It was good advice but difficult to follow because Beau didn't seem to have anything at all when it came to football. The team was doing fine. A swarming defense led by Marcus White, together with an offense with superb ball control and a powerful running game almost always got the job done. However, Beau felt removed from the team's success. He ran opponents' plays on the scout team and sat on the bench at home games but never got to play or accompany the team on road games.

The scout team's lockers were located in the rear of the locker room. Beau was sitting in front of his locker in the "scrub section" when he noticed the other scout team players had suddenly become quiet. Marcus White walked over and sat down next to Beau.

"Beau, could you do me a favor?"

One of the best linemen in the Big Ten Conference was asking a favor from a guy who couldn't even make the traveling squad. Marcus humbly asked, while making it clear he would understand if Beau was too busy, if Beau could help TD. Marcus explained he was worried because TD was falling into serious academic trouble and needed more help than what the athletic department's regular tutoring program provided. Marcus said they'd provide substantial one-on-one tutoring for a first-team player but not for an unproven sophomore like TD. And, even if the team did approve intensive tutoring, TD would be branded as a dumb player and Marcus didn't want him to have to carry that stigma.

Neither Marcus nor TD had money to pay a tutor for the many hours of work Marcus felt would be required. The solution was to find a qualified tutor who would be willing to work without pay—not an easy task. Marcus had heard of a graduate student who, if approached properly and neither rushed nor pressured, might agree to do it. Marcus said he needed Beau's help because the demands of football, along with his pre-med academic load, accounted for every second of his life. Marcus simply didn't have the time to approach and patiently seduce an unpaid tutor for TD.

The name of the fellow Marcus was talking about was Peter Paeker. He was said to be an academically gifted odd duck who loved sports and practically worshiped the star athletes—the kind of guy who varsity football players referred to as a "jockstrap sniffer."

Beau couldn't say yes fast enough. He told Marcus to leave the TD tutor problem in his hands. Marcus stood and shook Beau's hand; a gesture that struck Beau as oddly formal.

It was one of the last times Beau ever saw Marcus White.

As Peter Paeker wrapped up the Wednesday morning meeting of Economics 101, section C, Beau waited in the hallway. When the door opened at exactly ten o'clock, the students walked out and Beau walked in.

Paeker was gathering his papers and appeared to be in a hurry. The first thing Beau noticed was his suit. He'd never seen anyone actually wearing a bright-green suit before; but Marcus had warned Beau that Peter Paeker was an unusual fellow.

"Excuse me, Mr. Paeker. May I speak with you?"

"Not now. Not now. Can't you see I'm busy? Go sign up on the sheet outside my office. I'll talk to you during my regular office hours."

"I'm not one of your students, Mr. Paeker. I'd like to speak privately with you for a few minutes. Could we go someplace and have a cup of coffee?"

"Not one of my students? Well, of course not. I don't recognize you. What do you want?" He continued talking, not giving Beau an opportunity to answer. "Well, it doesn't matter what you want because I'm busy." He placed his papers in a scuffed leather satchel and started for the door.

Beau saw that Peter was going to walk away and leave him standing in an empty classroom. He had to grab Paeker's attention. "Coach Blieschroeder would like your help with an important matter." It wasn't exactly a lie. If Coach Blieschroeder knew about it, he would certainly like to have Paeker help TD pass his classes and remain eligible to play football. Maybe it was a stretch, but it was for a good cause. The important thing was that it worked. Peter Paeker stopped in his tracks.

"Gary Blieschroeder wants my help?"

"Yes, he does. Let's go somewhere where we can talk and I'll explain."

They found a booth in a coffee shop on State Street. As they settled in,

Beau wondered how he was going to finesse his lie. After a few minutes, it was clear that Peter enjoyed talking much more than listening and Beau didn't have to worry about explaining why the famous coach desired help from an unknown graduate student.

Peter was obviously starved for attention. As soon as the waitress left after setting their coffee cups on the table, he began telling Beau about himself. Beau listened attentively and studied the man sitting across from him. His job was to manipulate Mr. Paeker and anything he could learn might prove useful.

Paeker looked like a typical professor's assistant ... perhaps a little on the weird side but within the range. His slumped posture caused him to appear shorter than his actual height. He was a pretty big guy, but soft. He wore thick glasses with black plastic frames and a dark-green tie with his light-green suit. The hair around the sides of his scalp was long but he had a large bald spot on the top of his head.

Peter told Beau he was twenty-six years old, married with no children, a teaching assistant in the Economics Department, and a couple years away from receiving his doctorate degree. He said he had always been an A+ student and was confident he would be able to help TD. He also mentioned that he would love to have some extra money from working as a tutor.

When Beau delicately informed Peter there was no money involved, Peter's interest cooled but Beau was able to get him to agree to meet again to talk some more.

It took three meetings to convince Peter to work without pay. Beau used every argument: TD was going to be one of the finest running backs ever to play for Michigan. TD would flunk out of school without Peter's tutoring. Assisting TD would be a personal favor to Coach Blieschroeder. Peter would be thought of as a "friend of the football program." In the end, it was patiently listening to Peter's stories rather than Beau's arguments that turned the tide.

Peter considered himself to be an excellent athlete as well as a gifted student. He overcame the curse of his name, one can imagine what other children called a boy named Peter Paeker, and became one of the best players on his junior-high-school basketball team. He enjoyed other sports and was good at all of them, but basketball was his game. He had once scored nine points in an important seventh-grade game and there was no doubt but that he would have become a basketball star in high school and college had he not been cursed with poor eyesight.

Beau listened patiently and nodded in agreement. Paeker went on to talk about his academic achievements, which were real but failed to provide him with the respect he deserved. Just the other day, Peter said he overheard one of his students refer to him as Peter Pecker. Peter didn't lower himself to say anything. He merely changed the disrespectful little bastard's grade from an A- to a C.

The hours of rapt listening, along with a truckload of empathy, softened Peter and Beau closed the deal with four 50-yard line tickets to the remaining Wolverines' home games for the season. Peter could treat his wife and a couple of their friends to wonderful seats and he could let it be known the tickets were provided to him because of his special relationship with Coach Blieschroeder.

They shook hands and the deal was done: unlimited free tutoring for TD. Beau didn't have the tickets but he figured he had spent many boring hours with Peter Paeker and Marcus White could darn well supply the tickets.

Marcus supplied the tickets. Peter tutored TD. TD passed his courses and remained on the team. Michigan ended the season with seven wins and a second place finish in the Big Ten.

~

Janet Cunningham spent more time than Beau thought was desirable with a senior from Shaker Heights, Ohio; so Beau drifted along. And drifting turned out to be okay because Dizzy Hernandez floated over to Beau and drifted beside him.

Dizzy was a wonderful companion: bright, enthusiastic, confident, and definitely a free spirit. She enjoyed changing her look. One day, it would be a stylish outfit from an exclusive boutique and her beautiful, thick, dark hair falling to her shoulders; the next day, it was Salvation Army grunge with an experimental hairstyle created by one of her sorority sisters.

When Beau planned to meet her, he didn't know which Dizzy was going to show up but she always looked terrific and she gave every indication she thought he was a great guy.

The winter passed much too quickly. Beau enjoyed the occasional company of Janet and Dizzy, and the constant company of Dizzy. He concentrated on his studies, improved his grades, and enjoyed several months without football.

But, football was his meal ticket and, all too soon, spring practice intruded into his happy routine. Spring practice was about next year's team. The seniors were gone and it was time for the underclassmen to earn their places. Coach Blieschroeder installed Eddie as starting quarterback, Bobby as first-team left tackle, and TD as first string fullback. As usual, Beau Lightfoot was not on the roster.

It was hard not to be discouraged but Beau remembered Marcus's advice. He was on his way toward earning a degree from the University of Michigan. Still, it was hard.

The day before the end of spring practice, Marcus White, walked into the South Quad room shared by Beau and TD. "School will be over in a couple weeks. I don't know when I'll see you guys again, so I came to say good-bye."

TD said, "You'll be here next fall, won't you? I know you'll be busy with medical school but you'll still have some time for your old friends."

Beau had never seen Marcus appear to be anything other than enthusiastic, but he thought a flicker of sadness showed on Marcus's face. Maybe it was nothing except Beau's imagination.

Marcus explained he had not been accepted into medical school. The demands of football and pre-med academics had been too much and his grades weren't good enough for medical school.

TD said he was sorry about med school but thought Marcus could make some good money playing professional football. Marcus said he wanted to be a doctor, not a football player. He viewed the current situation as a temporary setback rather than a defeat. He'd graduate in a couple weeks and become subject to the draft. Since there was no way to avoid being drafted, he was going to enlist in the Army. Killing a human being was not something he would ever do but he could serve as a medic. He would help wounded soldiers, gain medical experience, and put away some of his pay. After being discharged, he would enroll in a postgraduate program in biology. He'd get top grades because he wouldn't have to spend time playing football. With "A" post-graduate work and service as an Army medic behind him, he would surely be accepted into medical school. Everything was going to be okay.

Spring practice traditionally concluded with a spring game. It was really a scrimmage rather than a game. The squad was divided into two teams that played each other in the Michigan stadium. The game was open to the public and was attended by about five thousand people. Coach Blieschroeder said everyone on the squad would get into the game for at least a few plays.

It appeared to Beau that the coaches had placed the first-team offense and second-team defense on one team, and the first-team defense and second-team offense on the other. The reserves such as Beau were divided more or less evenly between the two teams.

Eddie started at quarterback with the first-team offense and, as they had throughout spring practice, the coaches worked intensively with him. Eddie made some excellent plays but was sacked three times and threw two interceptions. Gary Blieschroeder had a straightforward method of motivating his players. When Eddie came to the sideline after being sacked, Blieschroeder screamed at him like a madman. "How many times do I have to tell you to throw the ball away? Don't take a sack and don't force a pass if no receiver is open! Throw it away! If you're too stupid to learn that, you're not going to be our quarterback!"

Eddie didn't say a word. No player dared to talk back to Gary Blieschroeder. Beau thought Eddie looked happy the game was almost over.

There was time for Eddie's team to run one more offensive series. An assistant coach looked over the players sitting on the bench and asked who had not had an opportunity to play. Beau jumped to his feet and was told to go in as a wide receiver.

The second play was a long pass. As soon as Eddie dropped back to throw, two defensive players broke through the line and began chasing him. While running for his life, he made a quick look downfield but didn't see an open man. Eddie was a lot of things but he was not stupid. He threw the ball away, high and long and out of bounds on the right side of the field.

Beau ran downfield along the right sideline. The football came in front of him and very high; it seemed sure to travel well out of bounds. Some of the other players saw the ball's trajectory and began to slow down. The play was all but over. Beau put everything he had into a leap. He went high and in the split second when one would expect him to begin to come down, he rose higher. He could feel the spirit of the deer within him as he reached his right hand far into the air, caught the ball on his fingertips, and sprinted thirty yards to the end zone.

After a few more plays, the game was over. It was as if his catch didn't matter. No one seemed to notice what he'd done.

Two people did notice.

As the players walked to the locker room, Gary Blieschroeder patted Beau on the back and told him he'd made a hell of a catch. Eddie Bartucci pushed his way forward to walk beside Beau and said, "I'm going to stay at the Cunningham's cottage this summer and I want you and me to practice pass plays every day."

For the first time in two years, Beau felt hope for his football future. He hadn't thought he would feel like going to the end-of-spring-practice party at the Sigma Alpha Epsilon fraternity house but that was before his impossible catch. Now things were looking up and going to the party was exactly what he wanted to do.

    The fraternity was rocking. The old brick house was about to vibrate right off of its foundation. After only an hour at the party, Dizzy led Beau away from the swirling crowd to a couch in a dark, quiet corner. She leaned her head against his chest and it felt natural for him to put his arm around her. She seemed tired and closed her eyes as she rested her head against him. She fit comfortably beneath his arm and he didn't feel a need to make conversation. Her light-blue cashmere sweater was soft to his touch. His fingertips touched just inside the V-shaped opening in the neck of her sweater. Her skin was cool and smooth. Her breathing was soft and regular. She didn't move when he touched her neck; he thought she might have fallen asleep.

    He moved his fingers slightly under her sweater. Nothing happened. He waited for a little while and then moved his hand a bit farther. He stopped and listened. Her breathing was still even. He slowly, very slowly, extended his fingers. He thought he felt the beginning of the gentle swell of her breast. He quietly moved his hand by the smallest of increments. He could feel the top of her bra. He gently put his fingers inside its top edge. He listened again. Dizzy's breathing remained even although his had become ragged. He waited until he felt a little calmer before his fingers continued their journey. They were inside her bra. He could feel the top of her breast. It was soft and warm. He began to reach farther.

"JESUS CHRIST, BEAU! Is this your idea of how to seduce a girl? Wait until you think she's asleep and then try to sneak your hand inside her bra?"

He could not have removed his hand faster if he had touched a red-hot poker. As he attempted to stammer an apology, Dizzy saw his distress and smiled. She stood and took him by the hand. "You know I like you, Beau. Let's find a place where we can do this properly."

He followed Dizzy out the back door toward some cars parked in a dark patch of shadows behind the fraternity house. She opened the front door of one of the larger cars. Beau said, "What are you doing? That's not our car."

Dizzy replied, "We're not going to steal it, Beau. We're just going to use it for a few minutes." She looked at the bucket seats and said, "Let's slide these seats all the way forward and get in the back."

It looked like it was going to happen. He'd never done it, but he was confident. He'd been thinking about it for years and he'd read the yellowed pages he'd torn out of a paperback so many times he'd memorized every word:

She gave a slight gasp as Trevor entered her. He moved slowly and pushed deeper with each stroke. At first she put her hands on his face and stroked his hair, a loving but controlled response. Trevor's slow rhythmic movement shattered her control and she began to utter a moan with each thrust. She opened herself to allow him to go deeper and he pushed farther into her with each stroke. She gripped him hard and pressed her body into his chest. Her moans became louder; her body tensed; and, as she reached her climax, she cried out, "Trevor, Oh! Oh my God!" He could feel her tension ease and he paused for a moment. But he didn't stop. His powerful strokes quickly brought her back to, and then far beyond her previous passion. Each thrust seemed to go farther into the core of her being.

She gripped him with all of her strength and gasped for breath. When she came, she was unable to speak. She uttered a deep groan and relaxed her iron grip on Trevor's body. Still he continued. His strokes were now becoming faster. She squirmed beneath him as if she were trying to get away, but there was no getting away. She was pinned as surely as a beautiful butterfly pinned to a collector's display board. She cried, "No. Stop! I can't take any more! Please, Trevor. You're killing me." But there was no stopping. Trevor felt a surge begin deep inside his body. The pressure was building and building. It was like an oil well about to blow. The rumbling began deep under the earth and grew stronger and stronger as the pressure built and the oil forced its way toward the surface until it rammed through the top of the oil rig and shot a hundred feet into the air. She responded to his driving strokes with an orgasm that took possession of her entire being. As she came, Trevor pressed far into her and exploded.

Yeah! That was the way he planned to do it.

With the front seats shoved all the way forward, there was plenty of room in the backseat. Dizzy put her arms around Beau's neck and kissed him. He reached under her sweater and moved his hand up her back until he felt the strap of her bra. It was held together by a complex fastening system of hooks and eyes; not something easily disengaged with one hand.

Her back felt warm to his touch and he began to notice that the "rumbling deep under the earth" had started. It had more than started; it was moving along briskly. As he fumbled with her bra clasp, Dizzy ran her hand over his crotch and the top of Beau's personal oil well blew off.

Oh! Oh, my gosh! This was embarrassing. Maybe he could pretend it didn't happen. Maybe he could fake his way through. No, it wasn't going to work. She was looking at the big wet spot that was spreading over the front of his pants. There was nothing he could say.

Dizzy patted his cheek. "It's okay. You just got a little too excited. We'll try again another time."

Beau felt overwhelming gratitude. D'Isabella Hernandez was one hell of a fine woman.

I WANT LIGHTFOOT

The northern Indian Tribes enjoyed playing a fast and rough lacrosse-like game called baggataway.

On a spring day in 1763, braves from the Chippewa Tribe were playing on a field beside Fort Michilimackinac. Soldiers from the fort relaxed in the fine weather and watched the game. One of the players sailed the ball high into the air and it hooked over the stockade. The sentries allowed the Indians to run into the fort to retrieve their ball. Once inside, the braves massacred everyone.

2013

A sound at the bedroom door brought Beau's head up. He was happy to see Eddie rather than Janet. It was ridiculous to feel uncomfortable about Janet walking in while he was recalling the long-ago intimate moment with Dizzy. It was nothing more than a distant memory ...

Eddie glanced at the old photograph that was still lying on Beau's lap. "I remember when that was taken. Cunningham and Bartucci, football heroes of the future. When we posed for that picture, we didn't know the real star was wearing a busboy coat." Eddie smiled and continued, "I'll never forget the unbelievable catch you made in the spring game. I decided right then that I was going to spend the summer in Wequetonsing so we could work out together. Remember those workouts?"

Yes. Beau remembered the workouts and that wonderful summer.

There were terrible problems in the world—but Northern Michigan in 1967 was the happiest summer of Beau Lightfoot's life.

WEQUETONSING, 1967

Beau mowed lawns by day and practiced football every night. The lingering summer sunlight in the far north provided plenty of light for evening football. After Beau finished working, Eddie, Janet, Bobby, and he headed to the Harbor Springs High School football field. Eddie threw passes, Beau ran the routes and caught the passes, while Bobby and Janet played pass defense.

Although Bobby didn't have the speed to stay with Beau, Janet proved to be a tough defender. She was quick and athletic; and she maintained that since she was a girl, normal pass-interference rules didn't apply to her. She tripped Beau; pushed him as he made his cuts; threw grass into his eyes; pulled his arms down when he was about to make a catch; and, when all else failed, she tickled him.

In spite of the fooling around, Eddie and Beau grew adept at working together. Eddie developed a feel for Beau's moves and learned exactly where to throw the ball. With hundreds of repetitions, their timing came together and they mastered complex pass routes. Beau's favorite was the "Z in and out." He lost Bobby on his first cut to the outside. Then, he cut back to the inside to shake Janet, and immediately broke back to the outside. It was an elegant pattern and Eddie lofted a perfect pass. Beau extended his arms to make the catch and BLAM! Janet jumped on his back and covered his eyes with her hands. Their legs tangled and, as they fell, he put his arms around her and twisted so that his body hit the ground first to protect her from a hard fall. They rolled over and her face ended up only a few inches from his. If Eddie and her brother hadn't been there, he would have kissed her. She seemed to know and gave him a teasing smile. "You're gonna be a heck of a pass receiver. You can't do much against me but I think you'll be able to run all over the competition."

While Beau and his friends were cavorting in Harbor Springs, the urban ghettos across America were smoldering with black frustration and anger. In Newark, New Jersey, clashes between young blacks and local police flamed into mob violence. Firebombs, gunfire, and looting tore through the city. Property damage was extensive and twenty-one people died. The confidence of the nation was shaken. The influence of moderate civil rights leaders, such as Whitney Young and Roy Wilkins, appeared to be waning and a combustible racial tension hung in the air.

The explosion came in the City of Detroit. Scores of homes and businesses were destroyed. More than forty people lost their lives and it took the combined efforts of the Detroit Police, National Guard, and U.S. Army paratroopers to restore order. A new, more militant, civil rights leader, H. Rap Brown, warned that future riots would make Detroit "look like a picnic."

In Ann Arbor, forty-three miles west of Detroit, Coach Gary Blieschroeder called his racially mixed University of Michigan football team together for their first practice. Gary's strict policy of treating all players equally was not enough to head-off racial tension on his team. During practices there were fights between white and black players. Hostility was always present. The team worked, but it didn't operate smoothly. The black players blocked for the whites ... but without enthusiasm. The white players afforded the same treatment to the blacks.

This lurching football machine was commanded by its new leader, Eddie Bartucci. The 1967 team, with the flashy Bartucci as quarterback, the overpowering Bobby Cunningham as tackle, TD Kowalski as a solid fullback, and the speedy Billy Wilson as halfback had the potential to be champions.

Although they won their first two games of the season by overpowering lesser teams, the Wolverines were not working together. It was as if they were two separate teams, one black and one white. Coach Blieschroeder knew his guys had to start playing together rather than acting like a bunch of guys who didn't like each other. Their third opponent was Notre Dame, and the Wolverines weren't going to be able to beat Notre Dame unless they were unified.

Monday's practice did not go well. On Tuesday, Blieschroeder stomped into his office at 6:00 a.m. and slammed the door so hard it caused the latest issue of a national news magazine to fall off the corner of his desk onto the floor. He picked up the magazine and glanced at the cover. It was one of the most famous photographs taken during the Vietnam War. Blieschroeder realized it was the solution to his team's racial antipathy.

When Beau arrived for practice Tuesday afternoon, the first thing he noticed was the large photo filling the entire locker room bulletin board. It was an image of three American soldiers on the side of a battered, muddy hillside. One of the men was black. Two were white. One of the white soldiers was on the ground; seriously wounded. The other white soldier was sitting next to his comrade; he looked stricken and was bent forward with his eyes staring off into nowhere. The black soldier's shirt had been partially torn away. He was kneeling beside the man on the ground and holding up an IV bag with a line running into the arm of the wounded man. The black medic was pushing the wounded soldier into the shelter of a small depression in the muddy ground while shielding him with his own body. The medic's face and look of indescribable anguish were clearly visible. It was Marcus White.

Coach Blieschroeder had written a few words below the photograph: "Any player who allows race to interfere with the success of our team, dishonors this man."

Every Wolverine walked by the bulletin board and quietly studied the dramatic, battle-torn hillside. No one said a word. Beau wondered how the team would react. They had only four more days to get ready for Notre Dame.

Coach Blieschroeder's biggest concern was Notre Dame's outstanding kick-return man, Charles "The Jet" Jensen. The previous Saturday, The Jet had scored on a 95-yard run to help Notre Dame beat Oklahoma. Blieschroeder told his team they were not going to allow The Jet to make any long runs against Michigan.

The coach added some new defensive schemes specifically designed to stop Jensen and drilled the kick-return defense for two hours. When he felt they were ready, Coach Blieschroeder lined them up to kick-off and called for the scout team to return the kick.

The scout team was assigned to impersonate the Notre Dame kick-off-return team in order for the starters to practice shutting them down. Beau's role was to pretend to be Jensen. The Notre Dame kick-return plays had been designed to take advantage of The Jet's unique ability. Beau took the deep-return position, a fake Jet Jensen, to give the starters some practice. The kick came right to Beau and, as instructed, he ran toward the left side of the field. While Beau ran left, the scout team blockers drifted to the right and established a picket line along the right sideline. It was nicely set up, a beautiful return play; but as far as anyone knew, the only player in America who could actually run it successfully was The Jet.

Beau Lightfoot reversed his left-side return, looped back to the right, sprinted past several pursuers, caught the protection of the picket line of blockers, and ran ninety-seven yards for a touchdown.

Blieschroeder screamed at his starters. His face looked like a giant tomato that was ready to explode. Beau had accomplished exactly what the new defense had been designed to stop. The starters were given some harsh remedial instruction and lined up to try again. This time, Beau started toward his right and looped back to the left before running for his second consecutive touchdown. Blieschroeder was speechless.

Notre Dame was dominating the game and had just scored another touchdown. Blieschroeder stormed up and down the sidelines, glaring at his players and chewing gum like a snapping turtle. He terrified the players, particularly Beau Lightfoot. Beau avoided eye contact and tried to blend in with his teammates on the bench.

Blieschroeder stopped directly in front of Beau. The game was almost over. With the score 24 to 7 against them, Michigan was all but defeated. The late-afternoon shadows were beginning to lengthen and the discouraged home crowd headed for the exits. Blieschroeder was muttering to himself. "Twenty-four to seven. Twenty-four to goddamn seven! Son-of-a-bitch! I'm gonna try the kid. Why the hell not? Nobody else is doing shit."

Coach turned around and grabbed Beau by the shoulder pads, lifted him from the bench, and ordered him onto the field to return the kickoff.

Michigan was using two kick-return men. As Beau got in position, Billy Wilson motioned for Beau to take the left side. Billy was an All Big Ten halfback and Beau didn't argue. The right-footed Notre Dame kicker tended to hook his kicks to his left. Wilson was likely to receive the ball. *The positioning is fine with me*, thought Beau. *Billy can return the kick.*

The Notre Dame kicker saw Billy Wilson line up on the right side and an unknown small guy in position on the left. The kicker booted the football high into the air toward Beau.

More than 100,000 people watched Beau settle into position to catch the ball. Janet and Dizzy were sitting with their Chi Omega sorority sisters in the stands about thirty rows up. Mr. and Mrs. Cunningham were in their 50-yard-line seats right in front of the press box. Eddie and TD were watching from the sidelines. Bobby was on the field, ready to clear a path for Beau. And two hundred and forty miles north of Ann Arbor a priest and a young woman sat at a table in the Holy Childhood School's kitchen listening to the game on the radio.

Beau waited on the goal line and watched as the football appeared to hang in the warm September haze. The people headed for the exits stopped to look over their shoulders and watch the kickoff. *Mr. Cunningham said I'd never play a down for Michigan. Well, here I am. I'll bet the old bastard is ready to have a heart attack.* Beau had spent years preparing for the next few seconds. Did he have the speed of a deer and the elusiveness of a rabbit? When the football settled into his hands, Beau felt their spirits. They were with him.

Notre Dame was a big, fast, and well-disciplined team that would finish the season as National Champions. With their golden helmets gleaming in the fading sunlight, they bore down on Beau in a solid wave.

He ran fast, right up the middle of the field. At the 17-yard line, two men simultaneously launched themselves at him. They smashed into air. A split second before impact, Beau put on an extra burst of speed. He ran between the two would-be tacklers, spotted an opening, and immediately made a sharp cut to his right. Just as he appeared to have some room, he was hit hard from his blind side.

He bounced like a ping-pong ball striking a brick wall, staggered but did not go down, reversed direction, and broke toward the left sideline. The rabbit was moving at full speed after one step. A Notre Dame defender got an arm on Beau but he slapped it away and sprinted for the side of the field. He outran all but one man who trapped him along the sideline and threw a body block that would either knock him down or force him out of bounds. There was no room to maneuver. The deer jumped and sailed over the rolling body. Beau Lightfoot scampered the remaining fifty yards to the end zone.

Beau's spectacular run came too late to save the game. The Wolverines lost to Notre Dame—but there was no time to dwell on the defeat. The next opponent, Michigan State, was as tough as Notre Dame.

With the team preparing to face the Spartans, everyone anticipated a hard week of practice. As Beau undressed in front of his locker on Monday afternoon, the loquacious scout team coach, Webster Wallace approached. Wallace had a stern countenance. (He made a point of always using big words such as *loquacious* and *countenance*.) Webster was an odd guy but his players loved him. He spoke to Beau in a harsh voice but appeared to be having difficulty maintaining a straight face. "You're off the scout team. Clean out your locker." No longer able to contain himself, Webster broke into a huge smile. "You're our first-team kickoff return man—Coach Gary wants you to have a locker with the starters."

The MSU Spartans were ahead by eighteen points and the huge Ann Arbor home crowd had become quiet. Michigan's only scores had come on a Beau Lightfoot kickoff return in the first quarter and on a long field goal just before the end of the first half. During the third quarter, Beau was assigned additional duty as the Wolverine's punt-return man, a nice assignment, except the Spartans didn't punt. They chose to methodically pound down the field for the touchdown that brought the score to 28 to 10.

The Spartans kicked off short to keep the football away from Lightfoot. The offensive team took over on the 35-yard line but failed to make first down and had to punt. The Michigan defense held the Spartans but precious time ticked away.

On the sideline, Eddie approached Coach Blieschroeder. As they stood talking, a photographer with a telephoto lens snapped a picture which, a few weeks later, would appear on the cover of *Sports Illustrated*. The photographer couldn't hear what Eddie said but made up the three-word quote that was reported and later repeated by broadcasters and sportswriters around the country: **"I want Lightfoot."**

Michigan State's punt rolled out of bounds on the Wolverines' 10-yard line. With poor field position and less than eight minutes remaining in the game, Beau took the field as a wide receiver. Eddie immediately went to the Z-in-and-out sequence of plays. His pass to Beau on a simple cut toward the sideline went for seven yards. On the next play, Beau ran the same cut toward the sideline and then broke back to the inside for a thirteen-yard completion. The stage was set. When he returned to the huddle, Beau was greeted by the famous Bartucci grin. Eddie said, "Let's do it."

After two consecutive completions to Beau, Michigan State shifted their pass coverage and Eddie saw that Beau was going to be working against the Spartans' best defensive player, James Washington. On the snap of the ball, Beau cut toward the sideline but Washington didn't fall for the fake. Beau broke back toward the center of the field. Washington was all over him but wasn't prepared for Beau's move back toward the sideline. Washington was out of position and off balance. He twisted his body and turned so fast he lost one of his shoes. It was a terrific effort but he was too late. Beau was gone. Eddie's pass hit Beau in full stride and he sprinted down the sideline for a touchdown. Bartucci to Lightfoot—a seventy-yard pass and, along the way, one of the finest defensive halfbacks in the Big Ten was literally faked out of his shoe.

The stadium came alive. Michigan fans in the process of leaving stopped in their tracks. Those still in stands were on their feet screaming for their beloved Wolverines. The crowd sensed a miracle finish.

The Spartans had other plans. They powered out two first downs before being forced to turn over the ball. They had gained a total of twenty-six yards in nine plays and burned valuable time before punting the football into the Michigan end zone.

When Eddie led the offense onto the field, more than 100,000 people stood and cheered. Eddie was calm. His first call was a fake pass with a handoff to TD on a delay. TD ran right up the middle for twelve yards. On the next play, Eddie faked a pass to Beau and threw to his big tight end, Willie Jefferson, for an eighteen-yard gain.

It was first and ten at midfield with slightly more than two minutes remaining. Michigan had to score quickly. Eddie chose a high-risk play that required him to hold the football for an extra three seconds. If he was sacked, the team would lose valuable yardage and even more valuable time.

Beau lined up five yards to the left of the formation. On the snap, he would stand up, step forward a couple of steps, and hesitate for three seconds. It took every bit of his discipline to stand still. "One Mississippi ... two Mississippi ... three Mississippi." While Beau counted, Eddie dropped back to pass and every receiver except Beau flooded the left side of the field. Eddie patiently waited for the play to develop. A Michigan State lineman broke through and came after Eddie, only to be flattened by TD.

The longest three seconds in Beau's life finally ended. Michigan State's defense was moving left. Beau ran at a sharp angle to the right. As he sprinted against the grain, Eddie dropped a soft pass into his hands. The defenders faced the impossible task of abruptly changing direction and catching Beau Lightfoot in full flight. Beau scored without being touched.

Michigan now trailed by only four points. The crowd remained on its feet. The noise was deafening. Every person in the stadium knew that if the Wolverines could get the football back, they would score another touchdown and win.

The rally began too late. The Spartans covered Michigan's onside kickoff and were able to run out the clock. Although Eddie and Beau didn't get an opportunity to try for the go-ahead touchdown, there would never again be a doubt of Beau Lightfoot's importance to the team.

The next challenge was Iowa; a team many had predicted would win the Big Ten Conference championship. Playing on their home field, the Iowa Hawkeyes were favored by seven points. The Wolverines came to Iowa City and blew the Hawkeyes out of the stadium. The final score was 45 to 7. Next, the Wolverines traveled to Madison, Wisconsin, and demolished a good Wisconsin team 52 to 10. Beau Lightfoot had provided the spark. Michigan was on fire!

Everything was working. Bartucci-to-Lightfoot passes were making mincemeat of defenses. Nobody was able to stop the combination. When opposing teams overcompensated in order to stop the passing attack, they became vulnerable to the inside power running of TD and the outside speed of Billy Wilson. Beau returned kickoffs and punts for touchdowns and the offense began to score forty to fifty points per game.

The Michigan defense, inspired by the success of the offense, began to dominate opponents. The Wolverines tore through the remainder of the season like an Emmet County snowplow blasting through fresh snowdrifts. Sportswriters called the Wolverines the hottest team in the country. The last game of the year was against Ohio State and would be played in Columbus.

Undefeated Michigan State would go to the Rose Bowl, but a victory over Ohio State would give the Wolverines momentum to carry into the next season ... when they intended to be national champions.

The University of Michigan campus was going nuts for its football team. When Eddie and Beau arrived to board the team bus for the trip to Columbus, Ohio, more than a thousand students were on hand to see them off. Somebody had printed T-shirts with the words "Bartucci to Lightfoot" written in block letters. As the line of buses pulled away, Beau looked out the window and recognized one of the self-important fraternity men who had made him sit on the losers' couch. He was wearing a Bartucci to Lightfoot T-shirt.

Beau set the tone of the game by returning the opening kickoff for a touchdown. Everything worked: Bartucci to Lightfoot. TD blasting off tackle. Bartucci to Lightfoot. Bartucci to Willie Jefferson. Billy Wilson around end. Bartucci to Lightfoot. It was beautiful. One of those Saturdays when the Wolverines couldn't do anything wrong. The final score was 56 to 13.

Beau ran into the locker room to celebrate with his teammates. The first man he saw was Coach Gary Blieschroeder. *What the hell was going on? One of the toughest coaches in America was slumped in a metal folding chair with his head in his hands, crying.*

SACRIFICE

A warrior can have no greater honor than to give up his life in order to protect others.

2013

Eddie patted Beau on the back and started to leave but hesitated at the doorway. "I almost forgot to tell you, Father Marcotte wants us to come to Mass with him in the morning. Is that okay with you?"

Beau nodded. "Sure."

He thought about the beautiful white church at the end of Main Street in Harbor Springs and how different it was from the church in Pittsburgh.

PITTSBURGH, 1967

Beau hoped they wouldn't find it but, of course, they did. You don't drive all the way from Ann Arbor to Pittsburgh and not find the church. They made a couple of wrong turns and got lost for a short while but, in the end, they found themselves in front of Ebenezer Baptist Church.

They had been driving since 4:00 a.m. Bobby, Eddie, TD, and Beau were in Bobby's new blue Pontiac hardtop with white-leather seats. Beau thought it was a wonderful automobile. Bobby said it wasn't a big deal because his father could buy Pontiacs at manufacturer's cost.

The young men shared the driving in order to keep fresh and make the trip go faster. Bobby drove from Ann Arbor to somewhere east of Toledo and Eddie took over until they reached Cleveland. Beau passed up his turn. He said he was tired but the truth was he didn't have a driver's license. He didn't know when his court-mandated driving suspension expired and he hadn't bothered to apply for a license. It was easier to say he was tired than to explain.

Why explain anything? Why bother talking at all? The best man any of them had ever known was dead. What the hell was there to say?

Ebenezer Baptist Church, three stories tall and covering more than half a city block, stood bravely against the ravages of urban decay. In an earlier time, she had been a grand lady. Now, her bricks were stained black from years of soot. The graceful, white, wooden arch above the front door was faded and streaked with grime. Her neighbors were a pawn shop, a liquor store, and a take-out restaurant named Catfish Corner.

Beau didn't want to enter the church. He didn't want to see Marcus White's flag-draped coffin. What empty words could he say to Marcus's grandmother?

Marcus can't be dead. It's not right.

Someone held the front door open and motioned for the boys to walk up the front steps. Years of footsteps from people of faith had actually worn deep depressions into each concrete step.

They were four of several hundred people who had braved the dark December afternoon's wind and sleet to reach the Ebenezer Baptist Church to mourn the loss of a good man. As Beau stepped through the front door he entered a different world. The interior was illuminated by three huge chandeliers and hundreds of candles that lined the walls. There was polished wood; gleaming brass; and clean, white paint. Flowers were everywhere. Marcus made a friend of every person his life had touched, and they now crowded the huge sanctuary. There were more than thirty men from the current Wolverine football team, several former players, Coach Blieschroeder, a large group of both white and black former classmates from Carver High School, many people from the church congregation and neighborhood, several local politicians, and a U.S. Congressman. There was a large choir clad in crimson robes and an honor guard of soldiers standing at rigid attention beside the coffin.

Since Marcus was to receive a posthumous award of the Distinguished Service Cross for exceptional heroism in combat, the honor guard was commanded by a full colonel.

The news director of one of the Pittsburgh television stations sent a camera crew and junior reporter Susan Kirschbaum to cover the funeral. Ms. Kirschbaum could not have known this routine assignment would afford her invaluable national media face time and jump-start her career. Susan pushed her way into position near a row of folding chairs that had been set up in front of the first row of pews. Near the chairs was a line of people waiting to speak with Marcus's grandmother.

Beau joined the line and moved slowly toward her. TD had said Marcus had been her only living relative. Now Marcus was gone and she was alone. Beau felt sorry for the old woman, but wished he didn't have to take her hand and try to speak words of comfort to her. The line moved forward. Why had Beau expected a frail old lady? This woman was more than six feet tall with broad shoulders. She had Marcus's perfect white teeth and beautiful black skin. Although she didn't look as old as Beau expected, there was something wrong with her right hip and she leaned on an aluminum cane. She took Beau's hand in a strong grip.

"I'm Beau Lightfoot, from the Michigan team."

She smiled. "Thank you for coming."

He said the words he had practiced fifty times in his head. "Mrs. White, I'm so sorry for your loss. Marcus was a fine man. I'm sure he is in a better place now." *There I've said what I wanted; now I've got to get out of here.*

He tried to move away but could not. She tightened her grip on his hand and surprised him with a glare of scorching anger. "HAVE YOU EVER BEEN DEAD, BOY?"

"Ah ... well, no, ma'am. I haven't."

"THEN YOU DON'T KNOW WHAT YOU'RE TALKING ABOUT, DO YOU? A BETTER PLACE! NONE OF US KNOWS ABOUT A BETTER PLACE! NONE OF US KNOWS ABOUT ANY PLACE AT ALL! THEY KILLED MY GRANDBABY AND YOU THINK YOU CAN COME HERE AND TELL ME HE'S IN A BETTER PLACE?"

"I'm sorry, ma'am. I thought you were religious."

The storm passed as quickly as it had surfaced. "I am a religious person and I've got no cause to be mad at you." She released her grip on Beau's hand, but before he could step away, she seized his arm. "I hope you'll forgive a foolish old woman. Come and sit with me." She leaned on his arm to support her bad hip and walked to the center of the front row of folding chairs. She sat down and pulled Beau into the adjoining chair.

So much for my plan to blend into the crowd in the back of the church.

The service began. The choir created the most beautiful music Beau had ever experienced; sad and unbearably sweet; changing in an instant to joy, redemption, and power that rattled the stained-glass windows. When the minister spoke, the congregation responded to everything he said. Beau had never experienced this before.

"Marcus White was a fine man."

"OH, YES!"

"He's gone to be with Jesus."

"AMEN!"

"I'm telling old Satin he better watch out because Marcus White is coming."

"YOU TELL HIM!"

"Marcus played on a football team. Now he's playing on a better team. Now he's playing on God's team."

"YES HE IS!"

Beau looked from the minister to the coffin with its honor guard and American flag comforter. The soldiers stood still as posts; all sharp creases, polished brass, dress uniforms, white gloves, and spit-shined shoes. Mrs. White patted Beau's arm and said, "I sing in the choir and I'm going to stand up right here and sing the next one with them. It's a hymn for Easter but I asked them to sing it because it's Marcus's favorite."

The choir rose and she stood in front of her chair. Her voice was calm, controlled, strong, and beautiful: "Christ the Lord is risen today ... Hal ... a ... loo ... ou ... ya."

When the hymn concluded, everyone sat down, quieted in their seats, and turned to watch the colonel, who rose and began to read the account of Marcus White's exceptional heroism in combat which led to the Distinguished Service Cross. As the colonel spoke, Beau glanced at Mrs. White. Her control was impressive but her rock-like stillness and absolute focus on the colonel seemed unnatural.

The colonel had been sent from Washington, D. C. to make the posthumous presentation of the medal. He had obviously performed similar duties many times in the past. He was proper and confident. He turned to face the mourners and spoke in a strong, compassionate voice:

"Marcus White's platoon was ambushed by a superior enemy force. Three soldiers were seriously wounded and separated from their comrades. The platoon retreated approximately eighty yards, formed a defensive position, and dug in. Because of heavy enemy fire, they were unable to move forward to rescue the wounded men.

Medical Corpsman White, with complete disregard for his own safety, emerged from cover and sprinted through enemy fire to aid his wounded comrades. Corpsman White carried one of the men over his shoulder and ran back toward the American's position. He was shot in the left leg and fell to the ground but got up and, with his comrade still on his shoulders, ran the remaining distance back to his platoon.

Ignoring his own wound, Corpsman White ran back to the remaining two wounded ..."

A movement drew Beau's attention to Mrs. White. She held the shaft of her aluminum cane in her left hand and the curved handle in her right. While she appeared to calmly listen to the official version of her grandson's heroism, she gripped her cane in her hands and twisted with such force that the handle bent and completely broke from the shaft. Her eyes never left the colonel.

"... with the second wounded soldier across his shoulders, Corpsman White staggered into the platoon's defensive line. He had been wounded three times and additional enemy troops had now arrived and joined the battle. Fearing the platoon was in imminent danger of being overrun, the lieutenant in command called for an air strike on the enemy position.

By this time the enemy had advanced close to the third wounded American and it was probable the soldier would be hit by the air strike. The officer made the correct but heartbreaking decision to sacrifice one man in order to save the platoon. Although he was seriously wounded and had been warned an air strike was coming, Corpsman White broke cover and ran toward the enemy line to rescue the third wounded man ..."

The colonel was interrupted by a low moan that had begun somewhere in the back of the church, gained in intensity, and now engulfed the congregation. Loud sobbing could be heard everywhere—but Mrs. White was dry-eyed. The colonel opened a black-leather case to reveal the beautiful Distinguished Service Cross and approached Mrs. White. Bright television lights came on and Susan Kirschbaum, together with her cameraman, moved closer to Mrs. White to record the poignant moment of the presentation of America's second-highest military honor to the fallen hero's grandmother and to capture a few of her words.

The colonel stood in front of Mrs. White. He was undoubtedly accustomed to presenting posthumous medals to crying spouses and families.

Mrs. White stood. She was bigger than the colonel.

He concluded his presentation: "I present this medal on behalf of the President of the United States."

Mrs. White spoke in a booming voice: "WHY SHOULD YOU PRESENT IT ON THE PRESIDENT'S BEHALF? MY GRANDBABY IS DEAD! WHAT'S THE PRESIDENT DOING THAT'S MORE IMPORTANT THAN BEING HERE?"

Susan Kirschbaum leaned in with her microphone. She was getting everything and had the good reporter's sense to keep her own mouth shut and let things play out.

The colonel remained calm. He was in a predominantly black church, at a service to honor a black war hero. There was a huge crowd of whites and blacks, a dozen local politicians, a U.S. Congressman, and television coverage. He damn well better remain calm ... and respectful. "The President is very busy, Mrs. White. I know he would be here if he could, but he just can't get away; so he sent me to represent him."

"THAT'S A BUNCH OF CONDESCENDING BALONEY AND YOU KNOW IT! WHY DON'T YOU REALLY TALK TO ME?"

"I'll be glad to talk with you, Mrs. White. What would you like to talk about?"

"THERE ARE A LOT OF PEOPLE HERE TODAY. MARCUS'S FRIENDS FROM HIGH SCHOOL, COLLEGE, OUR CHURCH, AND OUR NEIGHBORHOOD—BUT NO FRIENDS FROM THE ARMY. MARCUS TOLD ME HE HAD GOOD FRIENDS IN HIS ARMY UNIT. WHY AREN'T THEY HERE?"

The colonel was starting to look unnerved. "Mrs. White, the soldiers in Marcus's unit are still in Vietnam."

"COULDN'T YOU PEOPLE GIVE THEM SOME TIME OFF TO ATTEND MARCUS'S FUNERAL?" Her voice continued to boom.

Susan held the microphone and affected her best look of respectful concern for the camera. This was great stuff.

The colonel kept trying. "Mrs. White, they're fighting a war."

"I DON'T CARE! YOU SHOULD HAVE GIVEN THEM SOME TIME OFF!"

Beau noticed beads of perspiration along the colonel's hairline.

"What would you have us do, Mrs. White? Should we just stop the war for a week so that your grandson's buddies can come to Pittsburgh?"

"YES! OH, YES! YOU SHOULD STOP THE WAR! YOU SHOULD SAY, 'OH MY GOD! LOOK WHAT'S HAPPENED! MARCUS WHITE IS DEAD! THIS IS AWFUL! LET'S STOP THIS WAR!'"

Susan Kirschbaum's heart was racing. This was big. This was national network material.

The colonel tried to surrender. He extended the open case with the beautiful medal toward Mrs. White and simply said, "Here is Marcus's medal.

"I DON'T WANT A MEDAL! I WANT MY GRANDBABY! GIVE YOUR MEDAL TO CARVER HIGH SCHOOL. MAYBE THEY CAN PUT IT IN THEIR TROPHY CASE NEXT TO MARCUS'S FOOTBALL TROPHIES."

The colonel had nothing more to say. He probably would have turned and walked away but there was one more thing to be done. The honor guard ceremoniously removed the American flag from the coffin, folded it into a tight triangle showing only the white stars and blue background. One of the soldiers handed the flag to Mrs. White and said the officially prescribed words: "Please accept this flag from a grateful nation."

Mrs. White accepted the flag from the soldier's hands and immediately handed it to Beau. She leaned toward Beau and whispered, "A piece of cloth for my grandbaby. I don't want the damn thing! You take it."

The ceremony was over. Susan hadn't been able to capture Mrs. White's whisper. She grabbed Beau by his arm. "What did she say when she gave you the flag?"

Beau didn't answer.

She tried again. "I'm Susan Kirschbaum, Channel 7 Impact News." She still had his arm.

She's a good-looking girl. It would be rude for me to just pull away, but if I repeat Mrs. White's words to be broadcast on television it'll probably cause a shit storm. Beau paused to give himself a minute to think.

Susan gave his arm a little pat. "Well, what did she say?"

Beau stood erect, with his shoulders back, just like the soldiers in the honor guard. "I'm Beau Lightfoot, from Marcus White's University of Michigan football team. Mrs. White gave me the flag to fly over our stadium in honor of Marcus."

Susan turned to face the camera and put on her most dazzling smile. "There you have it, an emotional end to a remarkable memorial service. A player from the fallen hero's college team has accepted the flag from Marcus White's coffin to fly over the stadium where Marcus achieved so many great victories. For Channel 7 Impact News, this is Susan Kirschbaum."

It was too good of a story to allow any delay. Susan stopped at the nearest phone booth and called her news director. The drive to the station took only fifteen minutes but, when she arrived, there was already a phone call holding for her. The secretary said it was someone from Walter Cronkite's office in New York.

THE CONVENTION

Among the tribes of the Great Algonquin Nation, the position of War Chief was not hereditary. It had to be earned through bravery in battle, victories won, wise decisions, and oratory skill.

Unlike a European general, a war chief did not merely issue orders. He spoke with his warriors to convince them to follow his war plans which, if judged to be sound, would be accepted. The War Chief's leadership depended on maintaining the confidence of those being led and that confidence could only be maintained by wise actions and victories. If the warriors lost confidence in their leader, they stopped following him.

2013

Janet sat on the edge of the bed next to Beau and draped an arm around his neck. He remembered another time, more than forty years ago, when she did the same thing. He had been sitting on the cold, wet concrete steps of the graduate library.

ANN ARBOR AND CHICAGO, 1968

The gray dreariness suited Beau's mood. The antiwar movement was gaining force and it had picked up steam from the nationwide coverage of parts of Marcus White's funeral.

But, so what? It doesn't matter. Nothing has changed.

Beau remembered Marcus's warning that there were no free rides for poor boys like them. He slogged through the January slush, attended classes, completed all assignments, and told no one that the story about Mrs. White's desire for Marcus's flag to be flown over the Michigan football stadium was a complete fabrication.

The tight triangle of white stars and blue background had resided in Beau's dresser drawer until Coach Blieschroeder came by and picked it up. He told Beau a ceremony honoring Marcus White was planned for the first home football game. The details were yet to be worked out but the plan was for a moment of silence followed by members of the Army ROTC raising Marcus's flag on the huge flagpole at the south end of the stadium.

Oh, great! The lie I told has already been broadcast to millions of people across the country. Now, another 100,000 people are gonna be deceived in person. I didn't intend for anything like this to happen. I made up a story and now it's out of control. I don't know what the hell to do.

Beau ignored the mist and sat on the wide concrete front steps of the graduate library. During warm weather it was a popular place for students to gather, but today he was alone. He didn't feel the cold as he surveyed the large buildings; the sagging, dripping landscape; and the sidewalk that diagonally bisected the central campus. Three girls were walking toward the old Economics Building. They were the only people visible on the normally crowded "Diag."

One of the girls separated from the others and walked toward Beau. She climbed the steps, and looked down at him. "You look like a guy who could use a friend."

Beau turned his head and looked into Janet's soft, brown eyes. He took off his varsity letter jacket, folded it in half, and placed it over the cold wet step next to him so she could sit down. She draped her arm over his shoulder and he told her all about his lie about the flag and the terrible situation he had created. Maybe Janet could figure a way out of this mess.

"Is there any honorable way out of this?" he asked. "What should I do?"

She said he shouldn't do anything. "A good man who died as a war hero will be honored before a huge crowd. How can that be a bad thing?"

Beau interrupted, "It's bad because I lied about the flag."

"Beau, think about what you're saying! You lied. So what? Did you ever stop and think that maybe you did the right thing?"

"How can a lie be the right thing?"

Janet shook her head. "Mrs. White knows the American flag is more than a piece of cloth. It's a symbol of our country. And I'm sure Mrs. White doesn't hate America. She hates the war—and who can blame her for that? Do you know why you made up the story about the flag?"

"No. I just did it."

"You did it for Mrs. White. You did it because it was the right thing to do. Mrs. White disapproves of our country's actions and she expressed her contempt for our leaders, but attacking America itself by rejecting the flag would have been going too far. You saved her from something she would have regretted. You told me that everything she said was in a loud voice that carried into the back corners of the church but, when she handed the flag to you, she whispered. Somewhere in her subconscious, she knew it wasn't the right thing to do."

Beau straightened from his slouch. "Thanks, Janet. Maybe I'm not such a jerk after all."

Janet gathered her textbooks, stood, and smoothed her shirt. "Beau," she said, "you're one of the good guys."

As the sad month of January wore on, Beau spent many evenings talking with Bobby and Eddie about the war. Shocked by the death of Marcus White, they were now convinced the Vietnam War was a tragic mistake. Their student deferments would end upon graduation. They didn't want to follow Marcus into the war in Southeast Asia but there were very few options.

After exploring every possibility, the boys concluded there were three alternatives to being drafted. One apparently wasn't possible and the other two were unacceptable. The best one, the impossible one, was to join the National Guard. Very few Guard units had been called to active duty and, in the opinion of most political observers, President Johnson wasn't going to make a large-scale call-up of the National Guard. The problem was that Guard units were completely full and had long waiting lists. The two other alternatives were either to simply refuse to serve in the military and be sent to jail or to flee to another country, like Canada or Sweden, which sheltered American draft resisters.

Their best hope was that the war would be over before they graduated—and by late January, that possibility appeared promising.

The White House and General Westmoreland issued optimistic statements. "We are making excellent progress in Vietnam." "We have inflicted heavy damage on the enemy." "Their war-making abilities are depleted."

In a speech before the National Press Club, Westmoreland promised that "we have reached an important point when the end begins to come into view." President Johnson said victory was around the corner.

On the last day of that dreary January, the five friends—Bobby Cunningham, Eddie Bartucci, Dizzy Hernandez, Janet Cunningham, and Beau Lightfoot—spent the evening together. They ordered an extra-large pizza with sausage and green peppers and watched *Star Trek* on television. It was the night of January 31, 1968; Tet, the Vietnamese lunar New Year.

~

The supposedly all-but-defeated Communist forces launched a massive surprise offensive. A series of coordinated attacks struck South Vietnam's five largest cities. The United States Embassy was hit at 3:00 a.m. Saigon police guarding the embassy fled for their lives. The Vietcong commandos blasted through the embassy wall and killed several Americans.

Other forces attacked General Westmoreland's headquarters and the South Vietnamese military's offices. An ammunition dump exploded, creating a giant fireball that could be seen for miles.

Television brought the horror into American living rooms. Both military and civilian dead and wounded lay amid filth and rubble ... all broadcast in living color.

U.S. forces launched a counteroffensive that reclaimed all the territory the Communists had taken, but the size and ferocity of the Tet Offensive had destroyed the credibility of the Johnson Administration.

Antiwar protests intensified and a majority of Americans now believed the war in Vietnam was a mistake.

CBS-TV news anchorman Walter Cronkite concluded the war could not be won. Senator Robert Kennedy delivered a scathing attack on Johnson's war policy. A U. S. Air Force officer didn't help matters by explaining that American bombers had leveled a village thought to be occupied by Vietcong troops because "it was necessary to destroy the village in order to save it."

Senator Eugene McCarthy of Minnesota, running as an antiwar candidate, challenged LBJ in the New Hampshire Democratic Party primary on March 12, 1968. Voters rejected Johnson and his war policy. The "Dump Johnson" campaign was in full swing but the candidacy of Eugene McCarthy failed to inflame the University of Michigan campus.

Ignition came four days later, when Robert F. Kennedy announced he would seek the Democratic presidential nomination. The students were excited by the dynamic Bobby Kennedy, who condemned the war and rolled out a professionally organized campaign. The charismatic Kennedy hit the trail with evangelistic fervor. Bobby looked like a winner.

Janet saw it on television. It came at the end of President Johnson's March 31st nationally televised speech. "I shall not seek, and I will not accept, the nomination of my party for another term as your president ..."

Her first phone call was to her brother, Bobby. "Oh, my God! Johnson's quitting! Kennedy is gonna win! He'll get us out of Vietnam!" Her next call was to Beau, but she couldn't get through. Every telephone circuit on campus was jammed.

It was time to put up or shut up. On an ordinary, cold, and damp early-spring Tuesday night, Janet drafted the letter and Bobby, Eddie, and Beau signed below her decidedly bold signature, "Janet P. Cunningham." In the letter, they offered to do everything they could to help Senator Kennedy win the presidency.

They went to the post office together and before Janet dropped the letter into the mail slot, they put their hands together in a four-way handshake. Eddie said that they were the four musketeers and would not rest until Kennedy became President of the United States.

Beau felt good, but in his heart he wondered if their letter would mean anything. They might not even get an answer. Or, more likely, they would wait three or four weeks before receiving a form letter from someone on the campaign staff.

The telephone call came Friday afternoon. Bobby and Beau were studying in Bobby's apartment. Bobby answered, listened for a minute, and said, "Yeah, yeah ... I don't have time for this bullshit!" Then his face, still skeptical, became serious. He held the receiver away from his ear so that Beau could listen and said, "Would you please repeat that?"

"This is Billy O'Donnell speaking. I'm placing this call for Senator Robert Kennedy. Senator Kennedy would like to speak with either Edward Bartucci or Beau Lightfoot. Are either of them available?"

This might be real. It sure sounded real. Holy shit! Beau grabbed the phone.

"This is Beau Lightfoot."

"Please hold for Senator Kennedy."

Bobby Kennedy came on the line. The voice was unmistakable. "Beau Lightfoot. I'm glad ta have a chance to talk with ya. Thanks for your letta. I accept your offa. I haven't decided exactly how to use you guys, but I want ya onboard."

Beau replied, "You can count on us, sir. I didn't think I would have an opportunity to speak directly with you. I was surprised ..."

"Hell, Beau," Kennedy interrupted. "I saw your picture on the cover of *Sports Illustrated*. You and Bartucci are big heroes. You guys can help us win Michigan and that's what I want ya ta do. My people will be in touch. I'm glad ta have ya with me. With your help, we're gonna win this thing."

The phone call was over but Beau didn't replace the receiver. He sat there and looked at Bobby Cunningham. The four musketeers were going to help Kennedy carry Michigan and win the presidency! Bobby Kennedy would end the war in Vietnam.

But the dogs of war, once released, cannot be controlled or contained. The slobbering hounds of hatred, violence, and death had crossed the ocean and they were running wild. Their work in America was not finished.

The first blow came less than a week later. Martin Luther King, Jr. was shot while standing on the balcony of his motel in Memphis, Tennessee. Within hours, young blacks began to riot in more than one hundred cities across the U.S. The morning following the assassination, Chicago Mayor Richard J. Daley ordered flags to be flown at half-mast and presided over a City Council memorial service for Dr. King.

By afternoon, angry crowds began to gather in Garfield Park, an area of terrible poverty less than five miles west of the Loop. Hundreds and then thousands of people moved onto the streets, smashed windows, and looted stores. The first fire was started at approximately 4:00 p.m., and in less than one hour fires were raging up and down West Madison Street. During the next twenty-four hours, the Chicago Fire Department responded to more than five hundred fires. Mobs stoned sanitation workers as they cleared debris and a sniper shot a fireman.

Daley asked the Governor of Illinois to call out the National Guard; 1,600 troops were on the streets by midnight. The city became quiet but, in the morning, rioting broke out on the south side. Additional police and Guardsmen were unable to stop the looting and arson. Mayor Daley asked President Johnson for Army troops and several thousand were rushed to Chicago.

After forty-eight hours of rioting, the streets became relatively calm. Nearly one hundred policemen had been injured. The police shot forty-eight people and eleven blacks (only four of whom were shot by police) were dead. More than two thousand people were arrested and property damage was devastating.

Daley told reporters he was disgusted by the "kid gloves" handling of the rioters. He issued orders to the Police Department for tough new methods: "Shoot to kill any arsonist or anyone with a Molotov cocktail in his hand ... and shoot to maim or cripple anyone looting any stores in our city."

Attorney General Ramsey Clark, the American Civil Liberties Union, and church leaders said the mayor's "shoot to kill or shoot to maim" order was barbaric. Although Daley backed away from his statement, rank-and-file policemen understood his suggestion that the policy of restraint, never popular with the Chicago police, need no longer be strictly followed.

The news of King's murder hit the small city of Ann Arbor like a punch in the face. Rage, sadness, and a wretched feeling of pessimism sucked the oxygen from the air. Students seeking news gathered in front of television sets and were provided with live coverage of burning and rioting in cities across America.

There was one notable exception.

Bobby Kennedy, who was campaigning in Indianapolis when he received word of King's murder, climbed onto the back of a pickup truck and addressed a large crowd of blacks and whites. Kennedy's grief and humanity tempered the fires of hatred. Indianapolis was spared the rioting and arson endured by other cities.

The news of Kennedy's spontaneous act convinced Beau and his fellow musketeers that the country needed Bobby Kennedy more than ever and they renewed their pledge to do everything in their power to help him become president.

Senator McCarthy's supporters denounced Kennedy as an opportunist who entered the race only after McCarthy had successfully challenged LBJ in New Hampshire. The antiwar movement was split between McCarthy and Kennedy. Vice President Hubert Humphrey enjoyed the support of the Democratic Party establishment.

Kennedy won primary elections in Indiana and Nebraska. He lost in Oregon and the following day, Beau received a telephone call from one of the campaign staffers. He told Beau that Senator Kennedy wanted his help at the Democratic National Convention in Chicago. He said Bobby was going to win the California primary on June 4 and McCarthy would be knocked out of the race. The antiwar voters would consolidate behind Kennedy and he'd roll up a string of primary victories. The Humphrey forces would put up a fight at the convention and Bobby wanted Beau and his friend, Eddie Bartucci, to be on hand. The staffer wasn't sure what they were expected to do but he said that Bobby made a point of saying he wanted Lightfoot and Bartucci to be there with him.

Beau said, "It can't be only Lightfoot and Bartucci. There are four of us. If some of us go, we all go."

The staffer didn't hesitate. "Okay, we want all of you. I'll see you in Chicago."

On the night of June 4, Beau went to bed a happy man. With most of the votes counted, all three of the major networks had declared Kennedy to be the winner in the California primary.

Beau awoke to news of the assassination. His hero was dead. The man they were counting on to save the country; the man who had made a personal appeal for Beau's help, was gone. Beau couldn't wrap his mind around it. He felt like crying, but he didn't. He felt like screaming, but he didn't. He stumbled through the day as if he were underwater.

In the evening, some students who lived in one of the rental houses on State Street across from the football practice fields held a Kennedy memorial. Bobby and Janet Cunningham had already completed their semester examinations and had gone home but Eddie, Beau, and at least two hundred other students crammed into the old house. Some of them spilled out onto State Street and overflowed onto the neighbors' yards. Many people carried lighted candles and a few gave speeches about Bobby Kennedy. There was so much noise that it was difficult to hear and the speeches Beau did manage to hear were long-winded and incoherent. The primary method of honoring Senator Kennedy appeared to be smoking dope and getting stoned.

The memorial was rapidly devolving. Beau found Eddie and said, "This isn't a memorial anymore. Let's go home."

Eddie shook his head. "Beau, the problem with you is that you're a straight arrow ... Get it? An Indian guy being a straight arrow?! That's pretty good, don't you think?"

Beau looked into Eddie's eyes and saw an unfocused brightness that usually meant trouble was on the way.

Eddie affected an expression that he meant to convey deep feeling, but it missed the mark. "Beau, you know I feel terrible about Bobby Kennedy's death ... but we have to go on with our lives. Bobby wouldn't want us to go home now. Look at all the girls. Most of them are wasted and need comfort. Do you know what Bobby would do?"

"Eddie, this is a ridiculous conversation. I have no idea what Bobby would do."

"Well, he'd smoke a little dope and get laid—that's what he would do. Not after he was famous—I mean earlier, when he was our age and people didn't know he was going to grow up to be Robert Kennedy." Eddie looked at Beau for confirmation of this profound insight but Beau merely shook his head. Undeterred, Eddie continued. "I'm gonna give you a joint and I want you to smoke it. Indians smoke peace pipes. Think of the damn thing as a peace pipe."

He produced a bent marijuana cigarette from his pocket. It was a fat, nasty thing and Beau thought it looked like a weird cigar rather than a cigarette. Eddie put it in his own mouth to light it and then placed it between Beau's lips. "See how easy that is? The next part, the getting laid part, is just as easy. You just relax. Sit right here on the floor. Smoke that thing and watch me. See that tall girl over there? I'm gonna have my hands up her shirt in five minutes."

Beau sat and took a tentative puff. It didn't have the slightest effect on him. He took a few deeper drags while he watched Eddie approach the tall girl. Eddie walked up to her and put his arm around her shoulders. He moved his lips close to her ear and said something which she apparently found to be exceedingly interesting. He placed his left hand on her belt buckle, at the spot where her shirt tucked into her pants. He gave her shirt a teeny tug and winked at Beau.

Beau blinked and took a couple more puffs. The marijuana still had no effect on him but the smoke made his eyes water. He figured a few more drags while he watched Eddie wouldn't hurt anything.

Eddie's behavior is inexcusable. He's treating this young woman like a piece of meat. She is a person with feelings, a fellow student, somebody's sister, somebody's daughter. Oh, shit!

Eddie had his hand under the front of her shirt. Beau began to stand but his foot slipped and he sat back down with a thud. The joint he was smoking was more than half gone. He felt dizzy. He'd take one more little hit and then carefully get to his feet.

This time the other foot slipped and he was back on the floor. The tall girl was smiling and leaning into Eddie. His hands were all over her and it began to dawn on Beau that he didn't care what Eddie was up to. He took a few more deep drags of the joint.

In a situation like this, a young Bobby Kennedy probably would get laid. Eddie certainly was planning to. Why should I always miss out? That little blonde on the other side of the room is smiling at me and swaying to some music that only she can hear. I'll walk right up to her and put my arm around her—just like Eddie would do it. I don't understand why I held back in the past. This is going to be easy. The only problem is that I can't seem to stand up. My body isn't functioning properly.

Beau gave a final heroic effort; made it about halfway up and pitched forward onto his face. Although he could no longer move, things were really okay because his face was resting near a lovely hardwood floor. Everyone else was standing around and ignoring the beautiful wood. Beau's eye, positioned less than two inches above the floor, afforded him close observation of the interesting swirls in the grain of the wood. He wondered if they were the result of variations in the rainfall during the growing seasons. It was an important thought, definitely something to reflect on. He would give it some serious consideration. He lowered his head the final two inches and rested it on the magnificent but woefully underappreciated hardwood.

~

Beau couldn't identify the specific moment when they made the decision to attend the Democratic National Convention in Chicago. Events created a current that turned into a flood that swept them along. Bobby Kennedy's win in California did deliver a knockout blow to McCarthy and now, with Bobby dead and McCarthy having suffered at least a TKO, the nomination would go to Hubert Humphrey. Vice President Humphrey hadn't entered a single primary but, with the backing of LBJ, organized labor, and Democratic Party heavyweights, Humphrey was certain to win the nomination. And there was little doubt that Humphrey would continue Johnson's Vietnam War policies.

It wasn't right. It was time for action. They had to be heard and, although there was no guarantee of safety, the Democratic National Convention was the place. Beau didn't want Janet to risk being injured and tried to convince her to stay home—a predictable waste of breath. The four musketeers were in this together—and they were moving into dangerous territory.

Police and FBI agents reported that protest leaders, including several known Communists, were planning violent confrontations with the Chicago police. Mayor Daley was told Yippie leaders were prepared to "tear up the city." There were also rumors that protesters would put LSD in the city's water supply, block streets, set fires, vandalize buildings, invade downtown hotels, and storm the International Amphitheater.

At a press conference on August 16, Mayor Daley said, "People in Chicago behave themselves. It is only some people who might come to the convention from outside Chicago that might bring trouble."

In preparation, police officers were put on twelve-hour shifts and issued gas masks. They would ride three or four officers to a car. The mayor called for National Guard and U.S. Army units to supplement the police. He convinced Senator McCarthy to protect the safety of his people by urging them not to come to Chicago. Permits for marches were denied. Richard J. Daley was not going to allow a mob of outside troublemakers to disrupt the convention.

One of the first to arrive was Women for Peace, a moderate group of middle-class women. Buses had been chartered to bring the women to Chicago from cities throughout the country. Although several hundred members were expected, many of the buses arrived empty. The threat of violence had convinced all but sixty women to stay home.

Beau and his friends were not so easily frightened. Their mission was to protest the Vietnam War and the nomination of a man allied with President Johnson's war policy. Television coverage was essential. The immoral war and the unconscionable nomination of Hubert Humphrey had to be exposed to the entire world.

The Democratic National Convention convened in the International Amphitheater, located several miles southwest of the Loop. Security included a 2,000-foot barbed-wire fence, roadblocks that sealed off several blocks around the amphitheater, and hundreds of law enforcement personnel patrolling the area. The International Brotherhood of Electrical Workers was on strike and did not allow the equipment needed to broadcast live television to be installed outside the Amphitheater.

As Bobby's car traveled along the Chicago Skyway, Janet read aloud from a mimeographed page provided by the protest leadership: *the International Amphitheater is several miles from the central business district (referred to as the Loop), and no permit to march has been issued; many of the protesters are gathering (some planning to camp overnight) at the south end of Lincoln Park, which is located about two miles north of the central business district; Vice President Humphrey, most of the convention delegates, and the Democratic Party movers and shakers are staying at the Conrad Hilton Hotel, located on Michigan Avenue a few blocks south of the Loop.*

Bobby headed for Lincoln Park.

The police were on edge because of warnings of expected violence and did not allow Bobby to park his car anywhere near Lincoln Park. It was early evening by the time he found an open garage on Wells Street and the four friends were able to make their way to the park. When they arrived, there were already over two thousand people, most of them congregating in small groups. Most were white, between eighteen and twenty-five years old, and had long hair.

As night fell, bonfires were lit, people played bongo drums and guitars, danced, and shared drugs. By 9:00 p.m., this motley army was faced along the western edge of the park by a line of Chicago police in riot gear. Periodically, a police squad would charge into the park, stomp out bonfires, and shove people around. The youthful crowd began to scream: "PIGS EAT SHIT! PIGS EAT SHIT!" Some threw rocks at the police.

The policemen held their line for a short while, and then they rushed into the crowd with their nightsticks flailing and bashed every head in their path. Bloodied and terrified, the young people ran. A police car with a loud speaker drove through the park announcing that Lincoln Park would close at 11:00 p.m. and warning that anyone who failed to leave would be arrested.

The crowd taunted the police: "MOTHERFUCKERS! PIGS! SHIT-HEADS!" The beat of the bongo drums was drowned out by the Whoop! Whoop! Whoop! of the rotor blades of a military helicopter making low passes back and forth over the park. Some of the protestors put on helmets. Others screamed, "FUCK THE COPS! THIS IS OUR PARK! STAND AND FIGHT!" Another group opted to avoid bloodshed and began to leave.

Beau and his friends had come to Chicago to protest the Vietnam War and the Humphrey nomination—not to serve as fodder for an enraged police department. They walked out of Lincoln Park and joined a surging mass of people who headed toward the Conrad Hilton Hotel, located approximately three miles to the south and adjacent to Grant Park. In anticipation, network television crews and cameras had set up in front of the Conrad Hilton.

In Grant Park, a group of ministers had erected an eight-foot cross and announced their intention to hold prayer services in the park all night. The crowd marched to Grant Park to join the clergymen and, more importantly, to protest in front of the network television cameras.

About two thousand protestors gathered in the park directly across Michigan Avenue from the Conrad Hilton. Hundreds of police in full riot gear guarded the hotel. They were prepared for confrontation but the demonstrators were relatively peaceful. Deputy Police Superintendent James Rochford must have decided that attempting to clear the park of peaceful protestors in front of television cameras was a bad idea. He waived the park curfew and allowed the demonstrators to spend the night in Grant Park.

It was cold for August and, as the hours passed, much of the crowd drifted away. By dawn, the four friends were among a few hundred bedraggled protesters who had managed a few hours of peaceful but uncomfortable sleep.

Beau awoke stiff, sore, and tired. It was quiet. Most of the people in the park were still sleeping, including his friends. Beau was sleepy but he had avoided the various drugs that had been offered to him. He had gotten high a few weeks ago and was not ready for a repeat performance. He got up quietly and walked to a nearby restaurant for a cup of coffee. He arrived just in time to observe the conclusion of the morning's only excitement. Beau pushed forward to see what was going on.

The police had grabbed a guy who was eating breakfast and were hauling him out of the restaurant. The fellow being dragged toward a police van was an ordinary-looking, grubby, young guy with the word FUCK printed in capital letters across his forehead. People in the crowd said it was Abbie Hoffman, one of the Yippie leaders. The police arrested him for disorderly conduct.

The real action would begin in the afternoon.

By 3:00 p.m., more than ten thousand people had gathered around the Grant Park band shell for a rally to be followed by a march to the convention. Many in the crowd were older, nonviolent members of the antiwar movement who had come for a legal rally in Grant Park and a peaceful march to the convention. Others, already bloodied by the police in Lincoln Park, arrived wearing helmets and carrying pieces of broken concrete and balloons filled with urine.

Police moved through the area distributing leaflets warning that anyone attempting to march to the International Amphitheater would be arrested. Sometime after 3:30 p.m., a group of protesters removed the American flag from a flagpole near the band shell and raised a red shirt. Ten enraged policemen tore into the crowd. Although the nimble, young perpetrators ran away, the police clubbed several innocent bystanders.

The crowd taunted the police: "FUCK YOU, PIGS! FUCK YOU, LBJ! HELL NO, WE WON'T GO!" Police officers were pelted with rocks and beer bottles. Many of the policemen maintained their discipline, others did not.

A group of about twenty-five policemen attacked the crowd. They beat people to the ground and continued to club them even as they tried to crawl away. Most of the demonstrators had been peacefully sitting near the flagpole when they were attacked and beaten with nightsticks. The police quickly retreated and were followed by a barrage of curses, rocks, bottles, garbage, and urine-filled balloons.

Beau and his friends were on the opposite edge of the crowd and managed to avoid confrontation. They joined a group planning to make a nonviolent march to the Amphitheater. The police commanders had no intention of allowing the march to proceed and used their bullhorns to tell the demonstrators they would be arrested if they marched. A skirmish line was formed directly in front of the marchers to prevent them from moving.

One of the protest leaders told the marchers to stay put and wait for instructions. They sat on the ground and waited for almost an hour. Beau noticed that the police were bringing in vans and special vehicles for transporting prisoners. A sound truck repeated warnings of arrest. The police line began to edge closer.

Beau didn't wait to see any more. He grabbed Janet's hand and, with Bobby and Eddie trailing behind, left the line of marchers and began to look for a way out. Like many in the crowd, they weren't from Chicago and didn't know where to go. The police and the National Guard had blocked the park's exits. A frightened young Guardsman fired tear gas into the crowd. The mob surged back and forth seeking an escape.

Word spread that the Jackson Street Bridge had been left unguarded.

The four friends were part of a wave of protesters that ran across the bridge and flowed helter-skelter down Michigan Avenue toward the Conrad Hilton. Police formed one line to guard the hotel and a second diagonal line at the intersection of Balbo and Michigan Avenues to prevent the crowd from moving southwest toward the Amphitheater.

By 7:00 p.m., there were seven thousand people massed in front of the only television cameras outside of the Conrad Hilton. The crowd screamed: "DUMP THE HUMP! HELL NO, WE WON'T GO! HO HO, HO CHI MINH!" Several threw stones at the police. During the confusion, Eddie disappeared but Bobby, Janet, and Beau were in the front row. They didn't throw anything but they joined the chanting: "Hey, hey, LBJ, how many kids did you kill today?"

Everything suddenly exploded. Deputy Superintendent Rochford had ordered his men to clear the streets.

Beau and Janet tried to leave but the crowd behind them pressed forward. It was impossible to move back. Some policemen exhibited professional discipline. Others lost control and came screaming into the tightly packed crowd from all sides. Hundreds of people were indiscriminately beaten and maced. Even though Rochford used his bullhorn to order his commanders to "hold your men steady there," screaming police used their clubs to hurt people.

Some demonstrators hit back. They ganged up on isolated officers or picked an individual target from a line. Policemen were struck with rocks, punched, and kicked. Heavy doses of tear gas were fired into the mob. The crowd fractured in every direction. Many were vomiting. Others were temporarily blinded. Beau, Janet, and Bobby ran for their lives.

In order to avoid identification and individual responsibility, many of the officers covered their name tags and removed their badges. They surged into the crowd, clubbing everyone they could get their hands on—a middle-aged couple watching from the sidewalk, reporters, a minister wearing his clerical collar, newspaper photographers, a girl who was already lying bleeding on the ground, television crews, a medic in a white coat.

A black reporter waved his press credentials to a police officer who said, "That don't mean anything to me, nigger" and struck him with his nightstick. Television cameras recorded the violence. Some people chanted, "The whole world is watching. The whole world is watching."

The world may have been watching but it was difficult for Beau to see much or to understand what was going on. It was dark. Police lights were everywhere. Tear gas swirled through the air. People were running, screaming, crying, and half blind from the gas. A policeman on a three-wheeled vehicle raced through the crowd intentionally running over people.

Beau had lost track of Bobby but maintained a firm grip on Janet as they stumbled along. They almost tripped over a guy kneeling next to a girl with a gash on the side of her head. As he was trying to stop the bleeding with a torn T-shirt, she looked up in terror. A policeman took a swing at her with his club. The boy threw up his arm; he protected her but absorbed the impact of a terrible blow.

The cop turned toward Beau and Janet. "What about you, you little hippie fucks? You want some of this?"

They ran. Janet fell and got back up. Beau saw a statue standing on a large concrete base. It might afford some protection from the insanity. He pulled Janet behind the base. They hid on the ground and hoped no one would notice them.

It worked for a while. The crowd and the police swirled past the statue's base like it was a boulder in a fast-moving river. Then two big cops, who were running around on the side near Janet, came to an abrupt halt. One raised his nightstick above his head to strike Janet as she lay on the ground. Beau dove on top of her. As he tensed his body to absorb the blow, he saw a shadow moving toward them. It was Bobby Cunningham.

As the policeman raised his club, Bobby slammed his unprotected ribs with a right-handed punch that hit with the power of a Mack truck.

The blow landed with a thump and the cop wasn't able to make a sound. His mouth opened and closed. He gasped for air, sank to his knees, and slowly fell to the ground. The second cop got behind Bobby and was choking him with a nightstick pressed against his throat. The gagging Bobby was pulled backward and was being dragged toward Balbo Street where other policemen were waiting.

Beau looked for a weapon and found nothing. His foot touched the nightstick dropped by the policeman Bobby had punched in the ribs. Beau knew Bobby was being dragged toward a terrible beating. He was fast disappearing into an unreal world of darkness, flashing lights, and swirling tear gas. Beau grabbed the nightstick and ran toward his friend.

The policeman was a large guy, almost as big as Bobby. He wore riot gear: a helmet, Plexiglas face shield, and a protective vest. Beau grasped the club in both hands and, using the full force of both arms, smacked it against the officer's unprotected shin. The crack sounded like a Louisville Slugger connecting with a fastball.

The bone broke.

The policeman screamed.

Beau grabbed his choking friend and they stumbled away trying to disappear into the night. The confusion and flashing darkness made it impossible to see clearly but Beau and Bobby crawled in the direction they thought would take them back to Janet. Bobby was gasping. Beau guided him into a slight depression that had a pocket of clean air. Beau whispered, "Let's rest here a minute. After you catch your breath, we'll find Janet."

They couldn't see Janet, but Beau heard her voice. He looked in the direction of the sound and was able to catch brief glimpses of her through the swirling tear gas. They were only a few yards away. He could hear her talking quietly to the policeman Bobby had punched.

"Lie still," she said. "You're gonna be alright."

The guy moaned and clutched his side. "Oh, I really hurt! I think something is broken." His voice had an edge of panic. "I can't get enough air."

Janet adjusted his legs, bringing his feet a little higher than his head. She spoke in a soothing voice. "I think some of your ribs are broken. You have to lie still. Take shallow breaths. If you move, you might puncture one of your lungs." She took off her sweatshirt and placed it over him.

The young cop gave her a helpless smile and whispered. "You've got me now. You've captured a pig. You guys can do whatever you want to me and I can't do anything to stop you."

Janet smoothed her sweatshirt over his body and tucked it in around his sides. "You're not a pig. You're just a kid ... like me. Stay still. I'm not gonna let anybody hurt you."

The policeman was breathing a little more easily but he didn't say any more. She gently wiped some dirt from his face and asked his name.

"Mike Callahan."

"How old are you, Mike?"

He partially suppressed another groan. "I'm twenty-two."

Janet smiled. "My name is Janet Cunningham. I'm twenty-one. Do you live in Chicago?"

"Yeah. I live in the South Side. I've lived there all of my life."

Janet nodded. "I'm from a suburb of Detroit. You see? We really are alike. We're about the same age. You're a boy from Chicago and I'm a girl from Detroit." She paused and looked into his eyes. "And you were going to hit me with a club."

Mike swallowed. A tear formed in the corner of his eye. "Oh my, God, Janet. I'm so sorry. I'm so sorry." The pain, shock, and the realization of what he had tried to do, must have overcome him. Mike began to cry.

Janet wiped his face with the edge of her shirt. "Don't feel so bad. These are terrible times."

Janet shifted her position. "Mike, you didn't actually do anything. You were lucky that my brother was here. He gave you a smack you'll probably remember for the rest of your life—but he saved you from hitting a defenseless girl."

In less than an hour, most of the violence in Grant Park subsided. The tear gas had dissipated somewhat and Beau and Bobby were able to see well enough to make their way back to where Janet was sitting on the grass with the injured policeman. Sporadic fights continued to flare up and small bands of protestors ran through the Loop setting fires in trash barrels and shouting obscenities. By 11:00 p.m. there was a substantial National Guard presence in the park. When two Guardsmen walked nearby, Janet called out, "Soldiers! Over here. We've got an injured policeman. Do you guys have any medics with you?"

Mike was soon strapped to a board to prevent further injuries and Janet walked beside him as he was carried to an ambulance. The doors opened and as the medics prepared to slide him in, she took his hand. "Good-bye, Mike Callahan."

Mike pulled her to him and said something. The doors closed and the ambulance drove away.

News and television images of the violence in Grant Park reached the convention floor. Tempers were hot and many of the Democratic Party's leaders announced they would not support Humphrey in the general election. After the close of convention business, five hundred convention delegates marched to the Conrad Hilton and joined the demonstrators in Grant Park.

By that time, the exhausted Chicago police had been ordered to stand down. The National Guard patrolled the park's boundaries but allowed the people in the park to remain unmolested. There were small groups gathered around scattered bonfires. Hundreds of people carried candles and sang along with Peter Yarrow and Mary Travers: "This land is your land. This land is my land …"

Sometime after 3:00 a.m., they found Eddie. He was near the center of everything, sitting on a blanket with his back resting against a large elm tree. Of course, a girl was with him. She was a beautiful white girl with long dark hair that fell below her shoulders. She wore a fringed buckskin dress, moccasins, a beaded headband, and assorted bracelets and necklaces. Her name was Jennifer. She was a sorority girl from the University of Wisconsin.

Beau smiled. *Beautiful white sorority girls are dressing up and pretending to be Indians. What a strange world.*

A few hours later, when the sun was rising over the horizon, the four musketeers were in Bobby's car driving through Gary, Indiana. Beau and Janet were in the backseat; she was sleeping with her head on his shoulder. Beau wondered what they had accomplished. More than eighty million people had watched the protests on television. A majority of Americans believed the Vietnam War was a mistake. Hubert Humphrey was nominated on the first ballot but the Democratic Party was badly split. The presidency was probably going to be handed to Richard Nixon. Nixon said he "had a plan." Maybe he would end the war. If the war continued, Beau expected to be drafted soon after graduation. He would probably be sent to Vietnam and might lose his life.

But graduation wasn't until next June. Right now, he was headed toward Ann Arbor with his best friends and the most beautiful girl in the world asleep on his shoulder.

The sunrise was magnified and oddly more beautiful because of the air pollution from the Gary, Indiana, steel mills.

BETRAYAL

As Pontiac's warriors surged east, the Seneca, Mingo, Shawnee, and Delaware joined them. They swept up the Monongahela River Valley and destroyed every fort in their path until they reached Pittsburgh. Fort Pitt was well-defended but many of the soldiers were ill with smallpox. Chief Pontiac's formidable forces surrounded the fort and shot burning arrows into the interior.

An Indian runner was sent to the commander of the fort to request surrender. The commander said his men were capable of defending the fort but he wished to avoid unnecessary bloodshed. He urged the Indians to call off their attack. As a sign of friendship, the commander presented gifts for the runner to take back to the warriors: brightly colored beads, silver armbands, and blankets from the beds of the smallpox patients.

2013

A faint, gray light crept into the bedroom. It wasn't the first light of morning; just a hint the night was starting to give way. Beau eased out of bed and put on a pair of tan slacks and his faded blue shirt. He avoided turning on a light which meant he couldn't find his shoes or socks. Not wishing to wake anyone, he quietly padded down the stairs in his bare feet.

He opened the front door, maneuvered one of the white wicker chairs on the front porch to face east, sat down, and put his feet up on the railing. When the sun came up, it would appear over the Menonaqua dunes at the head of the bay. There was no wind and the lake was calm. The only sound came from small ripples against the shore. The air felt cool and had the sweet smell of pine. Beau remembered Pontiac's advice to take quiet moments to appreciate the natural world and to allow its healing powers into your heart. He leaned back to enjoy the solitude and to wait for the edge of the sun to peek over the dunes.

Shuffle ... clomp ... shuffle ... clomp. Then a whisper. "Hey, Beau, you want some coffee?"

"Thanks, Bobby. Coffee would be great."

"I'll go in and put on a pot. We can sit together and watch the sun come up." Shuffle ... clomp ... shuffle ... clomp.

After his injury, Bobby had had three surgeries on his right knee but the doctors hadn't been able to restore its normal motion. Beau had been only a few yards away when Bobby was cut down. He would never forget the sickening crack and Bobby's scream of pain.

ANN ARBOR, 1968

Eddie's confident voice called out, "Slot right. Motion left. Fly. On three—break!" The Michigan team that broke the huddle on that October afternoon was ranked as the number one college football team in America.

Beau took his position on the right side of the formation. Eddie crouched behind the center and called, "Set!" Beau took a step back and went in motion to his left. As the offense, Michigan was allowed to have one player moving before the ball was snapped and the play actually began.

The University of Illinois players were alert to Beau's movement and two defenders mirrored his motion. Illinois was a solid team in the middle of the Big Ten Conference standings, but undefeated Michigan was a 21-point pregame favorite. As Beau continued his motion toward the left side of the line, there were ten minutes remaining to be played in the third quarter. Michigan led by a score of 28 to 10.

The season had been phenomenal! Everything had gone so well, Beau felt like he was running downhill. Bobby was the best offensive tackle in the Big Ten. Both Eddie and Beau were potential All Americans. Beau had "bulked up" to 169 pounds and was said by many to be the best wide receiver and kick-return man in the country. Eddie had the swagger of a pirate and a throwing arm like a cannon. Beau believed Eddie could probably hit a sparrow in mid flight and knock it out of the air.

"Hut one!"

Beau moved through the backfield and let Eddie know where he was by slapping him on the hip as he ran past him. As he continued to move smoothly to the left, he took a quick look at the defense. Illinois was positioning a man on the line of scrimmage to hit him as soon as the ball was snapped, there was a defensive halfback about eight yards deep, and a safetyman was edging toward Beau's side of the field. It was a lot of manpower to stop one guy, but—*Let 'em try.* Everything was perfect. It was a crisp, clear afternoon in Ann Arbor; the Wolverines were rolling; more than 100,000 fans were howling; and Beau Lightfoot was running downhill. He didn't know the next ten seconds would change several lives.

"Hut two!"

Beau reached the left side of the formation, looked downfield, and waited for the snap.

"Hut three!"

Everything happened at once. The center snapped the ball to Eddie, who quickly retreated five steps before setting up to pass. Lamar Jones, the best pass rusher on the field, came crashing in from his outside linebacker position. Bobby Cunningham absorbed the force of Lamar's charge and smacked him in the chest. Lamar was knocked back a step but not stopped. He continued to charge but Bobby blocked his path. Beau dashed downfield. The Illinois defender assigned to hit him on the line of scrimmage was probably frustrated by his team's lack of success. His assignment was to bump Beau to throw him off stride and slow him down—but he took a vicious swing with his right forearm and lunged at Beau as if he wanted to kill him. He missed completely and Beau broke into the secondary at full speed. The defensive halfback retreated and the safety moved closer toward Beau's side of the field. The halfback played exactly as he had been taught. As Beau approached, he continued to move back. He maintained his balance. He stayed under control. He was alert for a fake and ready to move in any direction. Beau ran right by him. No fake. This was a fly pattern and Beau was flying.

The defender recovered but Beau was a step past him—and one step was all Beau Lightfoot ever needed. The safetyman had hesitated for a fraction of a second and would be too late. Beau knew Eddie would throw the ball to the outside, away from the defenders, where only Beau could catch it. He looked over his left shoulder. Eddie would drop the football into his outstretched arms just as he had done so many times before. Beau would be in the end zone in nothing flat and the band would strike up "The Victors." That's the way it always went. If he got one step beyond the defense, it would be a touchdown.

Eddie's throw was short. Rather than the usual tight spiral, the ball fluttered and floated into the hands of an Illinois defender. It almost looked like Eddie was trying to throw to him.

An interception is a dangerous play for the big offensive linemen. Their football lives are devoted to blocking others and they have had little practice defending themselves from being blocked. The interception instantly upset the field. The Illinois defenders became blockers endeavoring to clear a path for their ball carrier, while everyone on the Michigan team turned and went after him. Beau pursued from behind. He was ten yards away but closing in fast. Bobby, with a good cut-off angle, lumbered after the ball carrier with the intensity of a slow-moving guided missile. Beau saw the block coming but Bobby had no warning. The blow came from the right and the full force of the Illinois player's helmet connected directly with Bobby's knee. Bobby's right foot was securely planted and his knee, fully extended, supported the entire weight of his large body. There was no give. Bobby twisted, screamed, and fell like a shot bird.

Illinois scored a touchdown and Eddie played badly for the remainder of the game. Without help from Eddie, the Michigan offense collapsed. The defense allowed Illinois to score another touchdown, but held well enough to preserve a 28-to-24 win. It was the third game in a row in which the Wolverines had won but failed to cover the point spread. Gamblers who bet on Illinois and took the 21 points were winners.

In Ann Arbor, October afternoons end at an early hour. By the time Eddie and Beau arrived at the University Hospital, it was dark outside. The nurse said they wouldn't be allowed into Bobby's room until the doctors evaluated the injury and his knee was stabilized. Eddie asked how bad it was. She replied that the doctors would speak to everyone later. Her voice was neutral and professional but her pretty face conveyed a message of bad news.

Beau was not reassured when he and Eddie met the Cunninghams in the waiting room. Mrs. Cunningham had been crying and had a look of panic. Beth Cunningham's boy was hurt. Beau understood she was frantic with worry. He wasn't prepared for Buck Cunningham, though. Buck's clothing was disheveled and his eyes were wild. The hair along the edge of his scalp, which he always had neatly combed over his bald spot, had fallen to the side. He looked dazed.

This must be worse than an ordinary football injury. I should say something or do something—but I don't think I can.

Eddie could. He walked over to Mr. Cunningham and spoke quietly. Beau couldn't hear their conversation but saw Mr. Cunningham shaking his head.

Beau willed himself to approach. The only thing he could think to say was that he was very sorry. Buck didn't respond, but Mrs. Cunningham patted Beau's arm and said she was glad he was there. Beau stood self-consciously for a couple of minutes before retreating to sit on one of the yellow plastic chairs.

The chairs must have been part of a well-intended effort by the hospital to make the waiting room attractive and cheerful. The décor featured "uplifting colors" and bright florescent lights. The white linoleum floor was spotless and had been shined to a high gloss.

As Beau was contemplating the waiting room, Janet Cunningham, Dizzy Hernandez, and Mitch Caputo burst through the door. Janet ran into the arms of her mom and dad and, after only a moment of hesitation, Dizzy, who never restrained her emotions, joined in the hugging. Mitch stood back a few steps and then walked over to Beau and took a seat.

There isn't anything to do in a hospital waiting room. After the greetings and expressions of concern were completed, everyone sat down to wait. Bobby's family and best friends all sat in the molded plastic chairs and looked concerned. They were the only people in the large room. No one said a word.

Beau knew he should sit patiently and worry about Bobby but, after a while, it was hard to keep his mind focused on nothing but worrying. He glanced over at Mitch and the girls. Janet's light-brown hair was cut in a page-boy style and she had artfully applied skin-tone makeup to cover the scar on her cheek. She wore a white blouse, navy blue cardigan sweater with a silver circle pin on its upper left side, a muted-blue-and-red-plaid wool skirt, navy blue knee socks that matched her sweater, and a pair of polished brown penny loafers. Dizzy had a style all her own but it was impossible to hide the fact that she was a strikingly beautiful girl. Her dark hair was cut short and streaked with peroxide. The streaks had the distinct look of a homemade job and her haircut was uneven. Her football-game attire, which she was still wearing, consisted of jeans, a yellow T-shirt with MICHIGAN across the front, and a pair of black high-top tennis shoes without socks. Mitch looked like a gangster: slicked-back long hair, black pegged pants, pointy shoes with two-inch lifts, and a cream-colored shirt with its top buttons undone to reveal a hairy chest and gold chains. Although Mitch always played the tough guy, Beau found it difficult to take him seriously.

A vibrating scuffing sound distracted Beau from his observations. At the far end of the waiting room, a maintenance man was buffing the floor. As the man expertly maneuvered the buffer, Beau considered how the floors at Holy Childhood would benefit from such a machine.

A doctor came through a set of double doors that led into the waiting room and broke Beau's reverie. He approached the Cunninghams. "Your son has suffered a major trauma to his right knee. We've got the knee immobilized and have given him something to help with the pain. We want to take more x-rays and run some further tests but, as of right now, our plan is to operate on Tuesday morning."

In a soft voice, Buck Cunningham asked the question most on his mind. "Will Bobby be able to play any more football?"

"I'm sorry, sir. We're not thinking in terms of playing football. We're thinking about rebuilding your son's knee to allow him to walk normally and to avoid spending the later years of his life in a wheelchair. I don't mean to scare you. We're going to do everything possible to put him back together—but it is a serious injury."

Janet held her father's arm and asked if they could see Bobby. The doctor said they could see him but, after a few minutes, everyone except family members would have to leave.

All of the color appeared to have been drained from Bobby. He was lying on his back on hospital sheets that were only slightly whiter than his face. Clear liquid dripped into his left arm from an IV bag hanging from a stand next to his bed, through a tube and needle. His right knee and lower leg were raised and held in a sling-like contraption and a thin bloody liquid drained from his knee through a tube that emptied into a container under the bed. The head of the bed was cranked up part way. Bobby's eyes were open.

Although clearly showing the effects of the pain medication, Bobby was still Bobby. He managed a smile. "Did we win?"

His mom and dad hugged him and said some things that Beau couldn't hear. In a moment, probably remembering the others would soon have to leave, they stepped back to make room for Eddie.

Eddie's swaggering, confident attitude was gone. "Bobby, I'm so sorry. It's my fault. I never thought a thing like this could happen." He slumped in the chair next to Bobby's bed and hung his head.

Bobby patted Eddie's head and whispered. "Wasn't your fault. It was an accident."

Mr. Cunningham helped Eddie to his feet, as Janet and Beau came to the side of Bobby's bed. Janet looked as if she was trying not to cry. Bobby put his big right arm around both his sister and Beau and pulled them close. Janet whispered, "I love you, Bobby."

Bobby said, "I love you, Janet. I love you, Beau."

Beau felt like crying but, of course, he wasn't going to allow that to happen. He was overcome with emotion and his words came out without forethought. "I love you, Bobby ... I love you, Janet."

She didn't speak but turned to look at Beau. Her brown eyes brimmed with tears as she acknowledged Beau's words with a small nod.

Beau stepped back so that Dizzy and Mitch could talk with Bobby. A short while later, a nurse came into the room and asked everyone except the Cunningham family to leave.

The four friends stood on the sidewalk in front of the main entrance to University Hospital. Mitch turned to Eddie and said, "It's a sad day—but you understand this doesn't change anything about the football games, right?"

"Yeah, I understand," Eddie replied.

Then Mitch said he had something he had to do and said good-bye. Eddie, Dizzy, and Beau didn't have a destination but began to drift in the general direction of Eddie's apartment and the Chi Omega Sorority house. As they walked, Beau thought about Mitch's odd comment to Eddie: 'Doesn't change anything about the football games.' What the heck did that mean? Mitch had spoken directly to Eddie and was obviously trying to sound tough ... threatening.

Beau decided his imagination must be running wild. He simply couldn't buy Mitch's tough-guy act. Mitch threatening Eddie Bartucci—the very idea was absurd. But, yet ... there was something.

Eddie and Bobby shared an apartment in a new building at the corner of Washtenaw and South University Avenues. Of course, Bobby wasn't there. Eddie said he couldn't face going into the empty apartment and suggested they stop for coffee in one of the small restaurants along South University.

It was after nine o'clock. Beau didn't want coffee but he hadn't had anything to eat since the pregame breakfast with the team. He was hungry and his favorite coffee shop was just a block down South University from Eddie's apartment. He loved the little joint because it was cheap and they served wonderful pecan rolls. They cut the rolls in half, slathered butter over the freshly cut surfaces of both halves, grilled them with the butter sides down until the brown-sugar glaze was partially melted and began to bubble. They served them hot off the grill. Biting into one brought Beau close to heaven. The place didn't even have a name, just a straightforward sign that said EAT. It was the kind of restaurant one might find in Harbor Springs; not nice enough for the summer people but just right for locals like Beau.

There were no customers and the place looked like it might be closed, but the EAT sign was illuminated and the door was unlocked. They made their way to their favorite booth in the back corner. Eddie slid into one side and Dizzy and Beau sat facing him. Beau thought Eddie looked terrible and was about to say something when a waitress approached. Eddie ordered coffee and a cheeseburger. Beau ordered a grilled pecan roll and a large glass of milk. Dizzy ordered black coffee.

If there was ever a person who didn't need caffeine, it was Dizzy. She was the most turned-on person Beau had ever met. She had her own force field. He couldn't be near her without feeling the crackle of kinetic energy.

Eddie stared across the worn table top and mumbled something about how sorry he was. He looked as if he might start to cry. Beau told him it wasn't his fault. Eddie said it was, and tears began to run down his cheeks.

Then something astounding happened.

SMACK!

Dizzy had reached across the table and slapped Eddie's face, hard! Both Eddie and Beau were stunned. Since Eddie failed to react, Dizzy slapped him again. The sound of the smack filled the small restaurant. "Okay, Eddie. Let's have it. What the hell is going on?"

"Dizzy, I've gotten myself in serious trouble. And now, I've caused Bobby to be injured. I feel awful … about everything … I don't deserve to live."

Beau was horrified but said and did nothing.

Dizzy smacked Eddie again. "We're your best friends. If you're in trouble, you have to tell us about it."

Eddie didn't move or say anything; just sat there with tears streaming down his face. Dizzy slapped him again.

"Jesus Christ, Dizzy! Stop it! I feel bad enough without you hitting me."

"Yeah, well I'm going to keep hitting you until you tell us what's going on."

"I threw the interception on purpose … some bad people have got me and there is no way out. I've ruined everything! I should just kill myself."

Dizzy looked thoughtful. "That's an idea. You can always kill yourself.

Why don't you keep that in mind as an option? But right now, just tell us what's going on."

"It started after the Minnesota game," confessed Eddie. "Remember what a super game Bobby played? He didn't let anybody lay a hand on me. They have a good team and we demolished them. Anyway, I was feeling on top of the world when I happened to run into Mitch after the game. Mitch said we should celebrate and, as you guys know, I'm always up for a good time. He said he had a couple of friends, older wealthy guys, who were big football fans. He said they were anxious to meet me. They'd buy us fancy dinners at the Fox and Hounds over in Birmingham and introduce us to some beautiful models from New York who had come to town to work at the automobile show.

"Doesn't sound like an offer Eddie Bartucci would refuse, does it? Well, like a dope, I went with Mitch—and that's when the trouble began. Mitch's friends turned out to be a couple of low-level criminals who said they were representing 'important people.' They said I could earn $10,000 to $15,000 every week without hurting anyone. All I had to do was shave a few points from our football games. 'What did it matter whether Michigan won a game by thirty points or merely twenty points?' they argued when I said no way. 'All it would take is for a few passes to be slightly off target. No one would ever find out about it, nobody would be hurt, and there was a lot of money to be made.'

"Well, I didn't need money and was insulted by their proposition. I told the two thugs to get away from me before I called the cops. Mitch said he had no idea his acquaintances would turn out to be bad guys, and he apologized profusely. I was disgusted by his friends, but I told Mitch to forget about it. It was over; no harm done.

"Well, it wasn't over. At noon on Monday, when I was in the library studying for my Econ 201 exam, I was feeling sorry for myself because I'd had to skip lunch in order to make time for studying. The practice questions were a bitch. 'With A and B as defined above, it must not be assumed that certain primary characteristics of A will be consistently unlike those analogous characteristics of B. True or false? Give your reasoning.' I was the best quarterback in the United States and I had to miss lunch to try to understand this crap. I was starting to get a headache when Mitch sat next to me and offered me a Snickers bar. Mitch said it wasn't fair I had to kill myself playing football for the glory of the University of Michigan and still be required to contend with Professor Simon's bullshit. It wasn't my fault that Simon couldn't make normal use of the English language. Mitch said I deserved a break.

"Peter Paeker, one of Professor Simon's teaching assistants, had seen the upcoming exam and would provide the correct answers, through Mitch to me. Of course, I neglected to ask Mitch why Paeker wanted to help me."

Beau, of course, recognized Peter Paeker's name, but now that Eddie was finally talking, he decided not to interrupt him.

Eddie continued, "At first I said no, but then Mitch convinced me this was a special circumstance and it'd only happen just this one time. It was easy. The exam consisted of eight essay questions. I memorized the answers furnished by Peter Paeker and took the test on Wednesday. On Friday, the graded examinations were returned to us. A tall, odd-looking fellow, who I figured must be Paeker, handed back the exams. He told me my grade was an A but that I wasn't going to get my exam back until later. I was glad about the grade and didn't care about the test being returned to me.

"Later that same afternoon, when I stopped by the apartment to drop off my books before heading over to dinner with the team, Mitch was waiting for me. Bobby had already left. Mitch told me 'they' had me. I could either shave some points from the football game or be exposed for cheating. I grabbed Mitch by the throat and punched him in the face. Blood gushed from his nose—but before I could hit him again, he choked out what he called the facts of life: he was only a messenger and giving him a beating wouldn't change anything. Some very important people were behind the scheme and they had proof of my cheating. If I refused to cooperate, I would be expelled. Indiana wasn't considered to be a strong team and we were a 28-point pregame favorite. All I had to do was ease up a little. Nobody was asking me to throw the game. We could beat Indiana by fewer than twenty-eight points and no one would be hurt. Michigan would still win and I'd earn some easy money.

"On the other hand, if I refused to go along, I would be expelled from college and a couple of goons would work me over with baseball bats.

They'd make sure I never played football again. So, I agreed to do it this once and that I did not want the money. I told Mitch to tell them they could take their money and shove it.

"The next day, we beat Indiana 31 to 7. Nobody noticed my miscues, and I figured I was done. I had fulfilled my part of the agreement. But Mitch came to me again, before we played Purdue. We were favored by only nine points. Shaving points without giving away the game would be difficult and I told Mitch I wouldn't do it. But Mitch said he had secretly recorded our last conversation when I agreed to shave points on the Indiana game. If I caused any problems, the recording would be given to the police. The new deal for me was to cooperate or be expelled, beaten to a pulp, and thrown in jail.

"Fortunately for me, Purdue was a good team. I took a little off of my game and we won with a 21 to 14 victory." Eddie took a deep breath. "So that's the story. The third time I shaved points was this afternoon. I intentionally threw the interception, my best friend got hurt because of me, and here we are."

One part of the story puzzled Beau. "Eddie, how could they prove you cheated on the exam?"

"Beau, I've got to give those bastards credit ... they are clever. Peter Paeker is one of Professor Simon's teaching assistants. The professor asked his TAs to comment on the proposed examination and one of them noticed that question six pertained to material they had not yet covered in class. Simon changed the question—but Paeker had provided me with the answers to the original questions, including number six. The TAs graded the exams and Paeker made sure he got mine. He was able to both give me an A and insure nobody saw my answer to question six. When the exams were returned, he kept mine. Now I understand why he kept it. It proved I cheated because only a student who had seen an advance copy of the original questions, rather than the questions which were actually asked, could possibly have answered question six as I did."

Dizzy cleared her throat. Beau and Eddie waited for her reaction. "Eddie, that's quite a story. After listening carefully, I've changed my mind. I think you probably should go ahead and kill yourself."

The famous Bartucci grin slowly spread over Eddie's face. "Dizzy, you are some piece of work."

Dizzy gently patted Eddie's cheek and said, "Go back to your apartment and go to bed. You're not alone in this anymore. We'll figure a way out of this mess. Let's meet in Bobby's hospital room at noon tomorrow. Okay?"

The boys nodded in agreement and the three friends slid out of the EAT shop's back booth. As they were leaving, Eddie said, "Beau, I think you should walk Dizzy back to the Chi Omega house. It's a dark night. Some guy might attack her and she'll be forced to kick the living shit out of the poor bastard. If you walk her home, it'll save trouble for everybody."

After leaving Dizzy at her sorority house, Beau continued to walk down Washtenaw Avenue toward the big old house where he rented an upstairs room. Washtenaw was a busy four-lane street but, by ten o'clock at night, the traffic had thinned and it was quiet. Large fraternity and sorority houses with carefully tended lawns were set well back from the street. A full moon was partially obscured by tall trees that lined the parkways. The October night air was warmer than Beau had expected and the sweet aroma of smoke from burning leaves was everywhere.

The leaves that remained on the sidewalk made a pleasing swishing sound as he walked through them. Beau sensed a presence on his left. Chief Pontiac was walking beside him. Beau was so happy to see him that he forgot his manners and failed to wait for the Great Chief to speak. "Spirit Father, I am glad you're here. Eddie is in bad trouble and I have to help him. What should I do?"

Pontiac walked slowly at Beau's side. He walked through the dry leaves with his head down and appeared to be deep in thought. Beau maintained a respectful silence as they walked. After a few minutes, Pontiac turned toward Beau and spoke in his deep, slow, self-assured voice. "The way out of this trouble lies in the white man's world. Tell Buck Cunningham everything and seek his help." After a pause, Pontiac continued, "There is one more thing I have to say ... remember who you are. These troubles came from betting on a contest. Now there is a different contest: the beloved son of The Greatest War Chief Who Ever Lived against a few criminals and low-life gamblers. You'll find a way. You can do this."

~

Early Sunday afternoon, Mr. and Mrs. Cunningham, Janet, Dizzy, Beau, and Eddie were gathered in Bobby's hospital room listening to Eddie tell his story about being the victim of unscrupulous gamblers. Mitch Caputo was conspicuously absent.

As Beau heard the story for the second time, words other than *victim* came to his mind; words such as *selfish, lazy, arrogant, thoughtless,* and *cheater*. Eddie had taken the easy road and betrayed them all. Beau knew he would stick up for Eddie no matter what, but he sure was mad at his friend.

Everyone's attention was focused on Eddie as he told his tale of troubles. He concluded by asking what everyone thought could be done to extricate him from the situation. There was a moment of silence before Buck Cunningham exploded.

"SON OF A BITCH, EDDIE! *How* could you have done this? I'll tell you what we're going to do. We're going to call the police and the university authorities and tell them everything. You've brought this on yourself and now you have to suffer the consequences!"

"Wait a minute, Dad," said Bobby. "He's my best friend."

Buck was yelling. "BEST FRIEND? THE COWARDLY BASTARD CAUSED YOUR INJURY! FOR ALL I CARE, HE CAN ROT IN JAIL!"

After this outburst, Buck ran out of steam and everyone took a moment to catch a breath. What happened next was completely unexpected.

Beau approached Mr. Cunningham in a manner which he would have previously considered unthinkable. He put his hand on Mr. Cunningham's shoulder and addressed him as Buck. "Buck, Bobby's hurt and Eddie has screwed up, but best friends stick together. After Bobby's accident, we all stuck together. If we report Eddie, it won't only affect him; it will be a black mark on the reputation of the University and a disgrace to the football team. We've got to work together—we need you to be with us."

Buck turned to Bobby. "Is that what you want?"

Bobby nodded his head, held out his right hand, and his father took it. "Yes, Dad. I want you to help my friend."

Buck immediately transformed from a father into a business executive. He warned everyone to be careful not to break any laws or do anything that might make matters worse. Serious legal help was needed. He would reach out to his old friend and advisor Buford Gerard. He would ask Buford to come to Ann Arbor to meet with them on Monday. Between now and then, since Beau said he knew this Paeker fellow, he should talk with him and learn as much as possible about Paeker's involvement. It would be best if everyone else kept quiet about the whole mess until after they met with Buford on Monday.

Peter Paeker's phone number was listed in the Ann Arbor telephone directory. He answered on the fourth ring.

"Hello, Peter. This is Beau Lightfoot. I know everything. I want you to meet me in the cafeteria in the Michigan Union in one hour."

"What are you talking about? And what makes you think you can call me up and give me orders? I don't know what the hell ..."

Beau interrupted, "I have no time for any bullshit from you, Peter. You either meet me or I'm going to the police."

"Goddamn it, Beau. Just wait a minute—I've got written proof your buddy Eddie Bartucci cheated on the exam. If you go to the police, I'll turn him in."

"So what? Everybody will get what they deserve. Eddie will be expelled and you'll go to jail. Are you going to meet me—or not?"

"Okay—yes, I'll meet you," said Peter. "Don't do anything stupid. There is more to this than you know. The Union in one hour; I'll be there."

Beau felt good as he put down the receiver. He thought he had sounded like a genuine hard ass. Pontiac would have been proud.

Fifty-five minutes later, a clearly shaken Peter Paeker took a chair at Beau's table in a quiet section of the Union cafeteria. Peter was initially reluctant to talk, but Beau was insistent; little by little, he succeeded in pulling Peter's story out of him.

As Beau already knew, Paeker had played basketball in junior high school and thought of himself as a potential star who failed to make the high school team only because of poor vision. Paeker said he loved sports and felt he was so knowledgeable that he could make some good money by betting on games. At first, the results of his gambling were bad, and they only got much worse. Before he knew what hit him, Peter owed $25,000 to some unforgiving people. He was in a jam. His wife didn't know about his gambling debt, he had no money, and his creditors seemed deadly serious about getting their money. Two thugs paid him a visit and forced him to set a trap for Eddie Bartucci by making it easy for Eddie to cheat on the exam. They didn't give Peter any choice; there was nothing else he could do.

Beau had no sympathy. *There are too damn many jerks in the world who think only of themselves.* He asked Paeker if he would give him Eddie's exam in return for help in getting out from underneath his gambling debt. Paeker promised he would return Eddie's examination. Beau told him to contact his creditors and tell them he wanted to arrange a payment plan.

Beau knew some cash up front would be required before they could work out any kind of installment plan. He guessed at least $500 would be required. That presented a problem because he only had $23 in cash and these fellows weren't going to accept a check. The only thing to do was to ask Eddie for the money.

After an urgent telephone conversation with his father, Eddie was able to provide the money. Beau carried a brown envelope containing twenty-five used $20 bills when he and Peter went to meet the debt collectors. As instructed, they drove Peter's car to a seldom-used railroad parking lot on the north side of Ann Arbor.

Two men were waiting outside a black sedan—a gigantic fat guy with the flattened nose of a former boxer and a small pointy-faced man that looked like a ferret. Before Beau and Peter got out of their car, Beau handed the envelope to Peter and said, "These guys don't know me. You've got to do the talking."

They stepped outside of the car and Peter offered the envelope and said he could pay an additional $300 to $400 per month until his debt was paid.

Ferret took the money and laughed. "The vig is two points a week. What's here covers one week. You still owe $25,000. We'll be back for it."

For some reason, Peter Paeker chose this moment to make a stand. Maybe he'd accumulated too many disappointments during his life.

Maybe he'd just been ridiculed too often. Or maybe this was simply one insult too many. Regardless, Peter straightened his usually slumped-over posture and stood almost six feet three inches. He told Ferret he wasn't going to stand for any bullshit. He said two percent a week was usurious. It amounted to more than one hundred percent a year ... a criminally high rate of interest!

Ferret cracked a nasty smile and said, "Yeah, you're probably right." Then he pulled a pistol out of his coat pocket and shot Peter in the foot.

Peter was holding his foot, crying, moaning, and bleeding all over the front seat of his car as Beau drove to University Hospital. He felt sorry for the guy but he remembered that the reason he got involved with Paeker's problem was to get Eddie's exam. He wanted the exam and demanded Peter give it to him. Peter was hysterical and almost incoherent due to pain and fear. He kept repeating that Eddie's paper was his insurance against being murdered. Beau didn't see any reason why this would be true but Paeker was beyond reason.

Peter held his ground, and Beau wasn't able to get the exam. Instead, Beau drove to the emergency room entrance, got out of Peter's car, and left him to face his own problems.

That was Sunday night, less than thirty-six hours after Bobby had been injured. Things were moving fast.

Bobby's parents, Janet, Beau, Eddie, and Dizzy had become a tight group. Late Monday morning they again met in Bobby's hospital room. Perhaps it was wishful thinking, but Beau thought Bobby looked a little better.

While they waited for Buford Gerard to arrive, Beau told them about his adventure with Peter Paeker. He said two bad things had come out of it: he failed to recover Eddie's exam and they were dealing with guys who didn't hesitate to shoot people.

When Mr. Gerard walked through the door, the pessimistic atmosphere began to lift. The attorney listened carefully. He wanted to learn every detail of the situation before making a commitment to his old friend and client Edmund Cunningham. Finally he looked up and said, "Okay, I can help ... usual rules: you must tell me everything. No lying.

And everyone must follow my instructions." He paused and waited for each person to nod in agreement before he continued. "There are two separate problems: the illegal conduct and cheating on the examination. The illegal conduct carries the greatest risk; I suggest we deal with that right now.

"Our first step is going to be to confess everything to the proper law enforcement authorities." He stopped and looked at Eddie.

Eddie's body stiffened but he did not object.

"Good. Yesterday, after I spoke with Buck, I reached out to a man by the name of William Andreason. Billy is an old friend of mine who happens to command the Michigan State Police. I'm going to meet him at the Ann Arbor State Police Post this afternoon. Billy and I have an idea. I want Eddie and Beau to accompany me to the Post. Then we'll all meet back here about the same time tomorrow."

Bobby, who thus far had been ignored, said, "I'm having surgery tomorrow morning."

After several minutes during which everyone made a fuss over Bobby and offered their best wishes for a good result from his surgery, the time and place of their meeting was changed to Tuesday night at Eddie's apartment.

Beau thought William Andreason looked a heck of a lot more like a Commander than a Billy. He was a large man with an erect posture, a square jaw, spit-shined shoes, neat short hair with some gray around the temples, and a ton of gold braid on his uniform. Beau and Eddie sat in respectful silence as the commander explained his plan.

In exchange for his cooperation, Eddie would avoid criminal prosecution. The situation presented State Police detectives with an opportunity to roll up a major sports-betting ring and put some criminals behind bars. The plan was to arrest a low-level guy and then flip him with the threat of a long prison sentence coupled with a promise of leniency in return for help nailing the people above him. The detectives would flip one man; then the people above him, then the people above those people, and so on.

The individual on the lowest rung of the criminal ladder was Mitch

Caputo. The plan was for Eddie to set him up and for Beau to be a witness.

Eddie's hand shook as he used the telephone on Commander Andreason's desk to call Mitch. He said Beau Lightfoot wanted to get in on the point-shaving deal and arranged for the three of them to meet in the back booth of the EAT shop.

The conspirators spent fifteen minutes enjoying coffee and discussing shaving points in return for large amounts of money. When Beau felt he had heard an adequate amount of incriminating statements from Mitch, he gave the agreed-upon hand signal: a tomahawk-chopping motion, like the one used by Florida State fans. Beau thought it was a ridiculous signal that probably was meant as a put down for him but, if it made the cops happy, he would use it. Before he finished his third chop, several Michigan State Police detectives burst into the Eat shop and arrested Mitch.

~

When the group met in Eddie's apartment on Tuesday night, their foremost concern was the outcome of Bobby's surgery. The doctors had informed the Cunninghams that although the surgery had gone well, the damage to Bobby's knee was extensive and it was probable that a second operation would be necessary. This sobering news was greeted by silence but the story of Mitch's arrest was met with cheers. There had been little reason for cheering during the past few days.

Buford Gerard allowed everyone to release some tension before reminding them that Eddie still faced the prospect of being expelled for cheating. Since Eddie's incriminating examination still remained in the unstable hands of Peter Paeker, the only viable way out of the mess led directly through Professor Sidney A. Simon.

Buck Cunningham said, "Let's just buy off the son of a bitch! What's his price? Everyone has a price. It may not be money but there's always something. Where is his weakness? What does he want?"

Buford answered with a smile. "Buck, as usual, you're probably correct. I'm going to have my people investigate Professor Simon. We want to know as much as possible about the man before we decide how to approach him. Let's give my researchers a day to study Sidney Simon's life under a magnifying glass. We should meet again tomorrow night."

"Here's what we know." The group had assembled on Wednesday evening in Eddie's apartment to hear Mr. Gerard's report. "Simon is a tenured professor. He can't be fired; can't even be effectively pressured. He earns a nice living from his salary and from consulting fees. He has been married to the same woman for twenty-six years. No known vices. According to some of his colleagues, Simon considers himself to be a top-tier intellectual who hasn't been properly acknowledged. He seems to have a bit of a chip on his shoulder and has been heard to opine that the University of Michigan would be better off without a football team because the players are a bunch of brutes with no business attending an institution of higher learning."

Buck broke in, "This is a swell report, Buford, but this guy isn't superman. I want to know about his vulnerability. How do we get to him?"

Gerard smiled the smile of a man who always had answers. "He does have a vulnerability—his inflated opinion of himself. I've got an idea, something he'll find impossible to refuse … a seat on the President's Council of Economic Advisors. What do you think?"

Dizzy spoke for the first time. "Mr. Gerard, how can we get him an appointment like that?"

Gerard answered, "We're not offering the chairmanship, merely a seat on the council. I think we can swing it. Buck, do you remember Joseph Stockwell, from Grosse Pointe?"

"Sure. I haven't seen him for a while but at one time I knew him quite well."

Gerard continued, "As we all know, it appears almost certain, that in less than two weeks, Richard Nixon will be elected President of the United States. Mr. Nixon has already quietly started to establish a transition team and Joseph Stockwell is a key member of that team. I'm going to speak with Joe and put Professor Simon forward as an excellent prospective member of President Nixon's Council of Economic Advisors. I'm going to need some money to grease the wheels and help with the appointment. Please understand that I am not talking about a bribe or anything improper ... merely an eleventh-hour campaign contribution to assist a candidate we sincerely respect and deeply admire. Eddie, a campaign contribution of $100,000 won't be a problem, will it?"

Eddie flinched as if he had been slapped. His eyes were so wide he looked like a barn owl. "That's a lot of money! I don't have that kind of money."

Attorney Gerard affected a look of insincere shock. "I know you don't have $100,000. I also know the Bartucci family can easily afford to contribute $100,000 to an excellent presidential candidate." He paused and fixed Eddie with a look that could drill through kryptonite. "You haven't told your family about your situation, have you?"

"My father knows some of it."

"You better get the whole family together and tell them everything. Eddie, you screwed up and you need help. Get in your car right now, drive home, sit down with your family, confess every stupid thing you've done, and meet me back here tomorrow with $100,000 in cash. Why are you still here? I told you to go—right now. Go!"

Eddie left.

Buford Gerard was in full action mode. "When I get the money from Eddie, I'll speak with Joe Stockwell but it will be helpful if we can get some more push on behalf of Professor Simon. Buck, you and Beth know Governor Landry, don't you?"

It must have been a statement rather than a question because Gerard didn't wait for an answer. "Go pay the governor a visit, and do it right away. You have to convince him that University of Michigan Professor Sidney A. Simon is the greatest economist since Adam Smith. Call in a favor. Do whatever you need to do to motivate him to write a letter recommending Professor Simon to our soon-to-be President Elect Richard M. Nixon. ... What else? ... Representative Gerald Ford of Grand Rapids is the most important Republican in Congress. I don't know him. Does anybody here know him?"

Mr. and Mrs. Cunningham did not know Representative Ford which, of course, meant no one in the room knew him. Buford was moving too fast to consider the improbability of one of the college students being acquainted with Mr. Ford.

"Well, it would be better if somebody knew him but maybe he'll help us anyway. Let's ask him to recommend our favorite economist. Congressman Ford is a former University of Michigan lineman. I think Bobby would be the best person to speak with him.

"Janet, will you take charge of this? Explain everything to Bobby and help him get a telephone call through to Representative Ford. Bobby should say he's calling from his room at University Hospital where he is recovering from the serious knee injury that he suffered while helping the beloved Wolverines defeat Illinois. I'm sure Bobby can say it better than that—but you know what I mean. Tell Bobby to use his own judgment about how much to lay it on. I don't know if Mr. Ford will help us but it's worth a try." Gerard stopped talking and looked around the room. "Does everyone understand his or her assignment? Are there any questions?"

Beau thought there was a major detail that had not been addressed. "What about Professor Simon? Even if we are successful in securing this appointment for him, how do we know he'll accept it in return for letting Eddie off the hook?"

Gerard responded, "That's a good question, Beau. We don't know what he'll do. I'm going to pay a personal visit to Professor Simon. By this time tomorrow, we'll have our answer."

On Friday morning, Beau was startled from a deep sleep by the ringing of his telephone. After managing a weak hello, he was greeted by the energetic voice of Buford Gerard. "Sounds like I woke you. I thought you would be up and about by this hour."

Beau's bedside clock showed 6:30, not an hour when many undergraduates were up and about.

Gerard continued without missing a beat. "Are you a member of the University of Michigan's Young Republicans Club?"

"What—? No. Why would I be?"

"I'll explain later. Right now, I want you to get dressed in nice conservative clothes and go join the club. I'm staying at the Michigan Union. After you join the Young Republicans, meet me in my room. Try to be here before ten o'clock."

Beau had a lot of questions but he had learned that when dealing with Buford Gerard, it was best to just do as he was told.

Beau arrived at Mr. Gerard's hotel room at 9:45 a.m. with his Young Republicans Club membership card in his pocket.

"You're here, Beau. Good! I'm going to try to get a commitment from Professor Simon and, if I'm successful, I don't want him to be able to change his mind and worm out of it. That's less likely to happen if he makes his commitment in front of two of us, particularly if one of us is an upstanding member of the Young Republicans Club. All you'll have to do is stay in the background and observe."

Beau nodded his understanding.

Gerard motioned for Beau to sit in the room's one chair while he sat on the edge of the bed. "Before we get started, I want you to understand a few things, Beau. As an attorney, I am an officer of the court. An officer of the court must always be truthful. I think you already know, I never lie."

"Yes, sir."

"I'm not going to lie to Professor Simon. However, there are certain matters which are not clear and I'm entitled to interpret those matters as I feel most appropriate. Let me give you a couple examples. Joseph Stockwell told me that since Simon was 'our man,' he had no objection to my speaking with him. Whatever actual authority that may or may not have given me, I am choosing to interpret it as granting broad authority.

"Perhaps a better example has to do with Mr. Nixon's attitudes and desires. While I, of course, do not know Mr. Nixon's mind, Joe Stockwell has informed me that Richard Nixon is a person of compassion, intelligence, and utmost integrity. Since that is the case, when I undertake to state Mr. Nixon's point of view, although I don't have the advantage of firsthand knowledge, I will express the point of view I feel a person possessing those outstanding personal attributes would be likely to have. Do you understand?"

Beau's head was spinning. He didn't have any idea of the actual meaning of what Mr. Gerard had just said. He did however understand what he was expected to say. "Yes, sir."

"Good. Let's go."

Gerard had arranged to meet Professor and Mrs. Simon at their home. He had explained he wished to speak with them about a position which the soon-to-be President Elect considered to be exceedingly important.

When they entered the Simons' house, Gerard didn't explain why Beau was there. He merely introduced Beau as a leading member of the University of Michigan Young Republicans Club. The Simons cordially greeted Beau and didn't question his presence. Beau took a chair a bit to the side of the main action.

Buford Gerard explained that Richard Nixon always thought of a husband and wife as a team and when he considered a man for a high position, he wanted the man's wife to be a part of the decision process. Gerard's demeanor toward Professor and Mrs. Simon was deferential. His manner became almost courtly as he explained that Mr. Nixon's transition team was seeking an economist with an impeccable background and a record of high academic achievement to serve as a member of the President's Council of Economic Advisors.

Professor Simon made it clear he was pleased he was finally being appropriately recognized and it appeared obvious to Beau that Mrs. Simon was thrilled with the honor that appeared to be forthcoming. She also seemed delighted by the prospect of moving to Washington, D.C.

At precisely the point when Beau figured Mrs. Simon was completely hooked, Gerard said there was one matter he needed to discuss privately with the professor. As Mrs. Simon quickly left the room, Buford leaned close in order to speak sincerely to his new friend. "Sid, I'm confident the President Elect will be favorably impressed with your qualifications. (Beau noticed Gerard had left out the words "soon to be.") I feel that he would like to have you on his team—but he may have one reservation." The attorney paused in order to give this information a chance to sink in. "The President Elect believes one's humanity is as important as his expertise. He doesn't want to be surrounded with bloodless technocrats. He wants advisors who understand that well-meaning individuals sometimes make mistakes, and he wants the people on his team to have the humanity to forgive a mistake. Sid, do you believe you are that kind of person?"

Sid assured his new friend that he did, indeed, possess the requisite high level of humanity and could certainly forgive a mistake.

It was apparent to Beau that Gerard was moving in for the kill.

"Sid, there is a situation at hand which I feel the President Elect would consider to be a bellwether. One of your students has made the serious mistake of cheating on an examination."

Professor Simon furtively glanced at Beau. Buford, a man who never missed anything, noticed the glance. "It's not Mr. Lightfoot."

There were good-natured chuckles all around. Beau Lightfoot, a clean-cut Young Republican, certainly wasn't the cheater. Mr. Gerard continued. "The student deeply regrets his mistake and I'm convinced it will never be repeated. At some future time you may be made aware of the student's name and the details of the incident. You would then have within your power either to forgive the student or to have him expelled. This sad affair may never see the light of day but if it is brought to you, I believe the President Elect would like to know what you would do. I believe he will use your answer as an insight into an aspect of character that is important to him."

There it was. Professor Sidney A. Simon sat very still. Buford Gerard had said what he had come to say and waited quietly. Beau thought it was an uncomfortable moment. What was Professor Simon thinking? He was egotistical but he wasn't stupid. Was he thinking of his wife's disappointment if he failed to be named to the President's Council of Economic Advisors and they didn't get to live in a townhouse in Georgetown? Was he thinking he richly deserved the appointment? Was he thinking an opportunity for an important government position might never again come his way? Was he thinking that a bad deed by one of his unworthy students should not be allowed to stand in his way?

As Beau wondered, the silence dragged on. It continued to drag for what he thought was far too long; but Beau was a young man who had not yet learned a fact well known to both skilled attorneys and great chiefs: silence is a powerful tool.

Finally, Professor Simon stood. He extended his hand to his new friend and said, "At the end of the day, we're all just people and sometimes people make mistakes. Of course, I would forgive."

~

Seven days had passed since Bobby was hurt. So much had happened; it felt like seven months to Beau.

Mitch Caputo had dropped out of college and was assisting the State Police by wearing a wire to his meetings with the gangsters. Because of his cooperation, Mitch would be sentenced to probation rather than prison. That is, of course, provided the gangsters didn't discover the wire and kill him.

Bobby's doctors were optimistic that a second operation would allow them to reconstruct his knee well enough for Bobby to walk normally.

After meeting with Professor Simon, Congressman Gerald R. Ford declined to write a letter of recommendation. The former Michigan Wolverine center did, however, make a personal visit to Bobby Cunningham in his hospital room. Based on other recommendations and generous campaign contributions from the Bartucci family, it seemed likely that soon after the election Professor Sidney A. Simon would be selected as a member of the President's Council of Economic Advisors.

Peter Paeker confessed his gambling addiction to his wife, sold his car, took a second mortgage on their house, borrowed $8,000 from his mother, and paid off his gambling debt. He still had unpaid medical bills for the bullet wound in his foot and his wife was considering a divorce.

And Beau, kind of by accident, told Janet he loved her.

The Wolverines were on the field in East Lansing, facing a strong Michigan State team fresh from their upset victory last week over Ohio State. The Spartans were determined to knock off the Wolverines. Although they would be playing without their outstanding tackle, Bobby Cunningham, Michigan was a pregame 7-point favorite.

By game time, a cold, damp wind had begun to blow. Pages of newspaper and sundry pieces of trash were swirling in the corners of Spartan Stadium. Heavy, black clouds hung low but the field was dry and the footing was good. Michigan received the opening kickoff and, in eleven plays, drove the length of the field for a touchdown. Under the confident command of Eddie Bartucci, the Wolverines performed with the precision of a symphony orchestra.

Eddie didn't feel as confident as he looked. He was playing with a new left tackle, a big kid from Manistee, Michigan, named John Johnson. The cause of Eddie's concern was Johnson's assignment to block Ray Smith. Smith was a fearsome pass rusher for the Spartans—big, fast, and mean as a wounded grizzly. Eddie didn't want any part of him.

So far, the Michigan fans were encouraged that their team could lose a star player like Bobby Cunningham and keep rolling as if nothing had happened.

But not quite! A coach with an outstanding pass rusher like Ray Smith, will position his player in the team's defensive formation so that he can crash into the opposing quarterback from the quarterback's left side. A right-handed passer like Eddie sets up to throw with his left shoulder forward and his right shoulder back. He can see the pass rushers approaching from his right. His left side is blind.

Eddie used short passes that he could throw quickly. He had been able, thus far, to get his passes away before Smith had enough time to reach him. The Wolverines continued to play well and, early in the second quarter, were ahead 14 to 0. Beau had already caught five passes. MSU's left defensive halfback appeared to be afraid of Beau; not physically afraid, he'd like nothing better than to lay a couple of hard licks on Beau Lightfoot. He was afraid Beau would get behind him and catch a touchdown pass.

To avoid being embarrassed by a long-pass completion, the halfback had been lining up too far back and giving Beau too much room. Beau had already caught three easy passes right in front of him. Beau had seen the frustration on the defender's face and saw he was beginning to edge up. The pass receptions had all been along the sideline; if the halfback could get between Beau and the football, he could make an interception and have an open field for a touchdown.

Beau sensed the time was right. He and Eddie had played together so long they could communicate without words. In the huddle, he caught Eddie's eye and gave him a nod. The play would require Eddie to take the risk of holding the football for a few extra seconds, but he made the call. On the snap of the ball, Eddie dropped back five steps and set up to pass. Ray Smith made a feint to the inside, punched John Johnson's right shoulder, and spun to the outside. It was Ray's best move. Bobby

Cunningham was one of the few tackles in the Big Ten who could block that move. But Bobby wasn't on the field.

As Ray spun past Johnson and into the Michigan backfield, Beau Lightfoot sprinted toward the sideline as if he was going to catch another pass right in front of the defensive halfback. At the sideline, Beau raised his hands to fake making a catch. Eddie pumped his arm to fake the pass. The halfback roared in front of Beau for the interception. Beau made a sharp cut downfield and raced into the clear. He had his one step. He had two steps. Beau looked over his shoulder and there was the ball. Eddie had dropped it right into his arms. Beau caught the football without breaking his stride and ran sixty yards for a touchdown.

Eddie didn't see the touchdown. At the instant he threw the ball, he was hit from his blind side by the awesome force of Ray Smith. Smith lifted Eddie and smashed him into the ground. The full impact of the collision was absorbed by Eddie's right shoulder. The team doctor took him directly to the locker room and then to the hospital.

When Michigan was next on offense, Jamie McDonald, who had played very little, replaced Eddie at quarterback. The Wolverines, with a 21-point lead, became conservative and scored only one field goal during the remainder of the game. Michigan State fought back, scoring two touchdowns during the second half, but the Wolverines held on for a 24 to 14 victory.

Those gamblers, who bet on Michigan State and took the 7 points, were losers.

THE WOMAN DECIDES

Among the Odawa, a woman had power to choose her own husband. A brave had to win a young woman's heart before he could purchase her by making gifts to her family.

After dances, which usually lasted most of the night, the unmarried women of a village would return to their lodges. The braves, carrying burning torches, would enter the lodges and walk among the "sleeping" women. A young man would walk slowly and quietly until he felt a small tug on the hem of his robe. He'd hand the torch to his maiden and she would extinguish it on the earth floor of the lodge. Then she would edge to the side and open her blanket to make a place for him to lie beside her.

2013

"**Beau, here's your** coffee. You look like your mind's a thousand miles away."

Beau accepted the large mug of coffee. "Thanks, Bobby."

Bobby scooted a chair next to Beau on the porch and sat down. The two old friends sat in comfortable silence, resting their feet on the railing, and taking small sips from mugs of steaming coffee. There were some clouds to the east and the sky had turned red and gray and light blue. Stripes of bright orange shot through all of it. As the sun began to peek from between the wooded sand dunes at the head of the bay, Beau was reminded of one of his favorite Indian stories: *"In the evening, Mr. Sun goes down in the west. At night, while it's dark and no one can see him, he sneaks around to the other side of the world and in the morning he comes up in the east."*

As Beau pondered the sun legend, he realized Bobby was saying something about Janet coming downstairs last night and telling him about Beau staring at the photograph of the 1968 football team. "We had quite a team, didn't we, Beau?"

Beau smiled wistfully. "We had a wonderful team. We could have won it all. Things just didn't turn out the way we planned. I'm so sorry you got hurt."

"Things usually don't turn out exactly the way people plan. It was awful having my knee smashed up but, if I hadn't been injured, I probably wouldn't have gone to law school and I wouldn't have had the opportunity to become friends with Gerald Ford. It gave me a heck of a good start in politics to have the future President of the United States as my mentor. We didn't win everything—but we won a lot. I'll always remember the entire stadium cheering for you. Ohio State fans were on their feet cheering a Michigan player. I don't think that will ever happen again."

ANN ARBOR, 1968

Beau's most vivid memory was of being afraid. Although he was usually the smallest man on the field, playing football didn't scare him. He tried to avoid giving the big guys a clean shot at him, and took his chances. This situation was far more frightening. He had to face Dizzy and tell her the hurtful truth.

He should have been honest with her a long time ago but he couldn't stand to think of hurting her. In addition to being beautiful, D'Isabella Hernandez was quick, smart, confident, passionate, and tough.

Beau knew that hidden behind her hardened exterior, Dizzy had a soft heart. She was a loving person, generous, loyal to her friends, and always the first person to help someone in trouble. It was her passion that scared him. Dizzy was volatility personified: delighted laughter one minute; screaming anger the next. It seemed to him as if her moods were unpredictable, violent, and instantly changeable. Now he must tell this girl he didn't love her. No wonder he was afraid.

The worst part about telling Dizzy he didn't love her was that he did love her; just not romantically. He cared deeply for her and loved her in the way he loved Bobby Cunningham and Eddie Bartucci. It wasn't right to lead her on any longer. The honest thing was to be straightforward; just tell her how he felt.

Beau took a deep breath and picked up the telephone. One of the pledges answered. "Good morning, Chi Omega. May I help you?"

As he waited for Dizzy to come to the phone, Beau felt a surge of panic. He wished there was some way he could avoid facing her.

"Hello. This is Dizzy."

"Hi, Dizzy. It's Beau."

"Hi, Beau. What's up?"

"Dizzy, I think you and I should have a serious talk." *There, I've said it. I've given her a clear signal. Now there's no chance to back out.*

"Yeah, Beau, I guess it is time for a talk. I'll meet you in the back booth at the EAT shop."

Beau hesitated. The back booth at EAT was a quiet, out-of-the-way-spot ... too out-of-the-way. He didn't know how Dizzy was going to react and he feared the worst. She might yell and scream, or break down in a fit of loud crying, or even hit him. She might be more likely to have some restraint if they met in a busy place.

"I don't have time to get over to the EAT shop. I've got a class at one o'clock and after class I only have a few minutes before football practice. Let's meet in the coffee shop at the undergraduate library."

Dizzy answered, "That's awfully crowded and noisy, but if that's what you want, I don't care. I'll see you right after your class."

It was two o'clock. Dizzy was sitting at a table waiting for him. Beau had a weightless panicky feeling, like the feeling you would get if you drove your car real fast over the crest of a hill and the car went down while your stomach kept going up for a couple seconds before it started to fall. He bought two paper cups of bitter vending machine coffee for Dizzy and himself and sat next to her. His mouth was dry and his throat felt constricted. He decided to wait a minute and drink some coffee before he tried to say anything.

Finally he forged ahead. "Dizzy, there's something I have to tell you."

She gently placed her finger across his lips for quiet. "Beau, I'm in love." Dizzy was bursting with enthusiasm. "His name is Juan Carlo Francisco. He's kind and smart and very handsome. He's coming to the United States next week for an interview at Harvard Business School. I can't wait for you to meet him."

A feeling of profound relief surged through Beau. He relaxed into his chair and blinked.

Dizzy looked concerned. "I don't want you to feel bad about this."

He quickly responded. "Oh, no; I'm fine with it." As soon as the words were spoken, he knew they were wrong. "I mean, of course I feel bad, but I want the best for you—and I'm happy for you."

"That's sweet of you, Beau. Thank you."

"Who is this guy, Dizzy? I've never heard a thing about him."

"He's from Caracas. Our families have known each other forever. We played together as children. I'm sure he'll be accepted at Harvard Business School and I'm going to get a job in Cambridge so I can be with him. I thought it wouldn't be right to wait any longer before telling you about him. I know I led you on about our relationship, and I'm sorry. I had a great time with you, Beau. Every single bit of it was wonderful but it was just messing around. You must understand, it was always going to be someone like Juan Carlo—a young man from one of the important families in Venezuela."

Beau nodded. He did understand. He understood that a young woman might be involved with a boy who caught her fancy but, at the end of the day, she would choose to marry someone from her own class.

Football practice was an easy workout. Beau ran a few plays, and worked up a sweat; but there was no contact. There would be only one more practice before the last game of the regular season. If they won, the Wolverines would be Big Ten Champions and play in the Rose Bowl—but Ohio State was a formidable hurdle.

Michigan had won both of the games they played since Eddie

separated his right shoulder but they both turned out to be dog fights. Without Eddie Bartucci, the days of easy victories were over. Although the Wolverines were undefeated, no one expected an easy victory over Ohio State.

As Beau walked home from practice, he visualized the deer and the rabbit and how he could help his team win the last game he would ever play in Michigan's stadium. He was on the sidewalk that ran along the outside of a tall brick wall that surrounded the practice fields. The wall was weathered; some of the mortar had fallen away and a few of the bricks were crumbling. It had been standing for a long time.

Beau's hero, Tom Harmon, must have walked beside this same wall almost thirty years ago, before his Michigan team played Ohio State. Tom Harmon, the most famous player in Michigan football history, led the Wolverines to victory over the Buckeyes. Beau Lightfoot was walking in Tom's footsteps. Maybe he could do the same. Of course, Tom had his extraordinary blocker, team captain, and best friend, Forest Evashevski, to help him. Beau was going to play without Eddie Bartucci and Bobby Cunningham. As he traipsed through the cold November twilight and smoke from burning piles of dry leaves, Beau Lightfoot dared to compare himself with the great Tom Harmon.

Following the 1940 season, Tom won the Heisman Trophy, an award given each year to the best college football player in America. Eddie Bartucci had been the front runner for the 1968 Heisman Trophy but Eddie had screwed up. A halfback from the University of Alabama would probably win this year's Heisman.

Tom Harmon did everything. He ran, passed, kicked, and was an excellent defensive player. He was named to the All-American team in 1939 and 1940. Beau was a pass catcher and kick-return man. He did fewer things than Tom, but he did them well. The early-season talk of three All Americans at Michigan was now long forgotten but Beau hoped there might still be one.

In Tom's last game against Ohio State, he ran for two touchdowns; passed for two touchdowns; intercepted three passes, running one back for a touchdown; kicked four extra points; and averaged fifty yards per punt. Michigan won by a score of 40 to 0. Tom went on to become a decorated pilot during World War II. After the war, he married the beautiful young movie star Elyse Knox.

Beau had no desire to participate in the Vietnam War and he didn't want a Hollywood starlet. Janet Cunningham was his star.

Janet and her father were standing on the sidewalk in front of the Michigan Union and Beau, lost in his daydream, almost bumped into her. At the last second, he made a quick dodge and avoided actual contact with either Janet or her father. "Oh! I'm sorry. I guess I wasn't paying attention."

Buck Cunningham said, "Don't worry about it, Beau. I know you've got a lot on your mind." He must have assumed Beau was preoccupied with the upcoming football game because he immediately launched into a lengthy monologue about the likely outcome.

Something in Mr. Cunningham's manner caused Beau to sense the man was ill at ease. He seemed to want to communicate something important to Beau but he wasn't getting to the point. He continued rambling about the football game. Beau nodded politely. Buck Cunningham was a knowledgeable football fan but Beau didn't need his explanations.

Buck continued his one-sided conversation "... Jamie McDonald is a good little quarterback. He's a better ball handler than Eddie ... just can't throw the long ball."

Beau listened respectfully as Buck told him things he already knew.

"If Ohio State does beat us, we'll be tied with them in the conference standings and still be Big Ten Co-Champions. Of course, if they do beat us in a head-to-head match, they'll go to the Rose Bowl and we'll stay home."

As her dad was speaking, Janet took Beau's arm. Rather than putting one hand through the crook of his elbow, she wrapped both arms securely around the upper part of Beau's right arm. Buck's eyes caught this innocent but somehow intimate gesture and he concluded his pronouncements. "... so I came to Ann Arbor to have dinner with Janet." He inclined his head toward the Union building and said, "Bobby and Eddie are inside waiting to have dinner with the team. Those boys look like the walking wounded. Eddie's arm is in a sling and Bobby has crutches and a cast on his knee—but, as Beth always says, you can find some good in everything. Their injuries will keep them out of Vietnam." Beau thought Mr. Cunningham looked uneasy as he continued, "I'm going inside to talk with Bobby for a couple of minutes. Janet, would you mind waiting for me in the car?"

As Beau watched Mr. Cunningham climb the concrete steps and enter the Union, he felt he was looking at a man who had something to say but hadn't been able to get it out. Dinner wouldn't be served for a few minutes so Beau accompanied Janet to Mr. Cunningham's car.

It was a new Pontiac, parked on the street and partially protected by shadows. Beau leaned against the front fender and turned to face Janet. She walked right up to him, very close. He was wearing his light nylon jacket and felt cold. Janet was wearing a long, warm camel-hair coat with a stylish double row of buttons up the front. She must have noticed that he looked cold. She stepped between his outstretched legs, unbuttoned her coat, and put her arms around his neck so that her coat engulfed both of them. He could feel her body pressed against his but, rather than pulling away, she lifted her face toward him.

Beau kissed her gently. Her lips were soft and as they kissed, she parted them slightly; just enough to cause him to almost faint. Her mouth was sweet and he felt no need to breathe or to ever let go of her. They kissed again and again, only stopping when Beau caught sight of Mr. Cunningham approaching the car.

As Janet stepped away from Beau she smiled and whispered, "Did that warm you up?"

Her father was right there. Had he seen them kissing? He didn't say anything but he had a knowing smile. "Janet, would you like to invite Dizzy to have dinner with us?"

Janet looked relieved. "Sure, I'd love to have her."

Buck suggested she telephone Dizzy from one of the pay phones in the lower lobby of the Union. He said she could take her time because he wanted a few minutes with Beau.

"Beau, things have happened that have caused me to doubt the wisdom of some of my long-held convictions." They had moved inside Mr. Cunningham's new Pontiac and he had started the engine and turned on the heater. "It's difficult to explain—and I'm not good at this sort of thing."

Beau gave what he hoped was appropriately empathetic encouragement. "Of course, sir. Take your time."

Buck frowned as he continued. "My father told me everybody makes mistakes and it's no sin to have opinions that turn out to be wrong. The sin lies in failing to recognize your errors and refusing to make corrections. ... What I'm trying to say is I've been wrong." He paused and took a deep breath. "When I first met you, I was king of the hill; a wealthy man with a beautiful family. My son was going to be just like me—only better. I didn't make the Michigan football team but my son was going to be an All-American. ... And there was my lovely daughter, Janet."

Beau smiled at Mr. Cunningham and wondered what the heck was coming.

"Janet is beautiful, athletic, and smart as a whip. She was a bit rebellious but she loved her daddy and would never do anything to hurt me. She was perfect. You certainly weren't good enough for my Janet. I must have thought I was going to live forever and would always be around to take care of her." Buck shook his head as if to clear his thoughts. "Well, time passes and things change. Bobby's football days are over but he's a good man and I know he is going to accomplish something big in his life. I don't know what it will be but it's all up to him—not me."

The car windows were filming over with condensation on the inside and the interior was uncomfortably warm. Buck didn't appear to notice. "As you know, my dad passed away last month. At the end of his life he was a frail old man but he was still my protector. I don't think I really understood my feelings until after he was gone." Buck rubbed his face with his hands and took a moment to settle down. "There's no logic to it, but I felt that old man was protecting me from death. I couldn't die while my father was still alive. It wouldn't be my time. He was in line ahead of me. As long as he was there, I would be okay. Now, he's gone and I've moved to the head of the line ...

"We're all going to die. We all say we'll die someday. The funny thing is nobody really believes it. I'm not going to always be here to take care of Bobby and Janet. I think I did take care of them when I was needed. Now, it's time to step aside.... It's harder with a girl. Girls are smarter and stronger than boys but fathers think of them as soft and vulnerable. The reality is that Janet is a competent young woman. She has her own mind and makes her own decisions." He paused and turned his head toward Beau.

Beau nodded his understanding but felt he shouldn't interrupt.

"It is very hard for me to accept Janet being grown-up. She doesn't need any more guidance from me. Hell, I don't know what's best for her. The advice I gave her ... the advice concerning you ... was wrong. You've shown me that you're as fine a young man as anyone could hope to know. I want to correct my mistake and to tell you I'm sorry." Buck was struggling to communicate something that was obviously important to him. It had been hard for him to get started, but now that he'd almost reached the end, he was determined to finish. "I've told her that I was wrong to say you were unworthy of her. I know she's fond of you. Whether it's more than that will be for her to decide."

Buck extended his hand and Beau took it.

"Go have dinner with your team. You have to whip Ohio State—and you're going to need your strength."

~

Beau and his teammates stood in the dark tunnel that led from the locker rooms under the Michigan stadium out onto the playing field. Beau was ready to take the field for his last game in Ann Arbor. The players stood shoulder to shoulder and restlessly shifted their weight from one foot to the other, like draft horses waiting for the order to pull. The signal to go would come any second. The sound of the huge crowd was damped as it reached down into the tunnel where the team gathered. It sounded like the rustle of leaves in the wind.

Someone shouted, "LET'S GO!" and the Wolverines exploded from the dark tunnel into the bright sunshine. The roar of the excited crowd was overwhelming. Beau could actually feel their screaming. They were pouring out love for their team, and their team wanted to win this one for them.

It wasn't to be.

The Michigan team was good—but not good enough to win without two of its best players. Buck Cunningham's assessment was correct: Jamie McDonald was a good little quarterback but he couldn't throw the long ball. Without the threat of a long pass, the formerly unstoppable Wolverines stalled. Ohio State didn't worry about Beau going deep because they knew McDonald couldn't get the ball to him. They moved their players close to the line of scrimmage and jammed everything.

TD Kowalski had had an outstanding year running against defenses that were spread out to stop long passes, but when the Wolverines attempted to pound away with TD's powerful running, he failed to dent Ohio State's massed defense. They tried to throw long to Lightfoot but McDonald's pass hung in the air and was intercepted. They tried short passes but the tight coverage limited their success. Michigan's swarming defense played well but they couldn't do it all. They didn't get any help from the offense. The defensive players would use every ounce of their energy to stop the Buckeyes, only to see their offense run three plays and punt the ball back to Ohio State for another go at them.

The Buckeyes scored their third touchdown with less than two minutes remaining in the first half. With a 21 to 0 advantage, the player who kicked off for Ohio State must have felt confident. He ignored his coach's instructions not to kick to Lightfoot. Beau caught the ball on the 2-yard line and threaded his way through the entire Ohio State team for a 98-eight yard touchdown. Although it provided a ray of hope to the Michigan fans, their brief optimism faded as the game wore on.

Near the end of the third quarter, with the score standing at 28 to 7, McDonald called for a ten-yard pass play over the middle to Beau. The middle is okay for a big tight end but a dangerous place for a small guy. Beau flinched when he heard the play called but lined up to go for it. At the snap, he sprinted ten yards and made a ninety-degree cut toward the center of the field. The ball was thrown high and Ohio's murderous linebacker ran directly at Beau. It was his opportunity for a hard shot at the elusive Beau Lightfoot and he was coming with everything he had. He aimed for a spot just below Beau's rib cage and launched into him.

In a situation like this, the most important thing a receiver can do to protect himself is to stay on his feet. But a deer is a champion leaper. Beau jumped high into the air and made a one-handed catch. He sailed higher than anyone thought possible, much higher than the linebacker had calculated. The Buckeye aimed for Beau's midriff but hit him at the ankles, causing Beau to cartwheel in the air and bounce off the linebacker's back. Beau turned a complete somersault in the air and landed on his feet facing an open field. It was a fifty-yard touchdown and it happened so fast that Beau didn't know how he did it.

It was a virtuoso performance but it wasn't enough to turn the tide. The Buckeyes added another touchdown in the fourth quarter. During the last few minutes of play, Beau scored Michigan's final touchdown on a thirty-three-yard double reverse; a nifty bit of deception—but the game was all but over. Ohio State ran out the clock for a 35 to 21 victory over their bitter rival.

As Beau walked slowly off the field, the announcer was speaking to the crowd. Beau didn't catch the exact words, but it was something about Beau Lightfoot having completed his last game as a Wolverine. The Michigan fans rose to their feet and began clapping and cheering. Beau paused on the field. Several thousand Ohio State fans were seated together in one corner of the stadium, and when Beau looked in that direction, he couldn't believe what he saw. Those scarlet-and-gray clad people were standing and applauding too. They were some of the most partisan fans in America—but they were football fans and they were adding their benediction to Beau's college career.

~

On the morning following the game, Beau couldn't summon the energy to get out of bed. It was a cold and impossibly dreary Sunday morning. Rain was falling and the branches of the tall, old pine tree outside of his window sagged under the weight of accumulated moisture. The world was trapped between thick, damp fog that lay along the ground and low-hanging black clouds. Beau didn't want to see anybody and he definitely didn't want to read the Sunday sports pages. He decided he would just lie in bed and let his mind go blank.

It's a difficult thing to consciously let your mind go blank. After a while, Beau gave up and decided to relax and allow his thoughts to wander wherever they wished. They immediately focused on Janet Cunningham.

Her father was no longer going to be an impediment—but what would Janet decide? I know she's fond of me. But Beau remembered that Dizzy had said she was fond of him too—but in her heart she thought of their relationship as a delightful flirtation. *Janet probably feels the same way. We're from different worlds. Janet Cunningham can have any man she desires. She's going to choose a doctor or a lawyer or a business executive from a wealthy Bloomfield Hills family. It is ludicrous to think that a girl like her would settle for me.*

His depressing thoughts were interrupted by a voice coming from the chair next to his bed. "I came to speak with you. Please pull your head out from under the covers."

Beau quickly sat up. He didn't want to appear a weakling in front of his Spirit Father.

Pontiac spoke in his usual deliberate manner. "I see you are sad. What's troubling you?"

Beau said he was terribly disappointed by the loss to Ohio State but as he looked at Pontiac, he realized The Greatest War Chief Who Ever Lived wouldn't consider the loss of a football game to be an event of importance.

Pontiac looked perplexed. "You played well. Was it fun?"

Beau admitted that, although he hadn't been looking at it quite that way, the game had been fun. Then he waited for Pontiac to speak.

Pontiac waited for Beau to say something more.

The silence became uncomfortable and, eventually Beau realized it was foolish to try to outlast The Greatest War Chief Who Ever Lived.

"There is another thing, Spirit Father."

"I thought there was."

"It's about Janet."

Pontiac smiled. "Ah, yes. Janet Cunningham, a beautiful young woman; a bit headstrong but a lovely girl. Tell me about it."

Beau got directly to the point. "I'm in love with her but I don't know if she loves me. Things are very confusing. It must have been a lot easier when you were a young man. I read that Odawa girls got to choose their mates and the only thing a young brave had to do was walk around carrying a torch until a girl pulled on his robe."

Pontiac nodded. "Yes, that's the way it worked more than two hundred years ago. And it's also the way it works today."

"I don't understand."

"Beau, for an intelligent young man, you can be awfully slow. You haven't given Janet an opportunity to tug on your robe. If you want her, you have to carry your torch and hold it where she can see it. You have to go to her and stand beside her. You have to invite her to choose you."

Four days after his conversation with Pontiac, Beau was sitting alone in the backseat of a luxurious limousine as it idled curbside in front of Ulrich's Bookstore. It was a few minutes before noon and, if things went according to plan, Janet would pass in front of the bookstore on the way to her sorority house for lunch.

The plan began to form in Beau's mind on Monday, after Coach Blieschroeder told him he'd been named a Heisman Trophy finalist. The finalists would go to New York City on Thursday afternoon and the winner would be announced at a nationally televised ceremony at the Downtown Athletic Club on Saturday night. Beau was surprised to be chosen. Eddie Bartucci was the Michigan player who had been considered the likely Heisman Trophy winner.

Beau said he didn't think he had a realistic chance of winning. Coach Blieschroeder agreed it was a long shot. He thought the running back from the University of Alabama probably had it sewn up.

Beau said that since he was unlikely to win, he'd skip the weekend in New York. Blieschroeder said that was ridiculous and pressed him for his reasons. Beau tried to sidestep but finally admitted he couldn't afford the trip. Coach actually laughed out loud before explaining that being a Heisman finalist was a very big deal. The Heisman Committee would take care of everything; Beau wouldn't have to spend one cent of his own money. They would have him transported from Ann Arbor to the Detroit airport by limousine, fly him first class to New York City, put him up at the Plaza Hotel, introduce him to celebrities, and wine and dine him at fabulous restaurants. He could even bring two or three people with him; everything would be at the expense of the Heisman Committee.

Most players took their parents but Coach understood Beau didn't have parents to accompany him so he explained that Beau's guests could be anyone he wanted. He could bring his sister or even the priest from Harbor Springs.

Beau had laid some groundwork before asking the person he wanted to accompany him by telling her brother about his nomination and the upcoming weekend in New York, including the Plaza Hotel, Broadway shows, and fancy restaurants. Beau knew everything he told Bobby would be passed on to his sister.

Janet was walking fast as she came around the corner. It was her late-for-lunch walk. She was looking straight ahead as she cut in front of the bookstore and passed beside a large black automobile with its rear window rolled down.

"Janet," Beau said when she was right by the car.

She froze in mid stride and looked in the window. "Beau?"

"Yeah. It's really me in this limousine. Can you believe it?"

"I believe it ... but you sure surprised me."

He had planned to say everything slowly and carefully. He had rehearsed several times but now, at the ultimate moment, he was excited and spoke too fast. "Janet, I'm on my way to New York. I've been selected as a finalist for the Heisman Trophy. I don't think I'll win but it's going to be a terrific weekend in New York. Everything will be first class. All expenses will be paid by the Heisman Committee ... will you come with me?"

Janet stood still, looked at him with her beautiful brown eyes, and didn't say a word.

"I can have the driver take us to the Chi Omega house and wait while you throw some things in a suitcase." Beau then opened the limousine door and Janet Cunningham slipped in beside him.

CLASS OF 1969

Excerpts from The University of Michigan Alumni Association class notes, published on September 30, 1979.

EDWARD R. BARTUCCI, JR.

Eddie was chosen in the fifth round of the professional football college draft by the Detroit Lions. Although his shoulder injury had healed, his passes never regained their former zip and he was released by the Lions after the third pre-season game. After failing to be picked up by another team, he retired from professional football and joined the Bartucci Foods Corporation. Edward R. Bartucci, Sr., Chairman of the Board, told the financial press that his son would not be shown any favoritism. Eddie would have to start at the bottom and try to work his way up.

Apparently Eddie had outstanding aptitude for the grocery business. He advanced from the loading dock to Senior Vice President in eleven months.

ROBERT L. CUNNINGHAM

After completing Yale Law School and spending three years practicing corporate law, Bobby embarked on a career in politics. With the guidance of his friend Gerald R. Ford, he was elected to the Michigan Legislature in 1975 and the United States Congress in 1978.

REBECCA GOLDMAN

Becky continued her passionate involvement in the antiwar movement. She met her husband, the nationally known political activist Richard Reinstein, at the Vietnam Veterans Against the War Rally in Washington, D. C. The Reinsteins now live in Evanston, Illinois. Richard is an orthodontist and Becky teaches Social Conflict Theory at Northwestern University.

THADDEUS D. KOWALSKI

After graduation, TD enlisted in the Marine Corps. He emerged from the Vietnam War disillusioned but uninjured. Following his discharge, he was hired as a driver's training instructor and assistant football coach for the high school in St. Joseph, Michigan. In 1974, TD was named head football coach.

Adopting TD's enthusiasm and aggressive style of play, the St. Joe Bears are now a Michigan high school football powerhouse.

MITCHELL A. CAPUTO

Mitch left the University of Michigan prior to graduation and has not kept in touch. There was a report of him living in the Cayman Islands but your Alumni Association has not been able to learn his address.

D'ISABELLA HERNANDEZ

Dizzy moved to Cambridge, Massachusetts. One year later, she married Juan Carlo Francisco. The wedding, attended by more than five hundred guests, was held at the National Polo Club in Caracas and was said to have been the social event of the year.

Dizzy has maintained her friendship with Janet Cunningham and the two women meet in New York City at least twice a year. Over the years, Juan Carlo Francisco and Beau Lightfoot have become close friends. Aided by family connections and his Harvard Business School education, Juan Carlo proved to be adept at both politics and finance. In 1976, at the age of thirty-two, he was appointed Oil Minister of Venezuela.

JANET P. CUNNINGHAM

Janet graduated with a major in Art History and was elected to the Phi Beta Kappa academic honor society. She has continued her study of Art History as a graduate student at Columbia University in New York City and is an active member of the Metropolitan Museum of Art.

In June 1969, Janet Cunningham and Beau Lightfoot were married in a small ceremony held on the front lawn of the Cunningham family cottage in Wequetonsing, Michigan.

BEAU LIGHTFOOT

Beau was the first-round draft choice of the New York Giants but feared he wouldn't be able to join the team because he expected to be drafted and sent to Vietnam. It required only one telephone call from the Giants front office to put his anxiety to rest. The commanding officer of a unit of the New York Air National Guard which was known to have a long waiting list, discovered he did have one open billet for the New York Giants' first-round draft pick. The Air National Guard was not called to action in Vietnam and it was arranged for Beau to serve his required six months of active duty during the Giants offseason.

Beau played football for seven years and was named "All Pro" five times. As a star athlete in the media capital of the world, he was afforded numerous business opportunities; but the sports world was amazed when, upon retirement as an active player, he purchased eighteen percent of the New York Giants Football Corporation. There were rumors of a South American financial backer but no information was ever made public.

THE SCHOLARSHIP

HARBOR SPRINGS, 2013

It was Sunday morning, and they all agreed to attend Mass with Father Marcotte officiating. Beau hadn't gone to Mass for more than twenty years but it meant a great deal to the old priest. Everyone at Bobby's cottage went: lapsed Catholics, Protestants, one Jew (Eddie's new wife), and a couple of nonbelievers.

Bobby said a little religion would be good for all of them. Eddie said he wasn't fooled. He knew Bobby was only going to Mass so he could have some pancakes afterward. And that is what happened. When the service was over, everyone piled into Beau's roomy Mercedes and went to the Flap Jack Shack to feast on blueberry pancakes with pure Michigan maple syrup.

Beau and Janet walked up the broad front steps into Harbor Springs High School. It was time for a special school board meeting to award the Good Heart Scholarship. Beau and Janet had provided $4 million to establish a four-year, all-expense scholarship to the University of Michigan for one graduating senior each year from Harbor Springs High School. Recipients would be chosen on the basis of academic achievement and financial need.

Their son, Mark, a vice president of the J. P. Morgan/Chase Bank in New York, had set up the trust and established investment policy guidelines. Their daughter, the writer, Harriet Lightfoot Anderson, composed the letter to be given to the scholarship recipient.

Beau had directed Mark to draw the trust document so as to give the school board, with recommendations from the teachers, sole discretion in selecting the scholarship recipients. As he and Janet entered the auditorium for the award ceremony, he wondered who they had selected. After thanking Beau and Janet for their generosity and the usual introductory comments, the school board president made the announcement. "The first annual Good Heart Scholarship is awarded to Sofia Lechowitz. Would Miss Lechowitz please come forward?"

A student in the fifth row stood. She was an ordinary-looking, blue-eyed, eighteen-year-old. As she walked toward the podium, Beau noticed she was wearing a faded dress that had been washed, ironed, and mended in several places. He made a mental note to tell Mark to add some money to her scholarship fund so that it would provide a monthly clothing allowance. He wasn't going to send a small-town kid to a big university without proper clothes. He remembered how that felt.

The board president handed the letter to Sofia and everyone applauded. As the audience departed, Beau and Janet spoke briefly with the board members and learned that although Sofia had been raised in impoverished circumstances, she was an exceptionally bright student. Janet said it was a privilege to help such a deserving young person. There were smiles and handshakes all around as Beau and Janet made their way to the front door.

Beau stopped at the top of the stairs. Sofia was sitting on the bottom step. She evidently had been unable to contain her curiosity and was reading her scholarship letter. Pontiac, dressed for the occasion in his full chief's regalia, was sitting one step above her and reading over her shoulder. Neither Sofia nor Janet appeared to notice him.

Pontiac looked up at Beau and nodded his approval.

Dear Sofia:

Congratulations on earning the Good Heart Scholarship. It will pay all of your expenses for four years at The University of Michigan. There are no conditions.

I would like for you to know that this scholarship is given in honor of five people with good hearts:

Father Marcotte, who devoted his long life to the service of God.

Bobby Cunningham, who forgave his friend.

Fawn Lightfoot, who, as a child, had courage at a critical moment and then spent her adult years in the service of others.

Buck Cunningham, who admitted he had been wrong.

Marcus White, who sacrificed his own life to save his comrades.

My wish is for you to enjoy a good life in this beautiful world we have been given. Have a good heart.

                Respectfully,
                Beau Lightfoot

PONTIAC'S RULES

Always remember you are not an ordinary person.

Take time to appreciate the natural world.

If someone asks for your help, give it.

Be brave.

Be bold.

Try your best.

Think for yourself.

Give your love freely—you will never run out.

ACKNOWLEDGMENTS

My thanks to Barry Pierson and Dr. Jim Detwiler for sharing some of their experiences as real University of Michigan football players during the years when the fictional Beau Lightfoot was a star receiver.

I took a great liberty by using the name of my old friend Dr. Oliver Marcotte for the Harbor Springs priest. Ollie, I just could not come up with a name that fit as perfectly as Marcotte.

My editor, Mary Jo Zazueta, did a wonderful job of improving my manuscript while preserving the essence of Beau Lightfoot's story.

This book could not have been written without the support of my family. My daughters, Peggy Brown-Rezek, Dr. Julie Brown, and Katherine Emrich, endured many readings of early drafts and were unfailingly encouraging. Thanks to you guys.

And thank you to my wife, Ruthie, who has given her wholehearted support to every project I have ever undertaken. Without the slightest complaint, she spent innumerable evenings by herself while I sat at my computer with Beau Lightfoot and Janet Cunningham.

ABOUT THE AUTHOR

Rob Brown was a finalist in the Pacific Northwest Writers Association fiction competition. He studied creative writing at Richard Hugo House, the University of Washington, and Story Studio.

He earned freshman numerals at the University of Michigan as a tight end. Unlike Beau Lightfoot, he did not move up to the varsity and become a star.

He lives with his wife, Ruthie, and his bulldog, Gloria, in Harbor Springs, Michigan, and Chicago, Illinois.